MURDER AT SEA

Maybe it was Val's imagination, but she already felt as if the yacht was rolling and pitching less than it had earlier. She checked her watch. Just past nine. Hard to believe that little more than half an hour had gone by since the squall hit.

The silence in the room was more deafening than the exercise music had been. With the host missing, returning to the table for the rest of the gala *Titanic* dinner probably had little appeal, especially for those feeling motion sickness. Yet Val was sure food would do them all good, if they could manage to eat. She decided to set out the main course as a buffet. Tricky to reheat the beef without overcooking it. It was still warm, so she'd serve it that way. She reheated the vegetables, found serving bowls for them, and put the food on the counter that divided the galley from the dining area. She then collected the booklets from the table and stuffed them into a drawer in the galley.

Two minutes after she invited the guests to the buffet, Stacy started the procession to the table. Damian and Louisa followed her. Cheyenne joined them at the table. She and Bethany talked quietly instead of eating. Homer had no interest in food either.

Val cleaned up the galley t could have happened rboard, but how? He m n from the stairs, and

Or one of th t have pushed him.

Under the guise of a mystery game, Otto had accused them of crimes and misdemeanors. Their vehement denials suggested his accusations might have hit home. Could his fiction about a girl's fall from the *Titanic* have led to his fall from the *Abyss*?

Books by Maya Corrigan

BY COOK OR BY CROOK

SCAM CHOWDER

FINAL FONDUE

THE TELL-TALE TARTE

S'MORE MURDERS

Published by Kensington Publishing Corporation

S'more Murders

MAYA CORRIGAN

KENSINGTON BOOKS
KENSINGTON PUBLISHING CORP.
http://www.kensingtonbooks.com

KENSINGTON BOOKS are published by

Kensington Publishing Corp.
119 West 40th Street
New York, NY 10018

All Kensington titles, imprints, and distributed lines are available at special quantity discounts for bulk purchases for sales promotion, premiums, fund-raising, educational, or institutional use.

Special book excerpts or customized printings can also be created to fit specific needs. For details, write or phone the office of the Kensington Sales Manager: Attn.: Sales Department. Kensington Publishing Corp., 119 West 40th Street, New York, NY 10018. Phone: 1-800-221-2647.

Kensington and the K logo Reg. U.S. Pat. & TM Off.

First Printing: August 2018
ISBN-13: 978-1-4967-0919-6
ISBN-10: 1-4967-0919-5

eISBN-13: 978-1-4967-0920-2
eISBN-10: 1-4967-0920-9

10 9 8 7 6 5 4 3 2 1

Printed in the United States of America

ACKNOWLEDGMENTS

I'd like to thank those who shared their expertise with me as I researched and wrote this book. I'm particularly grateful to retired Captain Brian Kelley, United States Coast Guard. He generously answered my questions about how the Coast Guard would respond to a Mayday call from the Chesapeake Bay and conduct a search-and-rescue operation in that area. For details about forensic investigations into drownings and shootings, I consulted D. P. Lyle, M.D. I received helpful information about the effects of drugs from pharmacist and toxicologist Luci Zahray. Any mistakes in the book on those subjects are inadvertent and resulted from my misunderstanding.

While writing this book, I frequently consulted *Last Dinner on the Titanic* by Rick Archbold and Dana McCauley. It contains details about the menus on the ship, table settings, and recipes useful for those who want to hold their own *Titanic* dinner. If you would like to add a murder investigation to your dinner, I recommend the *Titanic* Murder Mystery Dinner Party Game by Printable Mystery Games. I'm grateful to the family members who assisted my research by taking part in that role-playing game: Chris and Jim Bruns; Regina Roman; George, Dan, and Greg Berman; Nora and

Mike Corrigan. That murder mystery game is a lot more fun than the game Otto devised for his *Titanic* dinner guests in *S'more Murders*.

Thank you to my critique partners, mystery writers Carolyn Mulford and Helen Schwartz. They brainstormed with me, read the book chapter by chapter, and gave me helpful suggestions at our weekly meetings. My thanks go to Paul Corrigan, Mike Corrigan, Cathy Ondis Solberg, and Elliot Wicks for reading and commenting on the book. Mike also answered my many questions about guns. Writing a book is a long process, and he stood by me all the way. Thanks, Mike.

I'm grateful to my agent, John Talbot, to my editor, John Scognamiglio, and to the team at Kensington Books who helped bring *S'more Murders* to readers.

To those who always crave some more murders—readers who enjoy detective and mystery fiction—thank you for your support.

Titanic! *Of all the remarkable incidents connected with the short life of that ship of destiny not the least was her name. If you look in your dictionary you will find: Titans—A race of people vainly striving to overcome the forces of nature. Could anything be more unfortunate than such a name, anything more significant?*

—ARTHUR ROSTRON, Captain of the *Carpathia*, the *Titanic*'s rescue ship, *Home From the Sea*, 1931

Chapter 1

"I want you to re-create the final dinner served on the *Titanic*. Ten courses for eight people."

Val Deniston stared at Otto Warbeck. Was he joking? Not visibly. The yacht owner had wrinkles in his forehead, but no smile lines. Not a man given to jests. When she'd agreed to cater a dinner for him on the Chesapeake Bay, she hadn't expected him to demand a custom-made feast, not to mention one with really bad karma.

She ran her fingers along the granite counter near the glass cooktop, cool and hard like everything on his yacht. "I've catered themed dinners before, Mr. Warbeck." Only a few, since catering was a sideline for her. "My clients have always selected dishes from my standard menu, which offers many choices." She reached into her tote bag for her catering menus.

He stroked his neat salt-and-pepper beard. "Your grandfather assured me that your dinner party menus were flexible."

Granddad would say anything to get her a client. She would walk away from this gig if it weren't for the termite damage to the house they shared. Granddad needed help paying for the repairs, so she'd try to reach an agreement with the yachtsman. "Let's sit at the table and talk about this, Mr. Warbeck."

"Call me Otto."

As she walked around the counter that separated the galley from the dining table, the floor swayed under her feet, reminding her that she wouldn't be cooking and serving on solid ground. The boat would rock even more once it left the Bayport marina for the open water of the Chesapeake Bay. Fortunately, she wasn't prone to seasickness. But if the dinner guests felt sick in rough water, they might blame her food for their nausea.

Otto held her chair as she sat down, a courtly gesture that went along with his formal manner of speaking. Standing only four inches taller than her five foot three, he tucked his hand, Napoleon style, into his navy jacket with brass buttons. He took the seat to her right, at the head of the table. "As a collector of *Titanic* memorabilia, I really look forward to this dinner. It has a special meaning for me."

"I can certainly prepare a special dish that isn't on my standard catering menu." *One dish, not ten.*

His frown lines deepened. "Your grandfather led me to believe you were creative in the kitchen. But you just want to make the same things over and over from a set menu. Where's your spirit of adventure?"

Val's jaw clenched. What an annoying man, putting her on the defensive when he was making an unreasonable request. "Catering isn't an adventure for me. It's a business. I offer creative dishes at fair prices. I know my clients will be happy because I've thoroughly tested the recipes. With only five days before your dinner party, I don't have much time to cost out an elaborate meal and experiment with dishes I've never made before."

He reached for the catering menus she'd put on the table, giving her hope that he was open to compromise.

He scrutinized them. "You don't need to price out anything. Let's say I want you to make a four-course meal of the most expensive items you offer. Adding up the prices and multiplying by eight people, the bottom line is . . ." He took five seconds to calculate the total and announced it.

"That sounds about right. So you'll be happy with a four-course meal?"

"No! I'll multiply the total by two and a half, because I want ten courses, not four. Then I'll double that figure because of the extra work involved in preparing dishes you haven't previously tried." He flashed a puckish smile. "Have I made you an offer you can't refuse?"

Getting there. "I'd love to give you your dream dinner party, but I can't possibly cook and serve ten courses to eight people all by myself."

"I expected you might say that. I'll pay your grandfather to serve as sous chef. He told me his Codger Cook newspaper column features easy five-ingredient recipes, but surely he can assist you with more complicated dishes. He knows his way around a kitchen."

Granddad's cooking expertise was like a soufflé: mostly hot air. He'd wangled the job of food columnist by tweaking her recipes. "Besides my grandfather, I could use another assistant. My friend Bethany has experience helping at the athletic club café I manage." A *Titanic* dinner was wacky enough to appeal to Bethany.

Besides, she owed Val after dragging her into hunting for a dead body with a borrowed cadaver dog.

Otto raised his index finger and moved it back and forth like a metronome. "I won't pay for another assistant."

Only fair, given how much he was forking over for this dinner. Val would pay for Bethany's services out of her own pocket. "I'll need time to test recipes. Can you postpone the dinner?"

"I cannot. The date, the place, and the guests have aligned for this occasion. Saturday is April fourteenth, the anniversary of the last dinner on the *Titanic*. I now own a boat that can accommodate eight for dinner here in the saloon." His sweeping gesture encompassed the sitting-eating-cooking space that landlubbers would call a great room.

For the first time since she boarded the yacht, Val focused on the sitting area, two steps down from and aft of the galley and the dining space. Picture windows along the sides made the saloon look larger than it was. The cherry wood paneling and matching cabinetry gave it a welcome hint of warmth. "The saloon is elegant, like a lounge on an ocean liner," she said.

"In miniature. My wife is going to add decorative touches that suggest the *Titanic*. I even have tableware in patterns used on the *Titanic*." He pulled a card with rounded corners from his breast pocket. "Here is the first-class dinner menu from that fateful night."

She gaped at the gilt-edged card he'd passed to her. On a surface barely larger than five by seven inches, the menu listed around twenty-five dishes. "This is a restaurant menu."

"And I don't expect you to turn the galley into a

restaurant kitchen. Just choose one of the options listed for each course."

The menu included dishes she'd never heard of— Consommé Olga, Punch Romaine, and Waldorf Pudding. "I'll have to do research to find recipes for these dishes."

"There are no surviving recipes for the dishes served on the *Titanic*, so you have leeway with the recipes, as long as you come up with something similar to what's on the menu."

Hooray, a chink in his armor. Val tried to picture what it would be like to cook and serve the dinner in such close quarters. She saw a potential problem. "Your guests will be sitting steps away from where I'm preparing the meal. You'll have cooking odors that the first-class dining room on the *Titanic* didn't have."

"They can always get up between courses and go outside for fresh air." Otto pointed to the door in the dining area. "That will give the guests easy access to the side deck. You can do much of the cooking ahead of time. Half the dishes on the menu are best served cold—even the consommé and the salmon."

Val didn't mind serving salmon cold, but she drew the line at jellied consommé. She glanced at the other end of the saloon. The L-shaped sofa, three chairs, and built-in cabinetry didn't leave much open floor space for a meet-and-mingle cocktail party. "Where do you want me to serve the hors d'oeuvres?"

"Weather permitting, on the large open deck above us." He pointed to the ceiling. "I'll show you."

They went out the sliding glass door from the sitting area to the aft deck. A door just outside the saloon led to a tiny powder room, which Otto called a *head*. Val called it a step up from an outhouse. They took the stairs to the open area on the top deck. Perfect for serving drinks and hors d'oeuvres unless it rained. The only indoor space on this deck was the glass-enclosed bridge, equipped with three leather chairs facing the helm.

They'd just returned to the saloon when a young woman slid open the door from the aft deck and swept into the room. Val recognized her from the Protect the Bay Barbecue the weekend before last.

The woman flung her leather jacket on the sofa in the saloon. "Getting windy out there." She finger-combed her golden brown hair back into place. It grazed her shoulders and turned under neatly.

Val didn't bother trying to smooth her own, less tame, hair. After its wind treatment on the upper deck, it probably looked like a cinnamon-colored clown wig.

Otto stood up and hugged the young woman. His daughter, perhaps?

He steered her toward the table. "Come and meet the caterer for our dinner. Val, this is my wife, Cheyenne."

Ah. The trophy wife. She looked to be in her late twenties, at least five years younger than Val. "Hi, Cheyenne. I'm Val Deniston. We were both helping the children make s'mores at the picnic a week ago." Though Cheyenne had done more eating than helping.

"They were so yummy," she gushed. "It was like being back at summer camp. Fun times around the open fire. Can we have s'mores at the dinner party, Otto?"

He winced. "Even if s'mores existed in 1912, they wouldn't have been served on the *Titanic*. You know I'm striving for authenticity with this dinner. I don't want the ambiance of a backyard barbecue."

"I saw a classy tabletop s'mores maker that uses chafing dish fuel. We could serve the s'mores as an ice breaker," his wife said, unmoved by his objection. "You need something like that, or the guests will stand around stiffly in their formal clothes. It'll be deadly dull."

"I doubt that." He looked at Val as if he expected her to reject his wife's idea.

The last thing this dinner needed was another dish, but Val saw how she could turn this one to her advantage. "In addition to the sweet s'mores, we could do savory ones as one of the hors d'oeuvres. Melted Brie on a cracker with sun-dried tomato pesto." She smiled at Otto. "The assistant I mentioned could be in charge of that. She was a camp counselor, an expert at making s'mores."

"Okay." Otto touched his wife's cheek and then turned to Val. "Add the pay for the s'mores expert to my bill."

After his concession on the s'mores, he allowed Val to tweak the meat-heavy menu. She proposed mushroom pâté as a substitute for pâté de foie gras. He agreed that she could skip the course of roasted squab—difficult to get locally—and add fresh fruit and cheese as a final course.

She took out two copies of her standard contract and filled in the price and terms they'd negotiated.

As Otto looked over the contract, Cheyenne offered to give Val a tour of the lower deck. They went down the curved staircase near the dining area. Doors from the lower hall led to three staterooms and the guest head, all decorated with a nautical theme.

When they went back to the saloon, Otto gave Val a signed contract and a check for 50 percent of the total as a down payment. She tucked it in her shoulder bag. By preparing dishes wholly or partly ahead of time, she could pull off the dinner that had seemed impossible when he first brought it up.

Once off the boat, she walked along the dock, where sailboats and motorized yachts smaller than Otto's were moored. She turned to look back at his yacht and noticed what she'd missed earlier—the name painted on it. Otto's boat was called the *Abyss*.

She quelled a flutter of anxiety in her stomach. At least he hadn't named it the *Titanic II*.

Val pulled into the driveway at Granddad's gabled and turreted Victorian house, went in the side door, and looked around for her grandfather. He was in the front room, known as the courting parlor when the house was built. Instead of courting couples, it now held computers—Val's laptop and a new addition, the tablet her parents had given her. Her birthday fell during their annual sailing trip from Florida to the Bahamas, and they always sent a generous gift to make up for not celebrating with her.

Granddad stopped pecking on her keyboard when she joined him. Tufts of white curls fringed the sides and back of his otherwise bald head. "You usually come home earlier than this. Did your afternoon helper at the café show up late?"

"No, I got together with Otto Warbeck, the man you met at the Protect the Bay Barbecue, the one who needs a caterer." In the year since she'd moved in with her grandfather, he'd thrown several jobs her way, as if she didn't have enough to do managing the Cool Down Café. But she enjoyed catering small dinner parties as a change of pace. "The fancy yacht you saw at the marina yesterday belongs to him. That's where he wants me to make dinner. I wouldn't agree until I saw the kitchen on the boat. It's small but efficient and equipped with the latest appliances."

"Why didn't you tell me you were going on that yacht? I would have gone with you to see what it's like inside."

"You'll have your chance. Otto said he'd pay you as the sous chef."

Granddad grinned. "A chef on a yacht! I can do that."

"Assistant chef and server," she corrected. Nothing daunted the man. After taking an online course in private investigation, he'd added *sleuth* to his résumé. And despite little cooking experience, he was eager to turn his newspaper column into the *Codger's Cookbook*— with her help, of course. "Otto asked me to re-create the last meal the *Titanic* passengers ate."

Granddad's eyes bugged out behind his wire-rimmed bifocals. "Why does he want to do that?"

She shrugged. "He collects *Titanic* memorabilia. With this dinner, he gets to relive a piece of history."

"He's making a party out of a tragedy. It's like dancing on someone's grave. *Fifteen hundred graves.*" Granddad pinched the skin at his throat, a habit of his when something troubled him. "I don't want any part of it. And you shouldn't either."

She hadn't expected pushback from him. Who else could she ask to help her? Her cousin Monique would do it, but she'd just left for a two-week vacation in Hilton Head. So it was Granddad or nobody. "The yachtsman is willing to pay big money for us to make this dinner, enough to cover half the termite repairs. It would take me months to set aside that much from the café earnings."

"The house isn't going to fall down if we don't fix it right away." He waggled his finger. "Your mother wouldn't want you to do this."

Val had stopped listening to her mother when she went to college fifteen years ago, and she didn't plan to start again. "I signed a contract with Otto. I can't back out."

Granddad stroked his chin, the beard he'd had all winter now gone. "If you're giving that dinner party on his yacht, I have to go too. Your mother would never forgive me if anything happened to you. I'm going to make sure that boat doesn't leave the dock unless it has enough life vests, life rings, and lifeboats."

The yacht doubtless had all the safety equipment it needed, but if confirming that was enough to get Granddad to go, she was content. Obviously, fear of tempting fate, also known as superstition, contributed to his negativity about the *Titanic* dinner. "Otto's willing to pay for two assistants. I'm going to call Bethany."

"Call Gunnar instead. He'll be more help in an emergency."

"But not with cooking and serving." Though her boyfriend liked to eat well, he had few kitchen skills. "Anyway, he's too busy."

"With what? His next role as an *amateur* actor?" Granddad's intonation conveyed his scorn for Gunnar's acting ambitions.

"No, he's swamped with work from his accounting clients. Income taxes are due in a week. By the way, did you mail your tax forms?"

He nodded. "I earned more money than in any year since I gave up my video store."

But not enough to pay the bills by himself. "I'm glad to hear it. By the way, I'm going to need your help testing *Titanic* recipes this week. And you'll have to learn how to serve a formal dinner."

"No big deal. I'll watch reruns of *Downton Abbey* and see how it's done."

Late Saturday afternoon, Val parked her Saturn near the marina. As she and Granddad unloaded the food for the *Titanic* dinner, she spotted Bethany, who'd walked to the marina from her house a few blocks away. Granddad did a double take at the sight of Bethany in a sophisticated black dress. She usually wore bright colors, which clashed with her ginger hair, and styles that would look better on the first graders she taught than on a curvy woman.

With Val toting a large cooler, Granddad two smaller ones, and Bethany bags of groceries, they skirted around the waterfront crab house toward the marina.

Val stopped short when the dock came into view. The *Abyss* wasn't among the yachts at the marina. "Otto's boat isn't here yet." She checked her watch. Almost four.

Granddad set down his coolers. "You're sure we're here at the right time?"

"We're five minutes early, but the boat should be in sight by now." Val put down her cooler and peered down the river. No yacht approaching. "I'll call Otto."

She left a message on his voice mail and then shed her black jacket. With the weather unusually warm for April and the sun beating down on her, she was starting to feel the heat. The yacht's absence gave her even more reason to sweat.

Granddad took off his jacket. "These black duds make us look like we're bringing food to a wake."

Bethany laughed. "Your clothes are too hip for a wake, Mr. Myer."

"I haven't worn these since January, when I was the one with the rich client." He brushed imaginary lint from his black shirt and pants. "You're ready for a night on the town. Nice dress."

Val agreed. "You look elegant in a simple sheath. That style is very slimming. I'll have to get a dress like that."

"I only wear it when my choral group performs. Speaking of slimming, when you asked me to help with the *Titanic* dinner, I took it as a good omen for the diet I'm starting this week."

"*Titanic* and *good omen* don't go together," Granddad said. "What's on your diet?"

"Ice. When you're hungry, you chew ice. Eating it actually burns fat, because the body uses energy to melt it."

"It'll crack your molars too." He clacked his teeth. "Then you won't be able to chew real food, and you'll lose a lot of weight."

"No worries, Mr. Myer. I'm careful to pound the ice cubes into small pieces."

"So the diet involves exercise too," Val said. "It's perfect."

"Are you being sarcastic?" Bethany didn't wait for an answer. "I'm combining the ice diet with the raw food diet. They say you burn more calories than you consume when you eat a stick of celery."

A myth, but Val didn't bother to say so. She'd never succeeded in talking Bethany out of a fad diet.

Granddad pointed to the coolers. "What will you do with all this food if that rich fella doesn't show up with his yacht?"

"Have a feast with you two and then freeze the leftovers. We'll eat them for weeks. Weird as the *Titanic* dinner sounded to me at first, I'd be disappointed not to go through with it, after all the work I've done." Val craned her neck to look down the river. All she saw were a few sailboats and a motorized inflatable boat cruising toward the marina. "Come on, Otto. I was looking forward to the *Titanic* experience."

"So were the folks who climbed aboard in 1912," Granddad said. "And remember what happened to them. If Otto's yacht sank, I'm glad it happened before we got on it."

Chapter 2

An inflatable dinghy glided toward the dock where Val and her *Titanic* crew waited.

The young black man at the wheel shut off the motor. "You going to Mr. Warbeck's boat?"

"We hope so," Granddad said.

"I'll take you there." The young man tied the inflatable to a pier. "I'm Jerome Young."

Val introduced herself, Granddad, and Bethany to Jerome.

While Granddad and Bethany gaped at the small boat, Val answered her chiming phone.

Otto was finally returning her call. "The boat in the slip I reserved didn't leave when it was supposed to. Engine trouble. The marina will have a spot for the *Abyss* in an hour. I sent my crew member to pick you up."

"He just arrived in an inflatable."

"Best I could do on short notice. We're anchored down the river. See you soon." He hung up.

Val reported what he'd said to the others.

Bethany looked askance at the small boat. "Will there

be enough room for us and all this?" She gestured at the coolers and the grocery bags.

"No problem. The boat holds seven people." Jerome handed them each a life vest, though he wasn't wearing one himself.

The inflatable was the largest one Val had ever been on, about twelve feet long and six feet wide on the inside. Granddad occupied the rear seat, between the engine and the wheel, where Jerome stood. Val sat on a backless bench in front of the wheel and Bethany on the prow seat. She pressed on the curved sides of the boat every few minutes, presumably to make sure the air wasn't leaking.

After Jerome left the harbor's boat traffic behind, Granddad said, "Is this your boat?"

"Nope. It goes with the yacht."

Val twisted around to look at Jerome. "Does the yacht have other boats?" Lifeboats, perhaps?

"Another inflatable, smaller than this one. Six people can squeeze into it. You gotta paddle that one. And there's also a kayak."

She could guess what Granddad was thinking. As long as those boats were filled to capacity, unlike the lifeboats on the *Titanic*, they'd make it to shore in an emergency.

He leaned back and relaxed. "You work for Mr. Warbeck, Jerome?"

"Tonight I do. I'll be at the helm while he parties."

Granddad continued to make conversation, asking where and how Jerome had learned to pilot a yacht.

The young man's terse answers gave way to lengthier ones as the river widened. "I've completed all the training for a captain's license from the Coast Guard, but I still need more sea time." The *Abyss* came into view. "You'll board on the swim platform aft. It has a ladder and a railing to hang on to. I'll give you a helping hand."

The platform, molded into the hull, spanned the width of the boat, which was about twenty feet, and added four feet to its length.

Once on it, Granddad pointed to the door between the twin staircases that led up to the main deck. "Where does that go?"

"To a storage area and the engine room," Jerome said.

As they climbed the four steps up to the main deck, Otto and Cheyenne came out of the saloon to greet them.

He beamed at them. "My wife has gone all out with decorations. You won't believe how different the saloon looks, Val."

He was right. Cheyenne had applied decorative static-cling film on the windows to mimic the leaded glass in the *Titanic*'s dining room. Without a view of the outdoors, the room felt smaller than it had five days ago. The hostess had set a beautiful table with a striking floral centerpiece. Bethany admired the *Titanic* replica dishes: white plates trimmed in cobalt blue decorated with gold filigree. Val noted that the four forks at each place wouldn't suffice. They'd have to wash and reuse two of them.

She hurried to the galley to unpack the coolers and get the food ready. The dinghy delay had eaten up the slack she'd built into the schedule. She was so busy she barely noticed the yacht motoring to the marina. She couldn't fail to notice the Warbecks' raised voices drifting up the staircase from the lower deck, though she couldn't tell what Otto and Cheyenne were saying. They'd just gone downstairs to dress for dinner. Their disagreement lasted less than a minute, or else they continued it in lower tones.

Shortly before seven, Val hurriedly filled a silver tray with bite-sized appetizers, her take on the *Titanic* menu's hors d'oeuvres. The salmon mousse atop cucumber rounds and the bruschetta with goat cheese and roasted red peppers looked colorful and tasty. She wondered if Otto's guests had arrived yet. If it weren't for the opaque film on the sliding glass door to the aft deck, she would have been able to see them as they climbed aboard. The hosts would then direct them to the upper deck, where Granddad was setting up the bar and Bethany stood ready to make s'mores.

Granddad opened the sliding door into the saloon. "The first bunch came aboard. A couple who look around fifty. They're gussied up like Otto and his wife, tux for him, gown for her. In his penguin suit, he looks like Cary Grant in *To Catch a Thief.*"

Val smiled. She'd seen that movie at least twice in the last year. Granddad had a collection of film classics from the video store he used to own, and he never tired of watching his favorite Hitchcock movies. "Did he bring Grace Kelly with him?"

"He brought his wife. Grace Kelly she ain't, but she has the tastes of a princess. She asked for champagne, the one thing I didn't have in the bar upstairs." Granddad took a bottle of bubbly from the fridge. "A sixtyish guy with a mustache also came aboard. He talks like he belongs in *Downton Abbey.* His wife was supposed to come, but she bowed out because of a migraine."

"So we'll have seven for dinner." Not a lot less work than eight.

Granddad wrapped the champagne in a towel and took it outside. A minute later Val left the saloon too. She carried her appetizer tray to the upper deck and was surprised to recognize the woman drinking champagne. Louisa Brown often stopped at Val's Cool Down Café at the athletic club. There, she replenished the calories she'd lost trotting on the treadmill and twisting in dance aerobics. Though fit, she verged on roly-poly. She stood barely over five feet tall.

"I didn't know you'd be here." Louisa popped a salmon-topped cucumber in her mouth.

"I'm catering tonight's dinner."

Louisa looked up at the tall man in a tux next to her. "This is my husband, Damian Brown. Damian's a lobbyist for the poultry industry. Val runs the café at the Bayport Racket and Fitness Club."

Damian flashed a smile, his teeth as white as his starched dress shirt. "Glad to meet you, Val. I'm looking forward to a wonderful dinner."

With his mild Southern drawl, he didn't sound like Cary Grant, and Val thought he looked more like George Clooney. Damian fit the mold of a handsome middle-aged man with dark hair touched by gray.

The older man with the British accent came over and introduced himself to the Browns as Homer Huxby, an antique dealer and *Titanic* enthusiast.

Cheyenne beckoned from the s'mores table on the other side of the deck. "We have a special treat over here to whet your appetite. Come on over, everyone."

Damian responded quickly and crossed the deck toward her, Louisa hot on his heels.

Val noted the contrast between her and Cheyenne. Otto's wife resembled a Greek goddess in a floor-length cream silk dress that skimmed her curves as it draped down from a low-cut neckline. Next to her, Louisa looked dowdy in her long gray tiered dress with beige lace insets at the bodice and cuffs. Her four-inch-wide purple satin belt with a rhinestone buckle added pizzazz, but the style didn't flatter a short woman. Val wondered if the dress was a leftover from the *Titanic* era. It might have survived because the moths had shunned it as too drab.

Val offered appetizers to Otto and the antique dealer. She then handed off the tray to her grandfather and went down to the galley to make up a cold dinner plate for Jerome. She filled the plate with canapés, poached salmon, asparagus vinaigrette, cheese, and grapes.

As she was leaving, she saw Otto on the deck outside the saloon, greeting the last two guests to come aboard. He introduced her to them. Stacy Turnstone, a slim, fiftyish woman, had come with her son, Trey, who looked to be in his early twenties. They both had dark blond hair pulled into a low ponytail, hers held with a small black velvet bow, his with a red rubber band—an unusual accessory with a tuxedo. He looked uncomfortable, touching behind his ear and rubbing the back of his neck. His mother, unlike Louisa, had made no effort to dress in *Titanic*-period clothes. She wore black palazzo pants and a silver sequined top.

Otto took the new arrivals to the upper deck. Val followed them and delivered the plate to Jerome at the controls. He thanked her profusely and said he'd eat it later.

Otto took her aside when she went back to the deck. "I need eight people at the table. Since one guest couldn't come, I asked Bethany to switch hats and serve as a guest." He peered at Val. "I can see you're not happy about that."

Commandeering her assistant wasn't the way to make her happy. "I counted on Bethany helping me in the galley during dinner."

"I paid for her to make s'mores, and she'll be finished with that once we sit down. I'll still pay her for the whole evening, of course. She said she'd sit at the table if that's acceptable to you."

Val fumed. He had no right to approach someone who worked for her before he cleared it with her. Why did he need eight at the table anyway? Val swallowed her annoyance and her question. She had no choice, as he certainly knew. "That's fine." She couldn't force herself to smile.

"Thank you. I'd like you and your grandfather to join us all in a champagne toast when we leave the dock."

A gesture to mollify her? She usually didn't drink alcohol when working, but she had two reasons to do it tonight: Otto wouldn't be happy if she turned down his peace offering, and she'd seen the champagne in the fridge. It was French and very expensive. She couldn't pass up a sip of it.

She picked up the platter of appetizers and looked around the deck. She'd expected the Warbecks and their guests to be chatting amiably in one or two circles by now. Instead, the group had broken into twosomes and loners, spaced out like pods on the open deck.

Otto and Homer stood near the railing on the port side, discussing auction prices for *Titanic* collectibles.

Louisa lingered near them, sipping champagne and staring—or was it glaring?—at her handsome husband, who was monopolizing Cheyenne. They sat on the built-in bench that ran along the back railing.

Trey and his mother stood on the starboard side of the yacht, talking to Bethany and sampling s'mores.

As Val approached the bench where Cheyenne and Damian were sitting, she saw that Trey had moved toward them, close enough to eavesdrop. Damian was talking about lobbying the state legislature to grant more permits for poultry farming. Val offered the tray to him and Cheyenne, who took the goat cheese bruschetta, bit into it, and gave her a thumbs-up.

Damian shook his head. "Thank you. I've been eating those cheese s'mores. Delicious." He turned back to Cheyenne. "It looks like we'll get some permits in spite of the efforts of the radical environmentalists to prevent it."

"We're not radical," Trey protested loudly. "We're protecting natural resources. Poultry farms are a leading cause of bay pollution."

Damian managed an indulgent smile. "Maybe that used to be the case, but we've come a long way in how we handle the waste. And the new farms will follow the latest guidelines."

Trey stabbed his index finger in the lobbyist's direction. "Those guidelines are too lax."

Val stepped back from the fray and stood next to Bethany, who held skewered marshmallows over the portable grill.

Stacy locked arms with her son. "Pollution isn't the only problem with poultry farms." She spoke slowly and calmly, in contrast to Trey's belligerent tone.

"Chickens are raised in cages so tiny that they can't move. It's cruel and immoral, and it should be illegal."

Bethany leaned toward Val and spoke softly. "Good thing you're not serving chicken tonight."

Louisa stormed across the deck. "My father has been in the poultry business for fifty years." She pointed to Stacy. "You want to outlaw a major business in this state and throw workers out of their jobs. You'll drive up the price of chickens so poor people can't afford them."

Val expected the host to defuse the conflict, but he merely watched it as though his guests were characters in a play.

Val whispered to Bethany, "Did you pick up any info on how the Warbecks know these guests?"

"I chatted with Stacy. She's Otto's ex-wife, and Trey is his former stepson."

Val shook her head in disbelief. "They must have had an unusually amicable divorce."

Cheyenne stood up and interrupted the chicken dispute. "Otto has an announcement to make about tonight's entertainment."

All eyes turned toward him.

"I planned to say this at the sail-away toast, but since Cheyenne jumped the gun"—he gave her a stony look—"I'll do it now. As you know, our dinner will re-create the last meal served on the *Titanic*. While we eat, we'll play a mystery game. You'll each assume the role of a *Titanic* passenger. Together we'll try to determine who's responsible for the death of young Annie Milner, who disappeared the night before the ship hit the iceberg. A thorough search revealed she was no longer on board."

Val saw her own surprise mirrored in the faces of Otto's guests.

The antique dealer fingered his handlebar mustache. "Did that really happen on the *Titanic*?"

Otto shrugged. "It could have. The big tragedy destroyed the records of any smaller ones that occurred on board. That said, tonight's scenario is indeed a fiction. You will not play a real person, but someone who resembles a *Titanic* passenger."

Trey sneered. "Are you playing a role too, or are you just the puppet master?"

Otto showed no annoyance, suggesting he was used to hostility from his former stepson. "I'll assume the role of Captain Smith. That's the name of the *Titanic*'s actual captain. I expect lively and even heated table talk, but it's all in good fun."

"Where did you get this game?" Louisa asked in her high-pitched voice.

"I adapted it from a *Titanic* mystery game I downloaded. You'll each play a role and act as witness, suspect, and detective. You'll have a script to follow with a few set lines, but otherwise you're free to accuse each other and defend yourself against accusations."

"That sounds ominous," Val whispered to Bethany. "A minute ago I was worried about a food fight at the table. Now I'm glad they won't have steak knives at their places."

"Relax, Val. I've played these mystery games before. The murder always happens before the game starts."

A chilly gust ruffled Val's hair. "Otto didn't say the girl was murdered."

"No, but I'll bet it turns out that way." Bethany put a mini round of Brie on a wooden skewer and held it over the flame. "This game is a brilliant way to keep the peace. One year, when my family was feuding before our Thanksgiving dinner, my mother took a murder mystery game from the closet. Instead of real arguments, we all had a great time getting into character, accusing each other of crimes, and defending ourselves."

Val shook her head. "Playing the game wasn't a spur-of-the-moment decision tonight. Otto planned it, like he did everything else about this dinner. The game was the reason he needed exactly eight people at the table." Val remembered what he'd said about the date, the place, and the guests aligning perfectly for his party. Why did he invite this odd assortment of guests? What game was he really playing?

Chapter 3

Val made another circuit of the deck with the tray of hors d'oeuvres and asked Otto's guests about food allergies and aversions.

"I'm a vegetarian," Trey told her.

"Then skip the soup course and ignore the meat in the fifth course. Is your mother also a vegetarian?"

"She eats everything except chicken."

Val continued her rounds and was relieved to learn that none of the other guests had special food requirements.

Cheyenne asked for their attention. "Would anyone like to see the rest of the boat? Otto can show you the bridge and tell you about the navigation gizmos. I'll give a tour of the other decks if you're interested."

Damian was interested in seeing the lower deck with Cheyenne. Louisa went with them. Otto led the others through the glass door to the bridge.

Val, Granddad, and Bethany headed for the bench vacated by Damian and Cheyenne.

Granddad sighed. "Feels good to get off my feet."

"Amen to that," Bethany said. "I expected sparks

tonight, but not about chickens. According to Cheyenne, she just met Otto's ex-wife for the first time and—get this—she only found out today that he'd invited Stacy."

Val gaped at her. "Otto wanted a perfect dinner party, so he invited wife one without clearing it with wife two? Go figure."

Bethany shrugged. "Cheyenne told me she didn't know any of the guests. They all knew Otto and no one else, except for the person they came with. Weird party."

"I knew it would be," Granddad said. "Is Otto the kid's father?"

Bethany shook her head. "Former stepfather. Otto insisted Trey wear a tux tonight, rented it for him, and had it delivered. I heard Trey say to his mother, *Are these suits always uncomfortable, or did Otto order double starch in my shirt?* He's not used to dressing up. He works for an environmental nonprofit and telecommutes most of the time."

"He's protesting the dress code with a ponytail held by a rubber band." Val checked her watch. Almost seven thirty. The sun wouldn't set for another ten minutes, but under thick clouds, darkness was coming on fast. "I'm going down to get the first courses ready. Dinner is scheduled to start in fifteen minutes."

She hurried down to the galley, warmed the consommé and made the garnish for it, snipping chives and slivering carrots. Then she made the mousseline sauce for the salmon.

Granddad came into the saloon. He left the hors d'oeuvre tray on the galley counter. "It's getting too cool up on the deck. Otto's moving the guests inside for the toast." He popped open two champagne bottles and poured generous amounts into eight glasses and a taste into two glasses. "These last two are for us."

They stood at the door to the deck and handed out the champagne as Otto shepherded his guests into the saloon.

When everyone was inside, he raised his glass. "Let's drink a toast to the victims and survivors of the *Titanic*."

"Hear, hear!" Homer Huxby called out. He raised his glass on high, the way the Statue of Liberty holds her torch.

Otto's lips barely touched the edge of his glass. He gestured toward the sofa and chairs. "Please sit down. Make yourselves comfortable."

Trey didn't move. He stood by the door to the deck, looking as if he wanted to bolt. The vibrations Val felt in the floor meant he'd lost his chance. The boat had pulled away from the marina. Otto remained standing, while his other guests found places to perch in the sitting area.

The champagne was as delicious as Val had anticipated. She and Granddad returned to the galley with their glasses to plate the cold salmon, the course after the soup. She glanced at Otto across the room.

He put his nearly full champagne glass on the coffee table. "I'd like to thank you for joining me and Cheyenne tonight for the *Titanic* dinner and mystery game. Here's how the game will work. You'll each get a booklet with a character sketch for your role and a script for the four scenes in our little drama. Your part in each scene consists of one question to ask someone and one answer you must give to a question you're asked."

"I'm glad to hear it's all written down and we don't have to ad lib," Louisa said. "I played a murder party game once, and I was terrible at it. Everyone was supposed to tell the truth. Only the designated murderer was allowed to lie. Someone accused me of being the murderer. Then the others jumped on the bandwagon. I wasn't the murderer, but I got flustered when everyone ganged up on me. So I said, *Okay, I confess. I'm the murderer.*"

Trey snickered. "Why did you say that?"

"They all wanted me to say it, and I wanted them off my back."

"You were coerced. That's how false confessions happen," Stacy said. "What was the result of your confession?"

Louisa looked sheepish. "I ruined the game, and everyone was annoyed with me."

Damian nodded. "Especially the guy who played the role of the murderer."

Otto took papers from the built-in cabinet in the saloon. "That can't happen in our game tonight. The character sketches and scripts don't identify who the culprit is."

Cheyenne frowned. "So the culprit doesn't know he or she did it? That's not very realistic."

Trey snorted. "Nothing about this whole night is realistic."

Otto didn't react to the barb. "I'd hate to deprive the guilty party of the chance to solve the mystery along with the rest of us. I'm sure many of you would enjoy playing detective. Once we've gone through all four scenes, you'll have all the information you need to identify the culprit. You'll announce who you think is guilty. Then I'll open the envelope containing the solution." He crossed the room and climbed up the two steps to the dining area. "The booklets will also serve as place cards. I'll put them on the table while you finish your champagne."

When he'd done that, he stopped to talk to Val and Granddad in the galley. "I don't want to leave you two out of the fun, so I have a small mystery for you to solve too. I challenge you to find the envelope with the solution. I hid it in this room. Where would you look for the conclusion to a *Titanic* mystery?"

When Otto rejoined his guests in the sitting area, Granddad said in an undertone, "It should be easy enough to find the envelope. It's not that big a place." He peered into a cabinet in the galley.

"There are also built-in cabinets near the sofa and chairs, Granddad. We won't have much time to search them while we're serving dinner." Val went around the counter between the galley and the dining area.

Each place at the table now had a small pen and a booklet, one-quarter of the size of letter paper, with an image of the *Titanic* on the cover. Val checked the seating arrangement. Otto would sit at one end of the table, with Louisa on his right and Damian on his left. Cheyenne was at the other end, with antique dealer Homer on one side and Bethany on the other. Trey and Stacy had the middle seats.

Once the guests were at the table, Val and Granddad served the soup.

"While you enjoy the soup," Otto said, "please familiarize yourself with your character's background and your question and answer for the first scene, but don't read any further. I'll tell you when to turn the page to the next scene. From now on, we are all dining at the captain's table on the *Titanic*."

Busy preparing the upcoming course, Val caught only bits of the table talk. When Otto asked his guests to introduce themselves in their *Titanic* personas, Bethany jumped into her role as a retired governess hired to chaperone young Annie back to America. Bethany sniffed and sighed, distraught that her good name would be ruined because the headstrong girl had vanished.

Later, it came out that the chaperone did not have a good name to ruin. Damian said she'd lost her former job for tippling. She'd been drinking heavily since boarding the ship. Bethany denied it and accused him of marrying for money and seducing young girls. She'd seen him plying Annie with drinks and drugs the first night at sea.

Val glanced at the table. Damian wore a game face, amused and detached. Louisa, whose back was to Val, fidgeted in her chair and rushed to her husband's defense. As Val focused on preparing the next courses, she heard insinuations of blackmail, jewel theft, and fraud coming from the table. Everyone protested the veiled allegations against them with a vehemence that surprised Val, almost as if they'd taken them personally. She wondered what was left for the upcoming two scenes. Possibly an accusation of murder, as Bethany had predicted.

The turmoil at the table mirrored the increased motion of the boat, from rocking to rolling.

Otto pushed his seat back from the table. "In the next scene we'll find out where everyone was when Annie disappeared. I suggest we take a break now so you can stretch and read the next section of your booklets." He stood up.

So did Cheyenne. She went up to him. "I hope you'll get the yacht back to calm water."

"We've hit a squall. I'll do what I can." He leaned toward her, spoke into her ear, and left the saloon.

She went over to the entertainment cabinet and cut off the mix of classical and ragtime music. It had played quietly in the background during dinner. The silence in the room didn't last long. Rap music blasted from the speaker, similar to what Val had heard coming from the aerobic dance class at the club. Cheyenne turned up the volume and moved with the beat, dancing in place. The music made conversation difficult, and maybe that was its point. She might have had her fill of small talk with guests she'd just met.

As Granddad took the plates from the previous course off the table, Val worried that he'd lose his balance with the yacht rolling. "Why don't you sit down and let me clear the table?"

He cupped his hand around one ear.

She shouted over the music, repeating what she'd said.

"I got better sea legs than you do," he yelled back.

But her bones wouldn't break as easily. She took the roast from the oven. It could sit for ten minutes before Granddad sliced it. He loaded the dishwasher with the plates he'd cleared, while she washed the used forks and put them on the table for the next course.

The guests took turns going out the sliding door, probably to visit the head. Trey and then his mother left. Cheyenne lowered the music long enough to announce that there was a guest head on the lower deck, nicer than the one on the aft deck. Louisa passed by the galley and went down the curved staircase to the deck below. When Bethany asked if she could help in the galley, Val could tell that the boat's motion was bothering her friend and suggested she sit down.

Homer, still at the table, looked ashen. Val didn't feel great either. The stuffiness in the room bothered her more than the motion, and her head pounded in time with the music.

As Louisa came up and Homer went down the stairs, Val coaxed Granddad to take a break. He went to the sitting area and took the chair near the sliding door. Louisa sat on the sofa next to her husband.

Val added cream to the carrots and stirred constantly until it thickened. As she was taking the potatoes out of the oven, someone turned down the music. Thank goodness. She glanced toward the sitting area and noticed Cheyenne had left.

Val tested the potatoes. Perfect. Any more time in the oven and they'd turn mealy. It was past time to slice the roast, but she was reluctant to do it until Otto came back. Where was he anyway? When she looked around the saloon, she saw that everyone had returned except Trey and the host.

Trey flung open the sliding door and burst into the room, his face bone white. "Something's wrong with Jerome. He's zonked out. Where's Otto?"

Cheyenne frowned, perplexed. "You mean he's not on the bridge?"

Trey shook his head. "Does anyone know how to pilot this yacht?"

Chapter 4

Cheyenne stood up and wrung her hands. "Otto can pilot. Where is he? We have to find him."

"He isn't on this deck or the one above. And we need a pilot now," Trey shouted.

The boat lurched, underscoring his message.

Granddad stepped forward. "I have navigation experience. I'll go up to the bridge and take a look."

Val gaped at him. *What navigation experience?* If it was anything like the cooking expertise he claimed, they were doomed. "Don't go up there, Granddad. The water's too choppy for you to take the stairs."

Cheyenne went over to a door between the dining and sitting areas that Val had assumed opened to a closet. "There's a built-in ladder in here. It goes to a hatch on the upper deck. Otto said it's for when the weather is really bad. We've always used the outside stairs." She opened the door to the vertical ladder.

Val kept Granddad off ladders even when they were on solid ground. With the motion of the boat, he could easily fall off.

He peered at the ladder. "I'll take my chances

outside. Did you call the Coast Guard, son?" When Trey shook his head, Granddad continued, "A Mayday call is our first mission." He left the saloon with Trey.

"Where could Otto have gone?" Cheyenne wailed. "Did any of you see him on the deck when you went out there?"

Head shakes all around.

Cheyenne paced from one side of the saloon to the other. "Maybe Trey didn't check the side decks for Otto. He must be out there somewhere." She loomed over Stacy. "Are you sure you didn't see Otto? You left the saloon right after he did."

Stacy took a moment to answer. "I left a minute or two later. I might have caught a glimpse of him when I first went out." She stood up. "I'll look for Otto on all the decks and go to the bridge to see what's going on there. Now where are the life vests?"

Cheyenne gasped. "Life vests? Aren't you over-reacting?"

"No. I'm going on deck with the boat bucking like a bronco. If a wave hits us sideways when I'm on the stairs, I could fall off."

Cheyenne removed the cushions from one end of the sofa, dropped them on the floor, and lifted the seat on which they'd rested. "The life jackets are stored here for anyone who wants to wear one."

Louisa stood up, clutching her middle. "I don't feel well." She rushed past the galley and went down the staircase to the lower deck.

Stacy donned a bright orange life jacket, tested the whistle, and exited to the deck.

Bethany whispered to Val, "That sounded like the whistle Rose used in the *Titanic* movie after the ship went under."

Val couldn't distinguish one whistle from another, but maybe Bethany, with her singing background, would recognize a *Titanic*-pitched whistle. Otto would love the connection she'd just made.

Hmm. If he wanted to give his guests the full flavor of the *Titanic*'s last night at sea, not just the last dinner, he'd strike fear into them. Maybe that's what he'd done. Val wouldn't put it past him to hide somewhere on the yacht and talk Jerome into acting zonked. Where would he hide? On the lower deck, perhaps. But he hadn't taken the indoor stairway down.

Val pointed to it. "Is there another way to the lower deck besides those stairs, Cheyenne?"

Otto's wife stared at her for a moment as if confused by the question. "That's the only staircase, but . . . I'll go to the lower deck to check if he's there."

Val followed her down the stairs.

"I'll look in the master stateroom and head," Cheyenne said. "You try the other two staterooms." She went into the room at the front of the boat.

As the boat rocked, Val steadied herself by holding on to the wall in the narrow corridor. She opened the doors on either side of the hall. No one in the bunkroom or the larger stateroom. Through the closed door to the head, she could hear the sounds of Louisa being sick to her stomach. How many of Otto's guests were having a taste of seasickness tonight?

Cheyenne came out of the master stateroom. "He's not there."

Val pointed to doorways in the narrow corridor between the two guest staterooms. "What's behind those doors?"

"A washer and dryer on the left. Straight ahead is

the engine room. There's an outside door on the other end that opens to the swim platform."

Ah. A secret passage that Otto might have taken. Worth a look. "Let's check it out, Cheyenne. Maybe Otto's working on an engine problem."

"I'm sure he would have told us, but okay." Cheyenne opened the door and called out, "Otto? Are you in there?" Silence. She shrugged. "I guess not."

"He might have gotten hurt while trying to fix something." They should make sure he wasn't there, either injured or hidden. But that didn't cover all the possibilities. He could also be dead in the engine room.

Cheyenne rubbed her hands over her silk dress as if trying to wipe off dirt. "Would you look for him there? I'm not feeling well." She rushed into the master stateroom.

Val paused before stepping into the engine room, her nerves on edge. If Otto jumped out at her, she'd give him a piece of her mind, but what if she found him unconscious or dead? Twice in the last year she'd stumbled on a body. She doubted it would be easier the third time.

She took a deep breath, went through the narrow doorway, and felt for a light switch on the wall. She flipped it on. No worry about grease or grime in this engine room. The machinery looked new, or at least recently scrubbed, and it occupied most of the floor space. Pipes and ducts went into and out of the engines and tanks in the room. Valves and meters lined the walls.

Not much space to hide or even to move. She felt cramped under the low ceiling and amid the huge machinery. Claustrophobia threatened her as she inched

along the narrow aisle between two engines. She felt
her heart thumping. She opened a heavy door in
the far wall and entered the storage room. Though
smaller than the engine room, it had more open
space. She breathed easier and crossed the room to
the door that must lead to the swim platform. She
opened it wide enough to get rained on and to see
that no one was out there. Then she closed it and retraced her steps.

When she emerged at the other end, Cheyenne was
waiting for her in the corridor.

Had she avoided going into the engine room because she'd really felt sick? Or because she couldn't
face searching for her older husband, fearing she'd
find him dead?

"Otto wasn't in the engine room," Val said. "Is
Louisa still down here?" If so, someone should check
on her too.

"She went upstairs a minute ago."

Back on the main deck, Cheyenne collapsed into
one of the armchairs.

Val went over to Bethany, who sat at the table, her
face pasty. "I'm sorry I got you into this."

Taking this gig had been a mistake, no matter how
much money Otto had offered her. Granddad had
been right about that.

Bethany pointed to the dazed Homer, who sat silent
and rigid at the dining table. "He looks like he could
use a shot of brandy."

Val went to the bar across the room, poured a
brandy for Homer, and brought it to him.

The brandy revived him enough that he voiced his
fears instead of holding them in. "I shouldn't have
come tonight, but I wanted to experience the elegant

last dinner on the *Titanic*. What irony if this dinner also ended with a disaster. If anything happens to me, I don't know what my wife will do. She needs me."

"I'm sure she does," Val said, "and you'll be fine."

Stacy stumbled into the saloon as the boat pitched, her hair wet. "It's pouring rain now. No sign of Otto." She snapped off her life vest and reported that Granddad and Trey had reached the Coast Guard. "A response boat is coming to escort us back to the marina, and the Coast Guard will search for Otto."

Cheyenne pressed her hands together as if praying. "Thank God. There's some hope."

The others in the saloon avoided looking at her. Not enough hope to go around. How long could Otto tread water, and what were the chances they'd find him in the dark? They'd better do it soon. The Chesapeake Bay was far warmer than the North Atlantic, but hypothermia would set in here too, just more slowly than it had for the *Titanic* passengers.

Stacy said, "Trey said the radar shows we're getting out of the squall. It should be calmer before long."

Maybe it was Val's imagination, but she already felt as if the yacht was rolling and pitching less than it had earlier. She checked her watch. Just past nine. Hard to believe that barely half an hour had gone by since the squall hit.

The silence in the room was more deafening than the exercise music had been. With the host missing, returning to the table for the rest of the gala *Titanic* dinner probably had little appeal, especially for those feeling seasick. Yet Val was sure food would do them all good, if they could manage to eat. She decided to set out the main course as a buffet. Tricky to reheat the beef without overcooking it. It was still warm, so she'd serve it that way. She reheated the vegetables, found serving bowls for them, and put the food on the counter that divided the galley from the dining area. She then collected the booklets from the table and stuffed them into a drawer in the galley.

Two minutes after she invited the guests to the buffet, Stacy started the procession to the table. Damian and Louisa followed her. Cheyenne joined them at the table. She and Bethany talked quietly instead of eating. Homer had no interest in food either.

Val cleaned up the galley and pondered what could have happened to Otto. He must have gone overboard, but how? He might have had a heart attack, fallen from the stairs, and pitched into the water.

Or one of this odd assortment of guests might have pushed him.

Under the guise of a mystery game, Otto had accused them of crimes and misdemeanors. Their vehement denials suggested his accusations might have hit home. Could his fiction about a *Titanic* passenger who went overboard have triggered a similar event tonight?

Chapter 5

Val and Bethany were standing on the aft deck with Otto's wife and guests when the boat docked. Doubtless, they all wanted to get off as soon as possible, but they weren't allowed to leave yet. An emergency medical team rushed aboard to assess Jerome's condition. Coast Guard officers and Bayport policemen also met the boat. Val knew the rookie Officer Wade, but was surprised that Chief Earl Yardley, Granddad's good friend, wasn't there.

Cheyenne greeted the first Coast Guard officer who boarded the boat and said she was the wife of the missing man. Chief Petty Officer Campbell introduced himself and sent everyone except her back inside the saloon. Five minutes later, he came into the saloon with her and Petty Officer Lopez. Another officer had gone to the upper deck, where Granddad, Trey, and Jerome remained.

The lanky Officer Campbell announced that a search-and-rescue mission was under way for Otto. "We know the time and the location of the *Abyss* when we received the Mayday call. We'd like to know exactly when Mr. Warbeck was last seen on the boat so we can focus our search in the right area."

Damian spoke up. "Last I saw of him was when he left the table, but I don't know what time that was."

"I do," Val said. "He left a minute or two before eight thirty." She'd been watching the time to follow Otto's schedule for serving the courses.

Cheyenne, seated next to Bethany on the long side of the L-shaped sofa, pointed at Otto's ex-wife, on the other end of the sofa. "You saw him after that."

Stacy tilted her head, as if mulling alternative responses. "I went outside a few minutes after Otto did. I glimpsed the lower legs of a man in black trousers at the top of the stairs to the upper deck. I took him to be Otto, but it could have been Trey, or even Jerome."

Cheyenne frowned. "Earlier you sounded more positive that you saw Otto."

"I have to be more precise because I'm giving information to the Coast Guard now, not speaking casually."

"Did anyone see him after that?" Officer Campbell said.

Heads shook in answer, but no one spoke.

The officer asked about Otto's behavior and condition that evening. Had he appeared ill? Drunk much alcohol? Shown signs of being under the influence of any substance, including prescription drugs? No one responded except Cheyenne. She defended her husband against any suggestion that he drank to excess or misused drugs.

The officer asked if any of them had interacted with Jerome after coming aboard the yacht. Stacy and Homer had seen him when Otto gave them a tour of the navigation area, but no one had exchanged more than a few words with him. Though not friendly, he'd come across as sober and serious.

Petty Officer Lopez went around the room, writing down names and contact information. The sitting area was compact enough that Val could hear what was said. The guests all gave Bayport addresses, except for Homer from Annapolis and Stacy from a Maryland suburb of Washington, D.C. She was spending the weekend in Bayport, where her son was house-sitting. Val made a mental note of the three Bayport addresses.

The officer asked Cheyenne to remain when he dismissed the others. No one was allowed to take anything off the yacht except personal items. They wouldn't even let Val pack up the leftover food. Though Granddad and Trey joined the group getting off the yacht, Jerome remained on board with the officers.

On the way home Granddad reported that Jerome had recovered enough to talk to the Coast Guard, but he had no memory of the squall. "Otto will surface one of these days. I don't expect the Coast Guard helicopter will locate him while he's still afloat."

Bethany sighed in the back seat. "Poor Cheyenne. She's in denial. She can't understand how Otto could have fallen off the yacht. He had a lot of experience on the water."

"Folks with experience sometimes take more chances," Granddad said. "They think they know it all. Otto was a know-it-all if I ever saw one."

"Did he drink much at the table?" Val said.

Granddad shook his head. "He asked me to keep everyone's wineglass full. I never had to top off his or Trey's. They didn't take more than a sip."

Bethany leaned toward the front seat. "Otto was

engrossed in his mystery game, watching everyone at the table as if they were real suspects. He even made notes."

"In his script booklet?" Val said.

"I couldn't see what he was writing on. His hands were just below the tabletop, like a schoolboy who doesn't want the kid next to him copying the answer."

"I jot things down so I won't forget them," Granddad said. "Otto probably made a note to call his broker on Monday or something like that."

Val pulled up at the curb in front of Bethany's house. "Thank you for coming along tonight. You were a big help to me—and to Cheyenne when she needed support."

"I feel sorry for her. I'll call her tomorrow to see how she's doing." Bethany opened the back door. "Sorry this didn't turn out the way it was supposed to, especially for Otto. I'll help the next time you cater a *Titanic* dinner, but only if it's on land."

"There won't be a next time," Val said as Bethany climbed out.

"There shouldn't have been a *this* time," Granddad grumbled.

Once Bethany went inside her house, Val pulled away and made a U-turn. "Do you have any idea what was wrong with Jerome?"

"Nope. He was out cold, but breathing fine. We kept trying to shake him awake. He started to respond about fifteen minutes before we docked. He wouldn't take the controls, because he felt funny, but he gave us navigation advice."

"Did you see any alcohol or smell it on him?"

"No, but he'll be tested for drugs. You get in trouble with the Coast Guard for operating a vessel while impaired—big trouble if someone gets hurt because of it."

Val turned onto Main Street. "It doesn't make sense for him to drink or take drugs if he wants to be a licensed captain. He must have had a medical problem."

"Addicts can't control when they use, but he didn't come across as an addict."

"Otto didn't think so either, or he wouldn't have trusted him at the helm."

"I didn't trust that other young fella at all. Surly at the table, like your brother when he was a teenager. I didn't expect Trey would be much help, but he surprised me. He figured out how to read the radar, adjust the autopilot, and get away from the squall. He knew a lot about the controls, but he was nervous about putting his hands on anything."

Val pulled into their driveway. "I couldn't figure out why he came to the dinner. Maybe the yacht was the attraction."

"Could be. When Otto gave a tour of the bridge, Trey stayed the longest. He must have picked up a few pointers from Jerome." Granddad climbed out of the car and went in the side door to the house. "I'm beat. Ready to turn in."

"Me too. Thanks for helping tonight, Granddad."

Val trudged upstairs and got ready for bed, expecting to lie awake for hours. But preparing for tonight's dinner, standing on her feet most of the day, and dealing with the stress of Otto's disappearance had left her exhausted. Her eyes were closing as she brushed her teeth. She fell into bed and slept soundly.

* * *

Val had forgotten to set her alarm. She arrived at the Bayport Racket and Fitness Club only twenty minutes before she had to open the café. Fortunately, she'd recently cut down on her Sunday hours, opening an hour later and leaving an hour earlier than on weekdays. The leftovers from Saturday included bread pudding and quiche—something to offer customers until the baked ham-and-cheese sandwich with béchamel sauce was ready.

She was busy for the first hour, preparing the food for the rest of the morning and serving the club members who exercised early. Not as many showed up on Sundays as on weekdays, but enough came so that she didn't have time to check for news about the search for Otto. When she had a free moment, she took out her phone and searched online for information. Nothing new on Otto. In this case, no news was bad news.

She looked up to see Gunnar striding into the café. A smile lit up his face and brightened her mood. With his large features and square jaw, he wasn't conventionally handsome, but a good build, a resonant voice, and a megawatt smile put him in the category of attractive, at least to her.

"Gunnar! I didn't expect you this morning. I thought you'd be poring over income tax forms."

"Almost done with the last two. I've been spending too much time in front of a computer, so I came here early to work out." He sat on a stool at the eating bar. "How did your dinner go last night?"

She poured him coffee. "The food was good. Not much else was."

"You're only responsible for the food. Speaking of food, got anything special for breakfast today?"

"Muffins, bagels with toppings, baked ham and cheese." As she expected, he chose the last item. Raised in the American heartland, he was partial to meat, potatoes, eggs, and cheese.

"While I was driving here, I heard on the radio that someone fell off a yacht. That wasn't—" He broke off as she nodded. "Tell me about it."

She put the baked ham and cheese in front of him, went around the counter, and sat next to him.

While he ate his breakfast, she gave him the highlights of the evening and the details of Otto's disappearance from his own party. "I have a bad feeling that he might not have fallen into the bay by accident."

Gunnar rolled his eyes. "I know the source of your bad feeling. You haven't had a murder to solve for three months. Your sleuthing muscles aren't getting regular exercise."

"They're gearing up now. The dinner and mystery game were bizarre. The host invited an odd collection of guests, made captives of them by taking them out on a yacht, and then demanded they sing for their supper. He forced them to do dramatic readings of accusations that sounded like poison-pen letters."

"Mystery guessing games always work that way."

"But they rarely end the way that one did." She climbed off the stool. "Excuse me, I need to wait on the two men who just came in."

She took their orders and went around the counter to the food prep area to toast bagels. After delivering their food, she sat down next to Gunnar again.

"I have some news too," he said. "Mrs. Z is coming back to Bayport."

His landlady. "Is she selling the place?" Maybe Gunnar

would buy it. Then he could move in with all of his possessions, instead of storing them, using Mrs. Z's furniture, and continuing with a month-to-month lease.

"She doesn't have a quick exit planned. She wants to go through her things, not rush into a move."

"But it's good news for you. Spring is usually the best time to find a house. When you came here last summer, you didn't have much to choose from."

"You found me an ideal place to rent, and I'm glad I didn't buy last summer."

Why was he glad he hadn't bought anything? Val waited for him to elaborate, but he didn't. "I can put out the word that you're in the market."

He ran his fingers through his thick, dark hair. "Hold off on that. I'm looking into some options."

Houses he'd already seen here and liked? Before she had a chance to ask about his options, two groups came into the café. She jumped down from the stool. "Gotta see to these customers. I'll be right back."

"My customers' tax returns are waiting for me." He stood up. "How about coming over for dinner tomorrow evening? We can celebrate the end of income tax season."

"I'll bring champagne." She looked forward to spending more time with him. The bulk of his accounting work for the year was done, and for a change, he wasn't involved in the Treadwell Players' upcoming production, though he'd auditioned for a role in it.

As Val was leaving the café at a quarter after one, a friend and tennis teammate, Althea Johnson, came in. She wore a royal blue pantsuit, low-heeled shoes, and a troubled expression. Tall and graceful, she resembled her namesake, tennis champion Althea Gibson.

Instead of carrying an athletic bag, as she often did when she came to the club, she toted her hefty lawyer's briefcase. "I know you've closed up for the day, Val. Do you have time to talk?"

"Sure. You want to sit on the veranda by the tennis courts?"

"Let's go over there instead." Althea pointed to the table in the corner. "More privacy."

Val followed her to the table, speculating that her friend might bring up a problem with their tennis team. When they sat down across from each other, Val noticed the deep furrows between Althea's brows. On the tennis court she could pass for a woman in her forties, ten years younger than she really was, but not today.

She tapped the edge of the table as if she were playing an agitated tune on a keyboard. "I heard what happened on the yacht last night. I'd like your take on it. Jerome is my nephew."

Ah. Val saw the family resemblance. Though Althea's skin was a couple of shades darker than Jerome's, she had the same body type and eyes. "I didn't realize you were related to him or I would have called you last night. How is he doing today?"

"On top of not feeling well, he's panicking, afraid that the drug test the Coast Guard ordered will come back positive and he'll be blamed for an accidental drowning." Althea took off her tortoiseshell glasses and massaged her forehead. "Jerome got in trouble for drugs when he was a teenager. That convinced him to go clean. He said you made him a dinner plate. Could someone have slipped drugs into his food?"

"Not before I brought it to him."

"He told me he set it aside to eat later. The plate was there when the guests visited the bridge. They crowded around him, asking questions about the equipment. He's convinced one of them tampered with his food or his drink then."

Val remembered the layout at the helm. Three well-cushioned pilot chairs faced big windows on the front and sides. They provided a view in all directions except aft. The wheel was in front of the middle chair, where Jerome had sat. People standing on either side of him or looking over his shoulder would have blocked his view of the surfaces where he might have left a plate of food. "I suppose somebody could have tampered with his food without anyone else noticing. When did he eat it?"

"After the guests went down to the other deck for dinner. He remembers eating, piloting the yacht from the river to the bay, and feeling sleepy. He saw a storm on the radar and tried to steer out of it. That's the last thing he recalls clearly. His next memory is of your grandfather and another passenger with him at the helm, trying to get the boat back to the marina."

"Why would someone drug the pilot of a boat they're on?"

"I asked Jerome that, but he couldn't explain it. Not only does he have memory gaps, he's too upset to think clearly about anything that happened last night. He said the party had something to do with the *Titanic*." Althea took a pen and a leather-bound notebook from her briefcase. Then she donned her glasses. "I'm hoping you can give me a rundown on who was there."

Val eyed the notebook, embossed with the words *Althea Johnson Family Law*, and felt as if she'd just been called as a witness in a deposition. "Otto Warbeck, a retired maritime lawyer and *Titanic* collector, hired me to re-create the final dinner the passengers ate on that ship. Granddad and Bethany were there to help me."

"Who came to the dinner?"

"Otto's much-younger wife, Cheyenne, and an odd assortment of guests. You may have run into one of them here at the club—Louisa Brown."

"I don't recognize the name. Describe her."

"She's fiftyish, about five feet tall, on the plain side, and fierce in her defense of chicken farmers. Her tall and handsome husband, Damian, is a poultry industry lobbyist."

The vegetarian attorney groaned. "The poultry lobby has had some recent legislative successes. Are the Browns old friends of the Warbecks?"

"New friends. Otto and Damian met at the Protect the Bay Barbecue a few weeks ago. Otto also invited old friends, or possibly old enemies. His ex-wife Stacy came with her twentysomething son, Trey. He was Otto's stepson. She's a fit fifty, an animal rights advocate. I'm guessing she and Otto divorced several years ago. She was polite to him, unlike Trey. He bordered on rude."

"How did the current wife get along with the ex-wife?"

"They avoided each other. Now we come to the oldest guest, Homer Huxby, a British guy whose wife was smart enough to have a migraine and stay home. He owns an antique shop in Annapolis and, like Otto, is an expert on *Titanic* memorabilia." Val searched her mind for anything else Althea might find helpful. "The hosts and most of the guests were dressed to kill: tuxedos for the men, gowns or dressy pants for the ladies. Hard to imagine any of them carrying drugs around, much less having a reason to drug Jerome."

Althea folded her arms. "I can think of two reasons. The first is prejudice. Someone didn't like the cut of Jerome's jib—or rather, the color of his skin."

Though racism as a motive hadn't occurred to Val, she couldn't rule it out. "I don't know Otto's guests well enough to say if any of them think like that. What would a racist gain by knocking the pilot out of commission?"

Althea looked up from her notebook. "What do anti-Semites gain by vandalizing Jewish cemeteries? Prejudice isn't rational. Inside the racist mind, the world is a better place with one less black man working in a white man's job."

Chalk up a win for the racist. If Jerome were found guilty of taking drugs while at the helm of a yacht worth millions, he'd never pilot a boat like that again. "Okay. Besides racism, what other reason could explain drugging Jerome?"

"One of the guests really wanted to ruin that party."

Val immediately thought of Trey. He'd carried his resentment of Otto on board with him. She could believe he'd drug Jerome to disrupt the party. Might he have gone a step further and pushed Otto overboard?

Val's phone chimed on the counter, where she'd left it. She jumped up to answer it before her voice mail kicked in.

Granddad sounded excited. "Drive straight to the marina."

"Why? Is this about what happened on the yacht last night?"

"Yes. Gotta go. I need to get there early." He hung up.

Val grabbed her shoulder bag. "Something's up at the marina. To do with the yacht. Granddad said to hurry."

She and Althea dashed out of the café.

Chapter 6

Val parked in the marina lot. She had to speed-walk toward the dock to keep up with Althea's long strides. "My grandfather didn't say where to meet him, but I bet we'll find him near where the yacht is docked."

They walked past a van from the Salisbury, Maryland, TV station. A few dozen people gathered in a semicircle near the *Abyss*. Its side was parallel to the dock.

Eight inches taller than Val, Althea craned her neck to see over the onlookers. "I see a cameraman and a woman with a microphone. Try to get closer. I have a good enough view from back here."

Val wormed her way into the group and ended up behind a man with two preschoolers demanding ice cream. When he gave in to their whining, Val took his place in the first row of spectators. A strong breeze carrying the scent of the bay ruffled her hair.

In front of the *Abyss*, a chubby cameraman conferred with a petite, baby-faced blonde wearing four-inch heels. Val's feet ached just looking at those shoes. Fortunately, her job managing a café in a fitness club allowed her to wear athletic shoes to work. She spotted Granddad in his stylish black shirt and pants, standing a few feet from the reporter. Val had an attack of déjà vu. Last summer an attractive woman with a microphone had left him speechless by telling him about a man's death. Would he get flustered again in front of a camera? He waved to Val, pointed to himself, and mouthed, *How do I look?* She gave him a thumbs-up.

The reporter faced the camera. "I'm Sissy Reynolds at the Bayport marina. Prominent maritime lawyer Otto Warbeck disappeared from his yacht, caught last night in a sudden squall on the bay. Search operations for him continue. Behind me is Mr. Warbeck's yacht, the *Abyss*, where he was hosting a dinner party that ended in tragedy. We have located the passenger who steered the yacht back to the marina under difficult conditions."

If the station had nothing exciting to put on the evening news, they'd settle for an interview with Granddad. But news about Otto's fate would bump the interview.

The reporter stepped toward Granddad, the camera following her movement. "Don Myer, the Codger Cook recipe columnist for the *Treadwell Gazette*, a celebrity in the small town of Bayport, was recognized as he disembarked from the yacht last night. We understand you were the hero of the evening."

Who had told the reporter that? Val hoped Granddad wouldn't succumb to flattery and crow about his achievement.

He spoke into the microphone. "My most heroic act was calling the Coast Guard." As some in the crowd laughed, he beamed.

A gust blew the reporter's long, blond hair into her face. She tucked it behind her ear. "You brought the yacht back to the marina in emergency conditions. I think you're being modest."

"No one else has ever accused me of that," he quipped, drawing more laugher. "The squall passed quickly. Another passenger and I managed to set the yacht on course to the marina."

"Are you a licensed captain?"

"No, but I've been on a lot of boats. I've lived all my life near the Chesapeake."

"Wasn't there a crew member aboard who could handle the yacht?"

Val realized now what the reporter wanted from Granddad—dirt on the man at the helm. Had she heard rumors about Jerome?

Granddad took a moment to clear his throat. "Yes. He wasn't feeling well."

"What was wrong with him?"

"I'm not a doctor. I couldn't say."

"What were his symptoms?" the reporter persisted.

"When I was on the bridge, I focused on getting the boat to shore. Nothing else mattered to me."

Val was amazed at how much better he was handling this interview than the one he'd had last summer. He was debunking the notion that an old dog couldn't learn new tricks.

"Can you tell us the crew member's name?" the reporter said.

"Learning the names of everyone on board wasn't in my job description."

"Your job description? I thought you were Mr. Warbeck's guest."

Kudos to Granddad for diverting the reporter's

attention from Jerome. The longer the young man could avoid standing in front of a camera, the better.

"I wasn't a guest. I was on the yacht to help my grand-daughter, Val Deniston. She was catering a ten-course dinner for eight people."

"Did you know any of the guests?" When Granddad shook his head, the reporter continued, *"Eight people.* Even a younger person than you would have trouble remembering that many names. No wonder you forgot the crewman's name." She waited to see if Granddad would contradict her.

Val caught Granddad's eye and shook her head, encouraging him to ignore the bait the reporter had dangled in front of him.

He shrugged. "It was a one-night gig. I had no reason to pay attention to anyone's name."

Bravo, Granddad. The Coast Guard apparently hadn't revealed the names of those on the yacht. One or more of Otto's guests might come forward and identify the others before long, but for now they could enjoy the calm before the media storm.

The young reporter said, "Sources told us that most of the people getting off the yacht last night were wearing tuxedos and formal dresses. Was the dinner to celebrate a special occasion?"

"A special occasion for Mr. Warbeck as a *Titanic* collector. He wanted to commemorate the night the unsinkable ship sank. He hired my granddaughter to put on the same spread the first-class passengers ate for their last dinner."

Val heard gasps and murmurs from the onlookers.

He continued, "Val and I made a meal to remember."

The reporter said nothing for two seconds. She was

probably deciding whether to explore this lifestyle topic or give up on Granddad to pursue hard news.

She took two steps away from him and faced the camera squarely. "A man threw a party on his yacht to commemorate a disaster at sea. How ironic that his party ended with him missing, presumed drowned." She segued into a sign-off.

When the cameraman stopped recording, Val gave Granddad two thumbs up and scooted back through the group of spectators. She would wait until the reporter left before talking to him. Otherwise, she might end up in front of a camera herself.

She waved to the people she knew among the spectators—the woman who ran the Then and Now secondhand shop and the bartender at the Bugeye Tavern—but she didn't stop to talk to them, because Althea was waiting for her.

"Your grandfather did a good job," she said when Val joined her. "I'm grateful he didn't give out Jerome's name."

"I'll tell him you said that. Let me know if I can do anything to help Jerome."

"Warbeck's disappearance and Jerome's drugging are fishy, if you'll forgive the pun. Use your brains to find out the truth. And your influence." Althea cocked her head toward a bear of a man in his fifties looking at the *Abyss* as intently as if he were planning to buy it.

Bayport Police Chief Earl Yardley wore aviator glasses and a gray Orioles baseball cap, partially hiding his face. A navy windbreaker covered his broad shoulders and barrel chest.

"My grandfather has more influence there than I do," Val said, "but I'll try."

As Althea headed to the parking lot, Val approached the chief. Earlier this month, he and Granddad had gone as usual to the Orioles' opening day game at Camden Yards, a tradition they'd started decades ago, when the chief was a teenager. After the chief's father died, Granddad had served as a substitute dad, cheering young Earl's efforts on the school baseball team.

The chief greeted her. "Hey, Val. I was out of town yesterday when I got a call about the yacht. Just drove back to Bayport and came to look at it."

"Did you know Granddad and I were on it?"

"I heard. Didn't expect to see him giving an interview. I'd like to talk to both of you when he breaks free of his fan club."

Val glanced at Granddad. The TV crew had left. He was nodding like a dazed man while two older women talked to him. "He probably wouldn't mind a little help breaking free." She called out to him and beckoned him to join her.

He hurried over, greeted the chief, and said, "Thanks for saving me from those two ladies. They were chewing my ear off." He pointed to the *Abyss*. "What do you think, Earl? Can you see how anyone could fall off that boat?"

"A child could duck under the railing, stick his head out too far, and lose his balance. The railings on the upper and main decks are high enough to keep an adult from going over . . . by accident."

Val could see how other areas of the yacht might be more treacherous. "Could you go overboard if you fell from a staircase?"

Granddad shook his head. "The stairway between the upper and main decks is a couple of feet away from the edge of the boat. If you fell, you'd hit the deck. You can't roll off it, because the side of the boat comes up like a half wall with the railing above it."

Val switched her attention to the staircase down to the swim platform. Stacy might have had those steps in mind when she asked for a life vest. Val pointed to it. "The stairs to the swim platform aren't as safe. If the yacht rolled to the side while you were taking that last step, you could fall off. There's a gap in the railing."

The chief shrugged. "Possible, but it would be a freak accident."

Val eyed the set of four railings on the back of the swim platform. Three feet high, they were shaped like upside-down U's, with a foot of open space between them. "If I stood sideways between those railings, and the yacht pitched, I could fall into the water. Otto Warbeck might have done that. He was on the small side for a man." Val realized she'd spoken of him in the past tense.

The chief took off his sunglasses and studied the yacht. "Only a fool would stand between the railings, especially if the water was rough."

Granddad stroked his chin. "He'd only have to stand near them. Then someone with muscles could shove him through the space between the rails. All the men on that yacht were bigger than he was, and some of the women looked pretty strong, especially his wife."

The chief glanced around. The crowd gawking at the *Abyss* had doubled in size just in the last few minutes. "What happened to him is the Coast Guard's business for now, not mine. Even so, we should talk about this in private. Let's find a bench at the other end of the marina." As they circled around the cove, he said, "Look at the sailboats on the river and the yachts docked at the marina. More than ten million recreational boats are registered in this country. Yet boating mishaps cause less than a thousand fatalities each year."

"A small percentage," Granddad said. "Are most of those drownings?"

The chief nodded. "And the vast majority of drowning cases go down as accidents. Just like people are innocent until proven guilty, a drowning is an accident until proven otherwise."

"Proven how?" Val said.

"Evidence that the person jumped or was pushed. A suicide note. Body trauma. Best of all, a witness."

Of those, Val considered body trauma the likeliest, but that wouldn't be apparent until Otto was found. "What if someone on the yacht had a reason to kill Otto and the opportunity to push him overboard? Would that trigger an investigation, or would his death still be chalked up to an accident?"

The chief sat on a bench partially shaded by an evergreen. "In the absence of evidence to the contrary."

Granddad, who'd chosen to look cool in his black shirt for his TV interview, now looked chilly without a jacket. He took the spot next to the chief on the sunny side of the bench.

Val plunked down on the chief's other side. No point in telling him about the mystery game played on the yacht. He'd dismiss any connection between the game and Otto's disappearance as speculation, not evidence. Instead, she told him about Jerome's possible drugging by someone on the yacht.

While listening to her, the chief took a pipe and a small pouch of tobacco from the pocket of his windbreaker.

Granddad said, "Jerome hoped to pilot boats for a

living. He wouldn't have done anything stupid like take drugs while he was at the helm."

The chief filled his pipe with tobacco. "It doesn't make sense for any passengers to drug the pilot unless they expected Otto to take over the navigation."

Granddad shielded his eyes from the sun. "They probably did. Otto said he'd piloted the *Abyss* all the way from Florida to Maryland. Maybe someone drugged Jerome to make him look spacey without realizing the drug would knock him out totally."

Chief Yardley puffed on his pipe. "You can't predict how people will react to drugs."

Val wrinkled her nose as the pipe smoke drifted her way. "Just like drugs don't work the same for everyone, 'innocent until proven guilty' doesn't work the same across the board. People who've previously gotten in trouble with the law are often guilty until proven innocent, especially if they're brown or black."

The chief took the pipe from his mouth. "Is Jerome from around here?"

"Crisfield," Granddad said.

Val had heard him talk about Crisfield. The southernmost Maryland city used to have an economy based on catching and processing seafood. That had changed as the health of the bay and the fish population declined. "Jerome's been staying in Bayport with his aunt, Althea Johnson."

The chief nodded. "The lawyer. Jerome's in good hands. For the time being, this is a matter for the Coast Guard. It can take weeks or months for a body to surface."

Val saw a possible way to involve the chief in the case of the drowned man before his death brought Jerome more trouble. "If it takes that long for Otto's body to come up, people's memories of what they saw and heard on the yacht may fade. If he was pushed overboard, it's worth knowing what happened before he disappeared. The Coast Guard didn't ask about that."

The chief took the pipe out of his mouth. "Were the folks on the yacht locals?"

"Otto and Cheyenne recently moved here." Granddad took off his bifocals and held them up as if looking for a smudge. "I talked to Otto while I was setting up the bar for the cocktail party. He got married about a year ago. He retired soon after, sold his place in Washington, and bought a yacht for himself. Then they went shopping for a house she could renovate."

Val figured Cheyenne would get rid of the yacht, and probably the house, as soon as she could. Hard to stay alone in a place you'd expected to share with someone. "Louisa and Damian Brown, the poultry people, haven't been here long either. They bought a second home in Bayport last spring. I see her at the club. They split their time between the place here and their other house, which is somewhere between Annapolis and Washington."

The chief reached into his pocket and took out his buzzing phone. "Excuse me." He walked far enough away from the bench that they couldn't hear what he was saying. He returned in less than a minute, his face grim. "I have to leave, but I'll be in touch soon. Very soon."

He hurried away from the marina, surprisingly light on his feet for a big man.

"Looks like his Sunday just turned into a workday," Granddad said. "How much you want to bet Otto has surfaced?"

Chapter 7

"Sunday afternoon isn't the best time to keep up with the news," Granddad groused as he channel-surfed from his lounger in the sitting room. He tried the radio. The station he counted on to update the news every half hour during the week was broadcasting a baseball game, interrupted only by commercials.

Meanwhile, Val searched online for the latest local news. Her Google search turned up nothing new. She visited the sites for the local media, the Coast Guard, and the county and state law enforcement agencies. On her second circuit through the obvious news sources, a bulletin popped up. The Coast Guard had found the body of a man in the Chesapeake Bay. Further details would be available after the man's identity was confirmed and the next of kin notified.

Val sighed. She'd hoped against the odds that a strong current had washed Otto ashore, where he'd collapsed, exhausted but alive. Cheyenne had probably nursed a similar hope, and now she'd have to identify her husband's body. Hard for any woman, but especially difficult for one so young. When Grandma

died, Val had been around Cheyenne's age. Losing
a grandparent had hit her hard. Until then, she'd
understood death in the abstract, but it hadn't touched
her personally.

She went into the sitting room. Granddad had
fallen asleep in his lounge chair. No reason to wake
him. She went upstairs to gather the laundry she'd
neglected all week while preparing for the *Titanic*
dinner.

Passing by the unoccupied bedrooms upstairs, she
thought about Gunnar's urgent need to find a place
to live. He currently used the living room of the house
he rented as a home office and met accounting clients
there. If nothing turned up that met his needs, would
he want to live here until he found a place? And what
would he do for an office?

Val moved her clothes from the hamper to the laundry basket. Most of the time, Granddad's house had
plenty of unused space. Her parents stayed in one of
the spare bedrooms a few times a year when they
visited from Florida. Her brother and his family occupied the other two on their annual Christmas trip
from California to the East Coast. But how would
Granddad react to the idea of Gunnar moving in?
Before she broached the subject with him, she'd have
to decide how she felt about the arrangement herself.
She and Gunnar saw each other often, but in small
doses. Having him around from morning to night
would test their relationship and might determine its
future.

Val was on her way back to the first floor with an over-
flowing laundry basket when the doorbell rang. She put
the basket down and opened the door. Bethany stood
on the front porch in Black Watch plaid leggings and

a purple hoodie with a sparkling pineapple on it—a typical outfit for her, though not one Val had ever seen before.

"Come in." Val led her into the sitting room and saw the excitement in her friend's bright green eyes. "You look like you could use a calming drink. Tea? Wine?"

"White wine, if you have it."

Granddad sat up in his lounge chair. "I could use a calming beer."

"Sit down, Bethany," Val said. "I'll get the wine and beer."

Granddad stood up. "No, let's all go into the kitchen. I gotta try a recipe for my column this week."

At least he was starting earlier than usual. He generally tested recipes on Monday, the day his newspaper column was due.

"What are you cooking, Mr. Myer?" Bethany said as they trooped into the kitchen.

"The dish you didn't get to eat last night. Waldorf pudding. But I'm not making the version Val planned. Too many ingredients. I found a simple recipe for it in an old cookbook behind the other ones on the top shelf." He opened the cabinet devoted to cookbooks and held up a tattered, cream-colored book. "The 1903 cookbook compiled by the Ladies' Aid Society of Calvary Presbyterian Church. I'm using Mrs. Milligan's recipe for the pudding."

"I'm impressed, Granddad. I couldn't find any Waldorf pudding recipe that existed when the *Titanic* sailed." Val couldn't hold back the news any longer. "I read online that the Coast Guard found the body of a man in the bay."

Bethany sat down at the table. "It's Otto. I was with Cheyenne when she got the news."

Granddad took apples and butter from the fridge. "It's good Cheyenne wasn't alone. Were you on the yacht when she heard?"

"No. She never wants to set foot on it again. We exchanged phone numbers last night. I called this afternoon to find out if I could do anything for her. She asked me to keep her company while she waited for her brother to get here from Pennsylvania. I went over to her house and spent most of the afternoon there."

Val took wine, cheese, and crackers to the breakfast table. "It was kind of you to do that." She'd made few friends in ten years of living in New York who'd been as good-hearted or as much fun as Bethany. "I'm sure it was a comfort for her to have you there."

"She was doing okay until the police came to the door. Chief Yardley, a Coast Guard officer, and someone from the state police. They told her that a search team had retrieved the body of a man in evening clothes." Bethany gulped down some wine. "Cheyenne has to formally identify him, though the police didn't sound as if they had any doubt about who the man was. Her brother's going to help her through the formalities."

Granddad took a swig of beer. "How did she react to the news?"

"With denial, at first. She questioned how divers could have found him so fast. The Coast Guard officer told her the branches of a floating limb had snagged the man. She lost it for a minute and whimpered like a puppy."

Val understood that reaction. "She had a mental image of what happened to him. That's when it became real."

Granddad washed three huge apples and took out

a knife. "Remember the scenes after the sinking in the *Titanic* movie? Some folks managed to cling to floating debris. By the time help arrived, they'd died of exposure. That mighta happened to Otto."

Bethany toyed with the stem of her wineglass. "They're going to do an autopsy to find out how and when he died. Cheyenne objected. She said she didn't want Otto cut up when it was obvious he'd drowned. The Coast Guard officer told her that the man they'd pulled from the bay had a head injury that could have caused his death."

Granddad looked up from the cutting board, his eyes wide. "An injury that happened before he went into the water?"

Bethany shrugged. "The police didn't say. I thought at first that he fell, hit his head, and rolled overboard when the yacht tipped sideways. But then the police told Cheyenne not to return to the yacht until they've had a chance to go over it. I wonder if they're looking for evidence of a crime."

"Maybe they think one of Otto's guests clobbered him and shoved him in the water." Granddad's knife thumped against the cutting board as he sliced an apple. "The police might find some blood that the rain didn't wash away, but they aren't gonna find a weapon. The person who used it woulda thrown it overboard."

Bethany put down her glass. "I just hope Otto isn't too smashed up. That'd make identifying him even worse for Cheyenne."

Grim news for Cheyenne might prove good news for Jerome. If a guest had attacked Otto before he went overboard, the police would grill everyone on the yacht, not just Jerome. For his sake, Val hoped that

Otto had entertained his own murderer on the *Abyss.* "The three of us were the only people who stayed in the room after Otto left. The rest of them trickled out, probably to use the bathroom on the aft deck outside the saloon. I mean the *head,* not the *bathroom.*" Val corrected her own nautical terminology as if Otto were there to notice.

Bethany put a slice of cheese on a cracker. "Otto could have fallen, hit his head, and then rolled overboard when the yacht was tipping sideways."

"A freak accident," Val said, repeating the words the chief had used today for a similar scenario. "I think the police will want to know who had the opportunity to attack Otto. I was so busy in the galley that I didn't pay attention to which guests left the saloon when. But if the three of us put our heads together, we could figure out if any of them were out there alone with Otto." She took a scratch pad and pen from a cabinet drawer and returned to the table. Meanwhile, Granddad layered the apples with bread crumbs and poured melted butter over them.

Bethany put down her wineglass. "Trey was the first to leave the table after Otto did. Then Stacy."

Val jotted down three names. "Otto, his ex-wife, and his former stepson, all on deck while everyone else was in the saloon. I remember Cheyenne saying the guest head on the lower deck was nicer than the one on the aft deck. Louisa went down the stairs."

"Then Stacy came back to the saloon and Damian went out," Granddad said.

Bethany shook her head. "I think he left before she came back."

Granddad looked skeptical, but didn't argue. He peered at the cookbook. "*Set in a moderate oven until the apples are tender.* What kind of recipe is this? Mrs. Milligan didn't give the temperature and the time for baking the apples."

"Don't blame her, Granddad. I doubt ovens had temperature dials in 1903. Just follow your own oven rule, the one you gave in your first interview as the Codger Cook." Val wasn't surprised by his puzzled look. Knowing nothing about cooking when he won the job of recipe columnist, he'd made up kitchen maxims on the fly and promptly forgotten them. *"When in doubt, set the oven to 325.* That's what you told your readers."

"Hmm. Good advice." He fiddled with the oven controls. "Okay, it's preheating. Now I can finish my beer."

Bethany jumped up. "Sit here, Mr. Myer. I have to leave soon."

Val tapped her pen on the scratch pad. "We have Otto, Trey, Damian, and Louisa all out of the saloon. What happened next?"

Granddad sat down across from Val at the breakfast table. "Damian came back, looking anxious."

"I was feeling anxious myself by then, Mr. Myer. The yacht was really bouncing around." Bethany frowned in concentration. "Then Louisa came upstairs and Cheyenne left. Or did Homer leave before her?"

Granddad scratched his head. "I'm not sure, but I know he went out to the side deck by the door near the galley. Trey was out of the room the longest. When the Coast Guard officer questioned him, he said he was on the bridge the whole time and Otto was never there. Jerome can't confirm or dispute that, since he has no memory of what happened."

"Where else could Otto have been all that time?" Val remembered the door to the engine room on the lower deck. "Maybe he went from the deck outside the saloon down to the swim platform and then walked through the engine room to the master stateroom."

Granddad nodded. "To use the head in his stateroom and leave the other ones for his guests."

That made sense to Val. "And when he retraced his steps and went back outside, someone bashed him and pushed him overboard."

Granddad went over to the stove and put his apple, butter, and crumb mixture in the oven. "This kitchen is full of things you can bash someone with. A cast-iron pan, a marble rolling pin, a wine bottle. But on a boat deck, there's not a lot of stuff to grab. You can't have stuff rolling around when the water gets rough."

Bethany tapped the canister of the fire extinguisher on the wall. "Was there one of these on the deck? It's heavy enough to crack a skull."

Val remembered seeing a fire extinguisher on the open deck. "Good point, Bethany. It's also possible that debris hit Otto in the water and caused the injury."

Bethany glanced at her watch. "I'll leave you two to puzzle it all out. Time for me to go home. Chatty's coming over to give me a free facial. I'm so glad she moved back to Bayport in time to play on our tennis team this spring."

"I'm glad too." Val walked Bethany toward the front door and refrained from saying that few people could resist buying Chatty's overpriced beauty products after her free facials. "Thank you for tracking the ins and outs of the guests with us. Our timetable might help the police figure out what happened."

As they reached the sitting room, the phone in Bethany's bag jingled.

She pulled it out and glanced at the display. "It's Cheyenne."

While Bethany had the phone at her ear, her eyebrows shot halfway up to her hairline. She listened for the next two minutes, her face as expressive as her few words.

"No! . . . Really? . . . Are you okay?"

Granddad came into the sitting room as Bethany ended the call with the advice, "Be brave."

She hung up and sighed. "Otto's head injury was a bullet hole."

Chapter 8

"So Otto took a bullet," Granddad said. "That shoots the accident theory. We're down to suicide or murder."

Bethany tucked her phone away. "The police told Cheyenne not to say anything about their findings until the autopsy confirms them. Then they'll make a public announcement. Until then—"

"Mum's the word." Granddad tapped his index finger on his lips.

Val remembered her cousin Monique's warning about Chatty's facials: *She spikes them with truth serum. She'll coax you into telling her things you've never told anyone else.* "Be careful, Bethany, that you don't tell Chatty about the bullet hole. It'll be all over town by morning."

Bethany turned to Val. "Do you think Otto was the type of person to commit suicide?"

"I can't say. I just met him. But I know he went to a lot of trouble to get every detail accurate for his *Titanic* dinner. Killing himself in the middle of the meal doesn't make sense."

Bethany started toward the hall and then stopped. "I almost forgot to tell you. After Cheyenne said she never wanted to go back to the yacht, I offered to pick up the leftover food before it spoils. That was fine with her. She didn't want any of it. Once the police are done with the yacht, I'll salvage anything edible and bring it here."

Val hated to waste food, but this was one batch she'd be tempted to dump. Otto's death would make it hard to enjoy the second half of the dinner he had planned. The aroma of baking apples wafted into the sitting room. "You'd better check the oven, Granddad."

He hurried to the kitchen. She saw Bethany to the door and then joined him.

He poked the baked apples with a fork. "These are perfect. Tender, but not too soft. The next step is combining milk, eggs, and sugar to pour on top."

"How about I do that? Mixing ingredients relaxes me and helps me think."

"Good. Leave dinner to me. I'll go fire up the grill."

She didn't remember buying anything they could grill. "What are we eating?"

"Ned picked up a big piece of sirloin and asked me to grind it. He gave me a hunk of the ground beef, enough for both of us to have burgers tonight and one for the freezer." He hurried out to the backyard, possibly to forestall any pushback on his dinner plan.

She wondered if he'd talked his friend Ned into buying that hunk of beef. Though she kept Granddad on the low-fat diet his doctor recommended, she suspected he cheated on it when he ate dinner with friends and when she left him to his own devices.

While whisking the milk with the eggs, she stirred

up questions in her mind about Otto's death. She had them ready when Granddad returned from lighting the charcoal. "If someone fired a gun on the yacht, wouldn't we have heard a shot?"

"Not inside the saloon. The windows and doors on that yacht are heavy and tight. Besides, the minute Otto left the room, Cheyenne turned up the music. It was so loud that I had to lower the volume on my hearing aid."

"But what about the guests who left the saloon? They might have been on a different deck from Otto and not seen him, but they couldn't have missed the sound of a gun firing."

"Someone using the head wouldn't necessarily hear any more than we did, what with noises from the exhaust fan and the plumbing."

Val added sugar to the milk-and-egg mix. "A gun means premeditation, not a spur-of-the-moment killing. A man could have come on the yacht with a gun in his tuxedo pockets. Women don't tote shoulder bags like mine while wearing gowns. They carry clutches or evening bags, not much bigger than a wallet and too small for a gun."

"An ankle holster works with trousers *and* long dresses." Granddad pointed to his lower leg. "Or maybe the gun was already on the boat. Only Otto or Cheyenne could have put it there. One of them is dead, and the other benefits from his death."

Val stopped mixing the dessert ingredients. Her grandfather had fixed on the obvious suspect when the victim is married—the spouse. "You're assuming Cheyenne inherits Otto's money, but that's not necessarily true. Given Otto's obsession, he might have earmarked his entire fortune for a *Titanic* monument or museum."

"It doesn't matter what his will says. As long as Cheyenne expected to inherit, she had a motive. That's number one." Granddad held up his hand with the thumb up. Then he extended his index finger. "Two, she covered the windows so no one could see what was happening outside on deck. Three, she turned up the music so loud that it could drown out the gunshot. Four, she sent Louisa to the downstairs bathroom to keep her off the deck where she might hear or see Otto's murder go down. And five"—Granddad's pinky joined his other splayed fingers—"she waited until everyone else had visited the head and no one was on the aft deck before she went out there by herself."

"But Homer went out to the side deck after that. He would have heard the gun go off if that's when Otto was shot."

Granddad tapped his ear. "Homer wears hearing aids like mine. They don't work right when it's windy, like last night on deck. Sometimes mine whistle so loud that I can't hear anything else."

Val poured the egg mixture over the apples. "You've decided Cheyenne's guilty and closed your mind to other possibilities. She didn't go out on deck until Otto had been gone for twenty minutes. Where was he all that time when no one saw him?" Val didn't wait for Granddad to respond. "I think he was already dead, shot by either Stacy or Trey. They were the first to leave the room after he did. No one saw him after that."

Granddad tilted his head from side to side as if weighing her theory against his. "They didn't act real friendly to Otto. I'll put them second on my suspect list, after Cheyenne." He stood up. "Time to slice the onions. What's a burger without fried onions?"

Val had just put the pudding in the oven when the doorbell rang. "I'll get it."

Granddad took an onion from the pantry. "I wish people wouldn't come visiting at dinnertime. I wanna put the meat on when the charcoal's hot, not after it cools down."

Val hurried to the front hall and opened the door to Althea's nephew. "Jerome!" He looked more young, vulnerable, and uncomfortable in his Sunday clothes than he had yesterday piloting the inflatable tender in his T-shirt and jeans.

He ran his finger under the collar of his crisp blue shirt. "Can I talk to Mr. Myer?"

"Of course. Come in."

As she closed the door behind him, he inhaled audibly. "Something smells—wow—great."

"An apple pudding is baking in the oven. My grandfather's working on dinner. Let's go into the kitchen."

He peered at the walls and high ceiling as she led him through the sitting room, the dining room, and the butler's pantry. "This is a big place."

Granddad looked up from slicing onions. "Howdy, Jerome."

The young man gaped at him. Understandable, because Granddad was wearing bright blue swim goggles with mirrored lenses and looked like a bug. Val signaled him by making circles around her eyes with her thumb and index finger.

"Oh, yeah." Granddad took off the goggles. "Forgot I was wearing these. I use 'em when I cut onions so my eyes don't burn."

Jerome relaxed and grinned. "That's a good idea."

The smile disappeared as quickly as it had arrived. "I can come back some other time if you're busy. I don't want to hold up your dinner."

"You won't hold us up, as long as you stay and eat a burger with us. We've got lots of beef, and the grill's almost ready."

"A burger." Jerome breathed the word as if it had magic power. "I haven't had homemade burgers in a long time. Aunt Althea doesn't eat meat."

"You've come to the right place." Granddad took the ground beef from the fridge.

"When I try to make them, they don't turn out so good. Maybe I can learn how to do it by watching you." Jerome joined Granddad at the kitchen island.

Val took dinner plates from the cabinet near the dishwasher. The breakfast table was too small to fit three comfortably and the dining room table too huge and formal for tonight's meal. The picnic table would be perfect. "Let's eat outside this evening."

"Our first cookout of the season." Granddad unwrapped the meat. "Now watch how I handle this beef. You hold it like a baby. You don't poke or press or smash it down, unless you want to turn that baby into a hockey puck. You gotta have nice pockets in the meat to hold the juice."

Val had never before heard Granddad's hamburger tips. She found an oilcloth cover for the picnic table and wrapped the utensils in napkins.

"Do you add barbecue sauce to the meat before you cook it, Mr. Myer?"

"Nope. Only pepper and salt. The kind with big crystals—kosher salt. You salt the meat right before you put it on the grill. Otherwise, you're pulling all the juices out before you have a chance to taste them."

After forming the three patties, he put them on a plate and made an indentation in the middle of each of them with his thumb.

"Why are you doing that?" Jerome said.

"Because the meat shrinks when it cooks. It can turn into a meatball. This dent keeps it flat."

Val credited Grandma with teaching her how to cook and Granddad with staying out of the kitchen. But, come to think of it, he'd served as the meat chef for barbecues during her visits here as a child. She hoped tonight's burgers would taste as good as the ones in her memory.

With Jerome's cooking lesson winding down, she decided to explore his memory of last night. "Althea told me you thought someone on the yacht slipped drugs into your food. What did you eat?"

"The dinner you brought me." He looked apologetically at her. "Nothing tasted funny. I liked the salmon a lot."

And probably the asparagus less. "That platter of food was all you ate?"

"I had some of those marshmallow and chocolate crackers. S'mores."

As far as Val knew, he hadn't been on the open deck where Bethany was making s'mores. "Did you leave the bridge to get some?"

Jerome shook his head. "I stayed at the controls the whole time. Otto brought everyone in to look at the navigation instruments. When they all left, the s'mores were in a dish, next to the plate you made up for me. Do you think there were drugs in them?"

Maybe. "That would be hard to prove. Unless you left a few on the plate and the police tested them."

"I ate every last one."

Whoever wanted to drug a young man could safely bet he'd gobble up warm, gooey sweets sooner than he'd eat cold salmon and asparagus.

While Val made a salad, Jerome meandered to the breakfast table. He slumped into a chair and stared at the wood floor.

Granddad put the sliced onions in a frying pan. "Something bothering you, son?"

Jerome looked up. "I haven't talked to Aunt Althea about this yet. Promise me you won't tell her." He glanced nervously at Val, apparently viewing her as a possible blabbermouth.

"We won't repeat anything," she said, "unless you give us permission." She just hoped he wasn't going to confess to a crime.

Jerome propped his elbow on the table and clutched his forehead. "It's my fault."

"What is?" Val and Granddad said simultaneously.

"What happened to Otto."

Chapter 9

Granddad signaled to Val to watch the onions and sat down across from Jerome at the table. "How is what happened to Otto your fault?"

"I should have been paying more attention to the radar. There was nothing to worry about one minute, and the next time I looked, the bad weather was almost on top of us. My head was all fuzzy. Otto told me to leave the autopilot alone, but I had to adjust it to change course. By the time I did that, it was too late to get out of the squall." Jerome gulped. "If I'd gotten away from the bad weather, no one could blame me for Otto falling off the boat."

Val's heart ached for him. She exchanged a look with Granddad. They both knew Jerome hadn't done anything on the yacht that made him responsible for Otto's death, unless he'd pulled the trigger on a gun. But they weren't free to share that information with him or anyone else.

Granddad stroked his chin. "Did Otto blame you for what you did about changing course?"

"No!" Jerome said loudly. "I didn't see him after he went down to the main deck for dinner."

"You have blanks in your memory," Granddad reminded him.

Jerome took a moment to respond. "If he'd come to the bridge, he'd have known I was having trouble. He would have taken over the controls."

Good point. Val stirred the onions. Jerome obviously feared his moment of inattention or indecision had done irreparable harm. How could she set his mind at ease without mentioning the gun wound? She chose her words carefully. "I can't tell you how I know this, Jerome, but nothing you did or didn't do when you were piloting the yacht caused Otto's death."

"Really?" Jerome sounded eager to believe her, but his face remained tense. "I know you're friends with Chief Yardley, Mr. Myer. Could you put in a good word for me? I have to be drug free to get my license. I wouldn't do anything to ruin my chances."

"I'll make sure he knows how much that means to you."

"Should I tell the police Otto said not to touch the autopilot without talking to him and I did it anyway?"

Val had no idea whether that mattered, but she knew the general rule that applied here. "You should talk to your lawyer before you tell the police anything. Is Althea going to represent you?"

"I guess so. I don't have the money to pay anyone else. She's free."

Granddad returned to the stove and took over the onions. "If you need a lawyer because you're suspected of a crime and you can't afford one, you get assigned a lawyer. You never know if that lawyer will be any good. But your aunt is one of the best around."

Jerome's jaw dropped. "She is? I mean, I love her and all, but she doesn't talk much about her work. So I don't know anything about it."

"You have to work at getting to know people in your own family." Granddad glanced at Val and moved the pan off the burner. "The fire should be ready. Let's go grill the meat."

Once they went outside, none of them mentioned Otto's yacht. As they ate at the picnic table, Granddad talked about the changes he'd seen in Bayport over the last fifty years and asked about Jerome's family in southern Maryland.

Later, after Jerome had left, Granddad loaded the dishwasher. "I like that young man, but he's got a big problem unless there's proof someone drugged him. When Otto left the saloon, he said he'd take care of getting the yacht to calmer waters. It sounded as if he was going up to the bridge, where Jerome was. That makes Jerome the last person to see Otto alive."

"And drug-related amnesia isn't the strongest defense." Val believed Jerome, but would the police? A few times in the past year, when she was afraid they were building a case against an innocent person, she'd brought their attention to other suspects. "If we want to help Jerome, we'll have to find evidence against someone else. Otto made everyone play a game in which they accused each other of wrongdoing. Maybe those accusations had a basis in reality and one of the guests feared exposure."

"Or maybe it was just a game." Granddad closed the dishwasher. "Didn't Otto say he'd found it online?"

Val dried the frying pan Granddad had used for the onions. "What he said wasn't necessarily true. I'll look online myself." She put away the frying pan and hurried out of the kitchen.

While Granddad watched TV from his easy chair, she sat at the computer in the study and searched for *Titanic mystery game.* Links to video games appeared on the screen. She scrolled through them until she saw a link to a downloadable *Titanic* dinner party murder mystery game.

Val followed the link. The site gave enough information about the game to convince Val that Otto had used it as the basis for his evening's entertainment. The game entailed eight people taking the roles of *Titanic* passengers and attempting to solve a crime over a dinner that re-created the final meal served on the ship. Each participant received a character sketch and a question-and-answer booklet with sections for four rounds or scenes. And each was a suspect in the crime. Otto had used the same format.

As Val read more about the game, she realized he'd made crucial changes. The mystery to be solved in the downloadable game was the murder of an officer on the *Titanic,* whereas the object of Otto's game was to determine responsibility for a young woman who went overboard. In the original game, the players assumed the parts of actual *Titanic* passengers, like "the Unsinkable Molly Brown." Otto hadn't done that. He could have used the downloaded game as is. So why had he gone to the trouble of changing the crime and inventing new roles for his guests to play? Val might be able to answer that question if she read all of Otto's scripts.

She called Bethany and suggested going with her to

pick up the leftover food on the yacht. "I also want to get the mystery game booklets."

"Good idea. I'd like to know what happens in the scenes we didn't get to play."

"By the way, did you see anyone fill a plate with s'mores and take it to the bridge?"

"Louisa put several on a plate, but she gobbled them up quickly. Trey took a plateful away from the grill, and so did Cheyenne. I don't know where they went with them because I was busy making more. Why are you asking?"

"Jerome visited us after you left here. He said someone had brought him a plate of s'mores. I wondered who."

Not that it mattered, unless there was a way to prove that the s'mores had contained drugs. Val would mention that possibility to Chief Yardley.

The next morning, the chief strolled into the café as Val's breakfast crowd was thinning and her lunch bunch had yet to arrive. She'd planned to stop by police headquarters on her way home from the café in the afternoon. The chief had saved her the trip.

He greeted her and sat at the eating bar. "I've got some time to spare before a meeting, so I came here for my coffee instead of drinking the sludge at headquarters."

She poured his coffee and plated a blueberry muffin for him. "Anything new on Otto Warbeck?"

"I just gave the press a brief statement. He took a bullet to the head, but I suspect your friend Bethany already told you that." He sipped his coffee. "Good stuff. Your granddaddy told me you made notes on the comings and goings of the passengers on the yacht."

"Based on what Bethany, Granddad, and I remembered, we came up with the order in which the guests went outside after Otto left the table. I can e-mail you my notes."

"Please do." The chief sipped his coffee. "What's the bottom line?"

"Granddad, Bethany, and I were the only ones who didn't leave the room. Trey was gone for almost thirty minutes. He told Granddad he was on the bridge all that time. Except for Louisa Brown, who used the inside staircase to visit the guest bathroom, the others all left the saloon to go out on the deck."

"Singly or with another person?"

"They left singly, but often more than one of them was on deck at the same time. If all they did was use the head on the deck outside the saloon, they wouldn't have overlapped. They'd have just passed each other, one coming back into the saloon and then the other going out."

The chief shrugged. "They could have stayed outside for a breath of fresh air."

"Or a break from the loud music in the saloon." Val stopped talking long enough to make what she hoped was a pregnant pause. "Or they could have grabbed the chance to shoot Otto."

"Was Otto left- or right-handed?" the chief asked.

His question surprised her. She'd expected him to ask how the shooter came to have a gun so near at hand, and she had no good answer for that. An image popped into her mind of Otto signing the catering contract. "He wrote with his right hand." A right-handed man would shoot himself on the right side of the head, so a bullet hole there meant either suicide or murder. But a bullet hole on the opposite side would suggest murder, not suicide. The chief didn't volunteer information about the location of Otto's wound. No point in asking. She'd find out when the information went public. But why had he asked *her* about Otto's dominant hand? "Cheyenne would know if her husband was a righty or a lefty."

"She hesitated when I asked her. So I went for a second opinion from someone observant." The chief raised his coffee cup as if toasting her. "What sort of man was Otto Warbeck?"

"He struck me as controlling and manipulative." Val remembered how skillfully he'd talked her into making an elaborate dinner on short notice. "He got me to cater that dinner with a combination of flattery and bribery. He appealed to my pride and my pocket-book."

"Two vulnerable spots."

"Exactly. He wouldn't postpone the dinner to give me more time to prepare. The date, the place, and the guests are in perfect alignment, he said. The date was the anniversary of the *Titanic* sinking, and the place was his new yacht, but the people he invited seemed anything but perfect guests. He barely knew some of them. He couldn't have come up with a less compatible bunch if he'd deliberately chosen people who would grate on one another's nerves."

"Like the ex-wife and the wife."

"For starters, but they at least ignored each other. Stacy's son ridiculed his former stepfather and picked a fight with the poultry lobbyist on environmental issues." Val waved to a trio of women who came into the café. "Take a seat. I'll be right with you." She caught the chief's eye. "I'd like to know why Otto's ex-wife and ex-stepson accepted his invitation."

"If someone invited me to a ten-course dinner on a yacht, I'd probably go. I don't know about the son, but the former wife might have been curious to see the new one."

Val doubted many women would want to meet their younger replacement. "To convince me to cater the dinner, Otto pushed my buttons and made me an offer I couldn't refuse. I wouldn't be surprised if he used similar tactics to get his ex and her son there." She walked around the counter. "Give me a minute to wait on these customers."

He'd finished his coffee and the last crumb of his muffin by the time she came back to the counter. She told him about the s'mores as the possible vehicle for drugging Jerome.

The chief looked skeptical, glanced at his watch, and stood up. "Gotta get to my meeting."

"Any idea when the police will finish going over the yacht? I want to pick up the leftover food before it goes bad."

"If there's evidence of a crime, it could take another day or two. Otherwise, they should be done by the end of the day even if they start late. I'll call you."

He hurried out of the café. Telling him about Otto's mystery game would have to wait until the next time they talked. By then she might have read the scripts and figured out if they meant anything.

Val usually tuned the TV on the café wall to a sports station, the preference of most of the customers at the athletic club, but at noon, she switched to the Salisbury, Maryland, station for the local news.

In the first segment the anchorman announced,

"Breaking news about Otto Warbeck, the man whose body was pulled from the bay yesterday. The retired yachtsman had a gunshot wound. When asked if it could have been self-inflicted, Chief Earl Yardley of the Bayport Police Department responded that the case remains under investigation. Stay tuned for an exclusive interview related to Mr. Warbeck's death after this short break."

The weather forecast and another commercial break occurred before the reporter who'd interviewed Granddad at the marina appeared on the screen with the promised exclusive interview.

"This is Sissy Reynolds outside the Bayport home of the late Otto Warbeck. Initial reports suggested that he fell from his yacht and drowned during a squall Saturday night. New information today indicates his death was no accident. I spoke to the victim's widow, Cheyenne Warbeck."

When the camera zoomed in, Val was taken aback by how haggard the widow looked. Otto's death had taken a toll on her.

"We're sorry for your loss, Mrs. Warbeck," the reporter said, "and appreciate your taking the time to speak with us. Earlier today the police revealed that your husband had suffered a gunshot wound. They didn't rule out that it had been self-inflicted. What's your reaction to that?"

Cheyenne looked directly into the camera. "Impossible. Otto wasn't the sort of man who'd commit suicide. He'd recently retired and bought a yacht. He was living his dream."

The widow's response sounded rehearsed. Cheyenne must have expected that question, Val thought. So much for Granddad's suspicions about Otto's wife.

If she'd murdered her husband and wanted to get
away with it, she would have welcomed suicide as an
explanation for his death.

Val made chicken Caesar salads for her customers
as she listened to the interview.

The reporter said, "You and your husband threw a
dinner party on your yacht Saturday night. Can you
tell us something about the occasion?"

"Yes, Otto collected *Titanic* souvenirs and knew
everything there was to know about that ship. Saturday
was the anniversary of its sinking. He hired a local
caterer to re-create the dinner the first-class passengers
ate right before the ship hit an iceberg. He insisted the
caterer—Val Deniston—make the dinner authentic
down to the last detail."

Val stiffened.

"That's you, isn't it?" one of the retired men waiting
for his Caesar salad called out.

She nodded. Everyone in the café was now watching the TV or staring at her.

Cheyenne wiped away tears.

"Did your husband throw a similar dinner party
every year on that date?" the reporter said.

"He did it only once before, in 2012, on the hundredth anniversary of the *Titanic* going down. That
time the dinner was on land. Having dinner on our
yacht, the *Abyss*, made it more authentic. We were all
dressed like passengers on the *Titanic*." She smiled
with effort. "He reminded me of a little boy looking
forward to his birthday party. Why would he shoot
himself during his party? We were only halfway through
the meal and the game he made up."

"The game?" the reporter prompted Cheyenne.

"One of those role-playing mysteries. We took the

parts of passengers on the *Titanic.* We were all suspects in the death of another passenger."

"Amazing. Life imitated the game. While your guests were playing the roles of suspects, your husband was shot." The reporter turned away from Cheyenne and faced the camera. "Now those guests are real suspects in Otto Warbeck's death—a death on the *Abyss.*"

Cheyenne opened her mouth as if she had something to add, but the reporter signed off. Val spent the next half hour fielding questions from café customers about the dinner on the yacht. She described the various dishes she'd prepared and avoided talking about Otto's guests or his mystery game by saying she'd spent the whole evening working in the kitchen.

At two o'clock she turned over the café reins to Jeremy Pritchard, her assistant manager's twenty-something son. Though he didn't cook, he made sandwiches, salads, and smoothies, which sufficed for the few customers who came into the café during the afternoon. His mother would take over at four and prepare the food for the café's evening customers.

Val's friend and tennis teammate, Chatty Ridenour, was waiting for her outside the café alcove. Chatty's turquoise shirt matched her eyes, thanks to her colored contact lenses. She had contacts in various shades to coordinate with her clothes. Her earrings echoed the blue-green of her shirt. Pushing forty, average in height and weight, with straight brown hair a nondescript shade of brown, Chatty wouldn't have attracted notice except for her flawless complexion, expertly applied makeup, and the constant gush of gossip from her mouth. Her nickname suited her better than the name her parents had given her, Charity—though at times, *Catty* would make a more appropriate nickname than *Chatty*.

"Ready for your massage?" Chatty peered at Val. "Don't tell me you've forgotten. I owe you a massage, and I won't let you postpone it again."

A free massage was Val's payment for supplying food for the grand opening of Chatty's massage and spa concession at the club. Last summer when she moved temporarily to Florida to take care of ailing parents, she'd left as an itinerant cosmetologist who gave facials in her customers' homes. She returned to Bayport seven months later as a licensed massage therapist and convinced the club manager that a storage room could become a profit center if she set up her massage table there. Judging by the number of club members who sported T-shirts emblazoned with *Chatty Kneads Me*, her business was going strong.

"I don't want to occupy your massage table space when you might have a paying customer on it."

"My next appointment doesn't show up until three. You'll get a nice long massage if you hurry. Last night Bethany told me all about the *Titanic* dinner. She said the two of you didn't know much about any of the guests—or should I say *suspects?* After this morning's news about the bullet hole in the body, I guess we can call them suspects." Chatty arched an eyebrow at Val. "I can tell you about one of them if you're interested."

"I'm all ears." Val knew she'd pay a price for this free massage in Chatty's currency—her friend would dispense information freely, but demand some in return.

Chapter 10

Chatty ran her hands along Val's upper back. "You're really tense, Val. By now you should be used to people getting murdered around you. How many times has it happened since you moved here?"

"More times than I want to count when I'm trying to relax." Val was lying facedown in a headrest the shape of a doughnut with a bite out of it, her nose in the center of the doughnut hole, her mouth in the opening left by the bite. She could breathe and talk, but couldn't see anything. Just as well. Chatty's work space, a windowless room smaller than many walk-in closets, awakened Val's claustrophobia. She fought it by focusing on the scents drifting her way from the oil in the aromatherapy diffuser. The room smelled of cinnamon, coconut, and vanilla, like cookies in the oven. She sniffed a floral scent too, but she didn't let it interfere with the aromas that made her mouth water. "Which of the yacht's guests do you know?"

"Louisa Brown. She comes here for a massage twice a week."

"She visits the café too." But usually at a time when

Val was too busy working to stop and talk. On the other hand, Chatty's work involved massaging and talking in equal measures. "Tell me about her. I know almost nothing, except that she has a taste for sweets."

"She's an only child, and she'll inherit Purty Poultry. Her parents maintain total control of the business for now, but in a few years she'll ascend to the throne."

Val remembered Louisa's reference to the family business. "I didn't realize her family's chicken coops had a throne connected to them."

"The company has farms in Delaware, all over Maryland's Eastern Shore, and in North Carolina. Haven't you noticed the Purty Poultry label in the supermarkets around here?"

"No, because I only buy free-range chickens from nearby farms." Val felt herself relaxing as Chatty continued to rub, this time in a circular motion. "How did Purty Poultry get so big?"

"The company grew slowly over several generations. It contracted with small farmers to raise chickens for its processing plant. TV ads lifted Purty Poultry above the competition. I remember seeing their ads when I was a teenager. One of them showed an elegant dinner party with a beautifully browned roast chicken on the table. The host is about to carve the chicken when a bumpkin in overalls bursts into the room and drawls, *That there's a mighty purty chicken.*"

Val laughed at Chatty's exaggerated country dialect. "That one commercial made the Purty company a big player in the chicken world?"

"It was part of a campaign, which included spoofs of their own ad. One of them won an advertising award. A stiff-upper-lip butler announces in a British accent, *Dinner is served, Madame, and it's . . .* He pauses, looks pained, and drawls, *a mighty purty chicken.* People started asking for Purty chickens by name, and the family business expanded by taking over small, struggling farms."

Val saw a chance to feed Chatty some useless information. "On the yacht before dinner, a heated argument started over the poultry industry gobbling up more land for chicken farms. Otto's former wife protested the inhumane way chickens were raised, and Louisa lashed out at her."

"I can tell you why she reacted so strongly. Animal treatment is a hot-button issue for the Purtys, going back decades. The animal rights folks ran a commercial that turned the tables on Purty Poultry. It started with a close-up of chickens crammed into cages where they can't even turn around. The same actor who played the bumpkin in the Purty-sponsored ads came into a huge building full of chicken cages and drawled, *Those sure are purty sad chickens.*" Chatty stopped kneading. "Tell me if I'm working your trapezius muscle too hard."

"I wouldn't know a trapezius from a trapezoid, but I'll let you know before you hurt me too badly. Did the animal rights ads hurt the Purtys much?"

Chatty moved her hands to Val's left leg. "Enough so that they pulled the mighty-purty-chicken commercials off the air."

The story of the ad war made Val wonder if Otto had known about Louisa's family feud with animal rights activists. Had he invited her and her husband in anticipation of a clash between them and his ex-wife? Why had they accepted the invitation of a man they'd just met? Chatty might know. "Did Louisa talk about being invited to dinner on the yacht?"

"She talked about nothing else last week. She was

thrilled with the invitation to a formal event she could brag about. Louisa's house is on Belleview Avenue, on the same block as Bayport's mayor, a state senator, and at least one Daughter of the American Revolution. Louisa expected to party with that crowd when she moved to the neighborhood, but it hasn't worked out that way."

"My great-grandparents moved here a hundred years ago. My grandfather is still a newcomer to the people who inherited houses on Belleview Avenue. Those families go back two or three centuries in Bayport."

"They don't snub all newcomers. I'll bet that when the secretary of state and the vice president bought houses on the Eastern Shore, the Belleview elite sent them invitations. A chicken heiress doesn't qualify as prominent."

The massage had relaxed Val to the point of drowsiness. "Poor Louisa. No welcome wagon for her."

"She did get one invitation from a woman on that block. Emily Adams, a Daughter of the American Revolution. I give her facials. Emily's always trying to recruit new members for the DAR's local chapter. She invited Louisa to tea, figuring farmers fought in the revolution, so a chicken farmer's daughter might just qualify for membership." Chatty moved to the other side of the table and kneaded Val's right calf. "Louisa *didn't* qualify, but they had a long conversation. Louisa gave Emily useful advice about prenups."

Val lifted her head. "How did that subject come up during a tea party?"

"Emily's son wants his daughter's fiancé to sign a prenup. Emily's afraid that will jinx the marriage. She's asked for advice from everyone—including me, when I was giving her a facial. Louisa defended prenups.

She said her husband had agreed to one and their marriage has lasted more than twenty-five years. Her prenup specified that, if they divorced, he got no money and only limited visiting rights to their children. That applied even if she divorced him."

"So he not only had to stay married to her, he had to keep her happy. I'm surprised he agreed to those terms."

"Louisa said that if more people had prenups like that, the divorce rate would plummet."

"And the discontent rate would soar," Val muttered. "I think people should stay married because they want to, not because it's in their financial interest." A thud came from the adjacent weight room, probably a barbell dropped by a bodybuilder. "Did you ever meet Louisa's husband?"

"Briefly, when I went to their house to do her makeup for the yacht party. You realize that when Louisa becomes the Eastern Shore's chicken queen, he'll be the prince of Purty Poultry. And he's already mighty purty."

Val laughed. "Especially in his tux."

"I'll say. I saw him in it as I was leaving. Except for his little bit of gray at the temples, he could have just stepped out of the wedding portrait that hangs over the sofa, where he's also wearing a tux. You'd never recognize Louisa from that picture. When she was younger, she had thick eyebrows and long, dark hair overwhelming her small head. Saturday night, with her brows plucked, her hair lightened, and me working on her face for thirty minutes, she didn't look half bad. Gotta wonder what he saw in her back then."

"Looks aren't everything." A lesson Val had learned the hard way when she found out her drop-dead gorgeous fiancé was cheating on her, at which point he became her former fiancé.

"Speaking of prenups, did Otto Warbeck and his wife have one?"

Val had thought they'd left that subject behind. "No idea, but it wouldn't surprise me if they did. Prenups and May-December marriages go together like horses and carriages."

"From what Bethany said, Otto treated his wife badly. Imagine asking her to entertain his ex-wife." Chatty worked her way up to Val's right arm. "We're in the home stretch now. Bethany said Otto made his guests play a mystery game. Tell me how it worked."

By the time Val had described the game, her massage was over. She jumped down from the massage table. "Otto called for a break halfway through the game, in the middle of dinner, and he didn't come back to the table. We never found out how the game ends."

"But you will. Bethany said you were going to pick up the game booklets. Are you going to the yacht when you leave here?"

"No. The police won't be finished there until late afternoon or evening." Val opened the door, glad to see the world beyond the massage closet, even if it consisted of exercise machines. "Thank you for the massage. I should give you an endless supply of that baking aroma oil. Then your clients will go from here directly to the café for something sweet."

Granddad was in the hall hanging up the phone when Val went into the house. "That's the third call today from folks who want you to cater for them." He ripped the top sheet off the notepad on the telephone table. "Here are their names and numbers."

"Three in one day? I usually get three in a month." Val glanced at the paper he gave her. No one she knew.

"They must have called because I talked you up in that TV interview yesterday. Free publicity. They all want you to cater a *Titanic* dinner for them. On land, not on a boat." When she groaned, he pointed to the second floor. "We could use some quick cash to pay for the termite damage up there. It'll be a long time before we finish the *Codger's Cookbook.*"

"You didn't like the idea of celebrating a disaster. Now you're all for it." She shouldn't be surprised at his about-face. Granddad relaxed his principles when it suited him. "I'm not catering any more ten-course meals."

"One lady said she wanted a four-course version. I'm sure you can talk the others into downsizing. You did the hard part of testing the recipes. You might as well reuse them."

Val felt her resistance ebbing. "I'll return the calls."

"I gotta get back to typing my recipes for this week." He went into the study and sat down in front of her computer.

She followed him into the room. "Did you catch the interview Cheyenne gave on TV today?"

"Nope. I was busy testing the recipes for my column. What did she say?"

"That Otto couldn't possibly have committed suicide. You'll have to come up with a new theory about the murder, Granddad. If she killed Otto, she'd have welcomed suicide as an explanation. Instead, she's claiming he was murdered."

Granddad pecked at the keyboard. "I'm sticking to

my theory. She's putting up a smoke screen. She rejected suicide because that's what an innocent person would do, and she's trying to look innocent."

Val couldn't argue with him, though she suspected Cheyenne didn't have as twisted a mind as his.

By the time he'd e-mailed his column with recipes to the *Gazette* and left to meet his friend Ned for pizza, she'd set up appointments to meet the catering clients who'd called earlier. She then worked on expanding her catering menu to include dishes served on the *Titanic*. She'd expected to hear from the chief. When he didn't call by six thirty, she assumed he must have forgotten to let her know when the police were finished with the yacht. She left him a voice mail, asking him to call her. Though she usually walked to Gunnar's house, she decided to drive, because she was a little late. She grabbed a bottle of bubbly on the way out.

Gunnar opened the door to the one-story brick house he rented. He looked more relaxed than he had for months. The last time she'd visited, the table in his combination living room and office had been stacked high with papers related to his clients' tax returns. Now it was set for two with the china his landlady had left with the house. "It's nice to see that table set for a romantic candlelit dinner. Your happy face means you're finished with taxes."

"The written part. I've been getting phone calls from clients who waited until the last day to look at their returns and ask me questions about them. I didn't have time to shop for groceries. Do you want to go out, or can you make do with an omelet and a salad, and then a long, leisurely dessert?" He wiggled his eyebrows at her.

"That sounds wonderful." She plopped down onto the love seat near the window. "After cooking elaborate dishes for the dinner party, I appreciate simple food cooked by someone else." She added, "I'll help, of course."

"You will not. You're my guest. Your job is to entertain me while we drink the champagne and I make dinner. What have you been doing since yesterday morning?"

They were halfway through dinner by the time she finished telling him about Althea's request for help for her nephew, Jerome's visit to Granddad's house, and Otto's body surfacing with a bullet hole in it.

He winced when she mentioned the bullet. "Yesterday I was joking about your exercising your sleuthing muscles. Now I'm worried you *will* exercise them. I hope you'll leave this one to the police."

"Of course . . . unless it looks as if they're going to arrest Jerome."

Gunnar put his fork down. "Has it occurred to you he might be guilty?"

"He had no reason to take drugs or to kill Otto."

"How about this for a reason? Otto leaves the table to go up to the bridge. When he gets there, he goes into a rage because Jerome turned off the autopilot and steered into a squall. Otto says he'll make sure Jerome never pilots another yacht. Jerome's plans for the future will go down the tube unless he gets rid of Otto. He drugs himself after shooting Otto. Then he can say he remembers nothing."

Val admitted to herself that Gunnar's scenario was plausible—but it still had weaknesses. "Jerome didn't come on the boat with a reason to kill Otto, so why would he have brought a gun with him?"

Gunnar shrugged. "It could have been Otto's gun. Maybe he kept it in a compartment on the bridge and Jerome found it earlier in the evening. He didn't intend to use it, but he knew where it was when he needed it."

"You make a good theoretical case, Gunnar, but you haven't met Jerome. Granddad and I have. We both think he's innocent, and he needs help to prove it."

"And you can't turn down pleas for help."

She leaned across the table. "Do you turn down any? We're cut from the same cloth."

"Proving Jerome innocent means proving someone else guilty. That could be dangerous. I said that the last time you went after a murderer, and you didn't pay any attention. I don't know why I bother." Gunnar downed the rest of his wine. "Let's talk about something else."

"Okay. What are you going to do tomorrow without income tax forms to fill in?"

"I'm getting up early to drive to Washington."

A trip he'd made often in the last few months. "More forensic accounting work?"

"No. Something else I want to pursue came up."

Val's phone chimed. She jumped up to pull it out of her shoulder bag. "Sorry. I need to get this." As she'd hoped, Chief Yardley was returning her call.

"We're just about finished at the yacht," he said. "The fish stink coming from the trash was real bad when the team went in there. They opened the doors to get a cross breeze, but once they close up, it'll get bad again."

"Ew." She'd planned to take the trash with her when leaving the yacht Saturday night, but after Otto disappeared, getting rid of garbage was far from her mind. "Why didn't they take the trash out?"

"Because they remove only items that might be relevant to a crime. Also, they've been in places that smelled a lot worse."

And the yacht would smell worse the longer she waited to go there. "Thanks for the warning. I'm on my way." She hung up.

Gunnar's eyebrows lowered, overshadowing his eyes like thunderclouds. "You're leaving?"

"Briefly, assuming Bethany's available. She has the key to the yacht, and we need to clear out some smelly garbage and leftover food." Val speed-dialed her friend. "Hi, Bethany. Chief Yardley said we can get on the yacht now. Okay if I pick you up in a few minutes?" Bethany agreed. Val tucked her phone away and faced Gunnar. "I'm sorry. I'll be back in less than an hour. Then we can have dessert."

He folded his arms. "Can't Bethany go to the yacht without you?"

Though Val felt bad about leaving, she'd have felt worse if she left the dirty work to her friend. "Bethany helped me with the dinner on Saturday night, when I needed her. I can't send her to deal with rotting food as if she's my servant."

Looking glum, he blew out the candles on the table. She gave him a quick kiss and bolted for the door.

It was dark by the time Val and Bethany boarded the *Abyss*. Val immediately put the trash out on the deck, hoping the fish stench would go away.

When she went back into the saloon, Bethany was lifting the cushions from the built-in sofa. "I'm looking for the envelope with the solution to the mystery game. I really want to know how it turns out. The compartment with the life vests would be a good place to hide it."

"I doubt Otto hid the envelope where he'd have to deconstruct the furniture to get to it. He'd make an Academy Award moment of revealing the solution, taking the envelope from his breast pocket or having Cheyenne hand it to him."

"I asked Cheyenne. She said she didn't know where the envelope was." Bethany put the cushions back on the sofa. "There's no hope if he had it on him. After a day in the water, it would be unreadable."

"I think we can figure out how the game ends if we have all the scripts." Val opened a drawer in the galley and spotted the scripts. "Right where I left them."

As she pulled the booklets from the drawer, a bit of paper fluttered from them to the floor. She stooped to pick it up.

Bethany came into the galley. "What are you doing down there?"

"Picking up Otto's business card. It must have fallen out of one of the booklets." Val stood up and read the card. "*Otto Warbeck, Maritime Law Consultant.*" She put the card on the counter next to the booklets.

Bethany fingered the card and turned it over. "Look. There's writing on the back. *Meet me, swim platform 8:45.* Otto must have written this and given it to one of the guests."

Val peered at the words inked on the back. A handwriting expert could figure out if Otto had jotted the note. She couldn't. She'd seen only his barely legible signature. "Wait a sec. Didn't you say you saw Otto writing during the dinner? If he made notes in his booklet, we can compare the ink and the writing to what's on the card." Val found Otto's booklet and flipped through it. "There's no writing in it."

"Then maybe he was writing that note." Bethany pointed to the business card. "He could have slipped it to someone at the table."

A spur-of-the-moment act by a man who'd planned the evening down to the smallest detail? Unlikely. Val had a different explanation. "He also could have written it before the party and tucked it into one of the booklets."

"Too bad you don't know which booklet the card came from." Bethany put the food from the refrigerator on the counter for Val to pack up. "If we figure out who went out on deck at eight forty-five, we'll know who met Otto."

"He left the saloon fifteen minutes before that and implied he was going up to the bridge. But that could have been an excuse to go on deck for his rendezvous."

Bethany continued to empty the fridge. "Stacy and Trey went out first. Then Damian. I'd say he left closest to eight forty-five. Cheyenne and Homer after that. Homer had an antique watch on a fob. I saw him check it a few times during dinner, like someone who had an appointment."

Val double-wrapped the leftover roast beef and put it at the bottom of the cooler. "A watch like that might not keep accurate time. If it ran slow, he could have gone out late to meet Otto."

She looked forward to showing the chief the note scrawled on Otto's business card. Maybe the police could lift fingerprints from it. Best not to touch it more than necessary. She rummaged in a drawer for tongs, nudged the card to the counter's edge, and grabbed it with the tongs. Then she dropped it into her jacket pocket.

Bethany shifted items in the refrigerator. "Why set up a meeting on the swim platform?"

"Privacy, I guess. People might have left the saloon to visit the head on the aft deck, but they wouldn't have had any reason to go down the stairs to the platform."

"Makes sense." Bethany closed the refrigerator door. "All the food that could go bad is out of the fridge. I left things like mustard and marmalade in case Cheyenne changes her mind about returning to the yacht." She opened the freezer. "Nothing in here except the sorbet."

"I hope you'll take it home. It's mostly shaved ice—perfect for your diet, if you haven't given it up."

"I'm still on it." Bethany picked up the booklets Val had left on the counter and flipped through them. "There are only seven. We're missing Homer's."

"I grabbed the ones that were left on the table after everyone got up for a break. Homer must have tucked his away." Val mimicked putting something inside a jacket pocket. "We'll have to try solving Otto's mystery game without all the clues. Can you come over tomorrow night? We can eat the leftovers, study the scripts, and brainstorm about Otto's mystery plot."

"I can come, but our brainstorming will be guesswork unless we find the envelope with the solution." Bethany searched the cabinet drawers and shelves without finding it. "Maybe he taped it to the underside of his chair or the table." She got down on her hands and knees to check. "No luck."

Val put the container of sorbet in the cooler. Then she collected the scripts. She had no room for them in her shoulder bag, so she set them on top of the food containers in the cooler. She glanced at Bethany, who was unpeeling the opaque film from a window in the saloon. "You won't find the envelope there. It would create a bulge in the film."

"I've given up on finding the envelope. I'm just checking how this decorative film works." Bethany stripped away more of the film and peered out the window. "Yipes! Someone's out there, lurking." She jumped away from the window and pressed the film back on it.

"What do you mean by *lurking*? Trying to hide?"

"No, but he—or she—is acting suspicious. Standing still on the dock, dressed in dark colors, wearing a hoodie."

"Nothing illegal about that." Val carried a cooler to the sliding door. "If you take the cooler, I'll grab the grocery bag and the garbage. We're done here. Let's go."

"Right now? When we know someone's lying in wait?"

Val had made fun of Bethany's jitters about zombies in a haunted corn maze last fall. Her fears this time weren't quite as groundless. Yet, they couldn't call 911 and ask to be rescued from someone standing on the dock.

Val reached into one of the many compartments in her shoulder bag and handed a small canister to Bethany. "Here's some pepper spray. If we delay, the suspicious person will have time to assemble a gang of lurkers. Now we're two against one. Later, who knows how many cutthroats we'll have to fend off."

"You're not taking this seriously, Val."

Not true. Val made sure no one was on the dock before they got off the yacht. And she glanced behind her several times as they hurried to the parking lot and loaded everything into the trunk of her Saturn. Once in the car, she relaxed.

After dropping Bethany off at home, Val checked her watch. She had enough time to move the food from the cooler to the fridge at home and dispose of the garbage bag before driving back to Gunnar's place. She parked as usual in Granddad's driveway, grabbed her shoulder bag from the floor behind her seat, and went around to the back of the car. As she was about to lift the trunk lid, she remembered the fish stench that would assault her. She put her bag down so she could hold her nose, opened the trunk, and reached inside for the garbage bag.

Something rammed into her shoulders and shoved her forward. She went facedown in the trunk. Her legs stuck out like a piece of furniture that wouldn't quite fit. Before she could move, the trunk lid came down on her calves. She yelped with pain.

The pressure on her legs let up as the trunk lid lifted, but it might come down again. To protect her legs, she rolled sidewise and curled up, knees to her chest. She glimpsed a figure in black behind the car. A second later the trunk lid slammed closed.

Chapter 11

Val broke out in a sweat and coiled herself into a fetal position. She could hear her heart pounding.

She had less room to stretch out than she'd have in a coffin. Her worse nightmares couldn't compare to this. In one of her recurring dreams, the elevator she was riding morphed into a runaway subway car speeding through tunnels and stations. At least she could see the world whizzing by her in that dream. Here there was only blackness.

She shuddered as the claustrophobe's demon took over her body. Only one way to exorcise it—Get out! But how?

She uncurled enough to check her pockets for the car keys. Not there. Oh no! They were probably dangling from the trunk door. Whoever shoved her into the trunk could drive her car somewhere remote and leave her there to die a slow and agonizing death.

A tremor seized her. Calm down, she told herself. The car hadn't moved. Maybe her attacker had pushed her into the trunk to buy time for an escape after stealing her bag.

She rolled over on her back and reached up to

touch the "ceiling" of her prison. Not enough room for her to sit. She might be able to crawl, but where? Hysteria bloomed inside her like a poisonous plant that would numb her limbs and brain. She fought it with action.

She pounded on the trunk door. "Help! Help!" She pounded some more. Then she screamed as loudly as she could.

No response from outside. Could anyone hear her shouts? Granddad would be back from pizza with his friend by now. He was probably watching TV with the volume on loud, only a few yards away from her. He wouldn't hear her cries through the thick walls of the old house. The best she could hope for was a dog walker passing by at the moment she was pounding on the trunk door or yelling. How long could she keep making noise? Her throat and her hands were already sore. They would find her in the morning, of course. Her body trembled at the thought of spending the night scrunched up here.

She had to find a way out herself. The car's back seat folded down and opened to the trunk. Maybe she could push on the seat back from this side and make it fold down. Then she could crawl into the passenger area. In total darkness, she felt her way toward the divider between the trunk and the rear seats. Her hands touched the cooler and the garbage bag. Only five minutes ago the reek of fish had concerned her. Now she couldn't smell it even when her nose was up against the bag. Either her senses were dulled by her terror or she'd gotten used to the odor.

When she reached the "wall" between the trunk and the back seat, she felt around for a latch or a strap. She found neither, but her fingers closed over a cable.

She tugged and pulled on it. Nothing happened. She tried again and gave up, but at least she'd stopped trembling. She'd regained some control of her body.

Her brain kicked into gear. The trunk lid must open from the inside. She wiggled on the floor to turn her body around and reached for the latch on the trunk lid. Her left hand grasped it. She jiggled the latch, but it didn't open. If she had any light, she might be able to figure out how it worked. In the dark all she had was her sense of touch. She gripped the metal mechanism and tried to move it up and down. It didn't budge. She pushed sideways on it and heard a click.

A crack of dim light appeared as the door un-latched. Dizzy with relief, she raised the door. She breathed blessedly fresh air and scrambled out of the trunk. Her knees, bent for what seemed an eternity, nearly gave way when her feet touched the ground.

Her keys dangled from the trunk door lock. She closed the door, removed them, and rushed into the house by the side door. She'd take the food and garbage from the car later, but first she'd call the police.

Granddad was snoring in his easy chair while a 1940s film noir from his DVD collection played on the TV screen.

She called 911 and reported the incident. When she hung up, she thought about the things in her shoulder bag. Her driver's license, phone, and credit cards—all gone. What a pain.

Granddad woke up when the doorbell rang. A middle-aged Bayport police officer with broad shoulders and a weathered face stood on the porch. She remembered him from last summer when she'd reported a prowler around the house. He'd blamed a raccoon for the noises she'd heard and suggested more outdoor light fixtures to discourage trespassers. This time he couldn't scapegoat a raccoon.

She invited the officer into the sitting room. He took the armchair, while she sat on the sofa near Granddad's lounge chair. She told the two men what had happened, without mentioning her claustrophobia and her frantic efforts to escape the trunk.

The officer took notes. "Did you see anyone walking in the neighborhood or an unfamiliar car on the street when you drove up?" When she shook her head, he continued, "What can you tell me about the person who shoved you?"

"Nothing. He came at me from behind." Val flashed back to the second before her attacker shut the trunk. "I take that back. I caught a glimpse just before the trunk door came down. I didn't see a face, just the torso."

"Man or woman?"

Val conjured an image of the shadowy figure. "Probably a man, but I can't rule out a tall woman in bulky clothes. Dark clothes, black or navy blue." *Like the figure Bethany had seen standing on the dock.* Val decided not to mention that her attacker might have followed her from the marina. She didn't want to worry Granddad.

He piped up. "You've got a good nose, Val. Did you get a whiff of the guy who pushed you?"

"Good question, sir," the officer said. "Did you smell anything, like cigarette smoke, perfume, or chewing gum?"

"I smelled nothing but two-day-old salmon from the trash bag in the trunk." The fish odor would be worse by morning. "I need to take the garbage out of the trunk. I also have coolers full of food that should come inside."

The officer grimaced. "Better not touch the trunk lid 'til we have a chance to check for fingerprints. If we get some, we'll see if your thief is in the system."

"I can reach into the trunk from the back seat."

"Okay. I'm going to check the neighborhood in case your thief is looking to snatch other purses."

Once the officer drove off, Val brought the leftover food inside, and Granddad dumped the trash in the garbage can behind the house. When he came back to the kitchen, he picked up the scripts she'd left on the counter. "So you got 'em."

"All but one. See if you can figure out where Otto was going with his mystery game."

Granddad sat at the kitchen table and spread out the scripts.

After storing the leftovers, she made him a cup of tea and joined him at the table. "Reach any conclusions?"

"Yep. It was Miss Scarlet in the dining room with the candlestick." He grinned at her and gathered the scripts into a pile. "I can match questions with answers. But there's so much information, it's confusing. You might have to make a grid with the suspects and the evidence and clues against them."

"It'll be less confusing if we act out the roles. Bethany's coming to dinner tomorrow. We'll do it then."

"We need another person so we're each keeping track of only two people. A good job for an unemployed actor. Ask Gunnar."

Gunnar! Val thunked her forehead. "I was supposed

to meet him for dessert two hours ago." He'd probably tried to call her cell phone, now stolen. The doorbell rang. "Maybe that's him now."

She rushed to the hall and flung open the door. The police officer stood there, his uniform glistening with rain. She hadn't even known rain was in the forecast.

"Is this yours?" He held out her shoulder bag. At her nod, he continued, "Found it lying near the curb three blocks away. I picked it up before it got too wet. Take a look inside and tell me what's missing."

She was relieved to see her phone and her wallet. Her driver's license and credit cards were untouched, but the bills were gone. "The only thing missing is money. Around fifty dollars."

The officer grunted. "Smart thief, taking only cash. If he used the credit cards or your phone, we'd have a good chance of tracking him down. I don't want to raise your hopes that we'll catch the guy. We don't have much to go on. No description. Probably no fingerprints on your cloth wallet and bag. The rain's washing away any fingerprints on the car."

And the police weren't likely to divert resources from a murder investigation to nail someone who stole fifty dollars. "I understand. Thank you for retrieving my bag."

As she closed the door behind the officer, Granddad came into the hall and said he was turning in. She told him she'd gotten her bag back, kissed him good night, and then checked her voice mail. Gunnar had called at nine thirty, when she was in the trunk. Too bad the phone hadn't been with her. She called him back.

He picked up the phone after three rings. "Val."

She expected him to be annoyed, but the coldness in his tone surprised her. "Sorry I didn't get back to your place. I had a really good reason."

"I'm sure you do. Save it for another time."

His words hit her like ice water in the face. "I was locked in a trunk, Gunnar."

He said nothing for three seconds. "A storage trunk? How did you get—?"

"A car trunk." She told him how she'd ended up there.

"Are you hurt?"

"My legs will be black and blue. I'll never buy another car with a trunk. Otherwise, I'm fine."

"I was worried when you didn't answer your phone. I went to the marina to make sure you were okay. Your car wasn't there, so I drove by your house and saw it in the driveway."

"Then what? You went home?" She concluded from his silence that the answer was yes. "Why didn't you ring my doorbell?"

"I assumed you forgot about dessert because you were busy solving your latest mystery."

His peevish reply surprised and annoyed her. "While you were driving by the house, I was screaming for help and banging on the trunk lid."

"You can't blame me for not guessing you were in the trunk."

True, but he should have known something was wrong. "I've always called when I'm running late, which isn't often. And I've never failed to show up." He had no faith in her—not a good sign for their future together.

"I'm sorry, Val. Tonight didn't turn out the way I planned. Can we start from scratch tomorrow evening?"

He'd suggested starting from scratch once before when he'd misjudged her. Would this be the last time they'd have to reset the clock on their relationship? "Tomorrow I'd like you to come here and eat *Titanic* dinner leftovers with Granddad, Bethany, and me. We'll do some role-playing too, reading Otto's scripts for his mystery game."

"I'll do it, if we can stage a redo of tonight's dinner on Wednesday, just the two of us."

"Agreed. See you tomorrow at seven."

Val trudged upstairs to her room, taking the booklets with her, but she was too tired to pore over them. She dreamed that the missing script had fallen down a well and that only she was small enough to ride down in a bucket to fetch it. Gunnar lowered her down, but the well was deep, and the rope broke. She snapped awake in a sweat. Trying to calm down, she planned how to get hold of the missing script without going down a well. When she finished her shift at the café, she would visit Cheyenne and, if necessary, take a trip to Homer's antique shop in Annapolis.

Val called Chief Yardley in the morning to tell him about the note on the back of Otto's business card. The chief's voice mail message said he'd be in an all-day meeting.

The café was busier than usual for a Tuesday morning. The TV interview Cheyenne had given the day before brought Val new customers, eager to hear about the dinner she'd catered and the *Titanic* collector's yacht. They also asked questions she couldn't answer about the investigation into his death.

Midway through the morning she noticed Damian

Brown in the club's reception area, outside the café. He looked buff in an athletic shirt that hugged his shoulders and biceps. He lingered near the café alcove until the three people at the eating bar left. Then he took the seat at the end and put his athletic bag on the seat next to it. If the café had been busy, Val would have asked him to move the bag, but he'd hit the slack time between breakfast and lunch.

He smiled across the bar at her. "Hi, Val."

"Nice to see you here, Damian. What would you like?" *Coffee, tea, information?*

"Coffee and, uh, one of those." He pointed to the biscotti under a glass dome on the counter.

Val poured his coffee and put the biscotti on a plate in front of him. "Louisa often comes to the café after her fitness classes, but I've never seen you at the club before. What brings you here?"

"Needed some exercise. If it wasn't for the rain, I'd be on the golf course. That's where I conduct a lot of business," he said, as if he had to justify his time on the links. "A week ago I was playing golf with Otto. Now the poor guy's dead. And it happened at his own party." Damian locked eyes with her. "Your food was the only good thing about that party."

"Thank you." Was he trying to butter her up or come on to her? An image of him flirting with Cheyenne popped into Val's mind. "You looked as if you were enjoying yourself early in the evening."

"Just being polite, but it wasn't easy." He stirred sugar into his coffee. "When Otto invited us to a formal dinner on a yacht, we thought we were going to be on a large boat with lots of prominent people. But there was nobody there except another *Titanic* fanatic, a chicken kook, and an eco-nut. Otto's wife was the only normal person at the party . . . not counting you and your helpers." He crunched down on the biscotti.

His wife had been more vocal than the fanatic, the kook, and the nut. "Stacy and Trey have strong feelings about the causes they believe in. Louisa's like that too. She got pretty heated when she talked about chicken farming."

He sipped his coffee. "An attack on chicken farming is an attack on her family, the Purtys. I learned long ago that Louisa always takes their side."

Val heard the note of bitterness in his honeyed drawl. Was he still stewing over the prenup he'd signed decades ago? Maybe, but saying his wife *always* sided with the Purtys suggested that the in-laws took precedence over him even now.

A man at one of the bistro tables caught her eye and raised his mug. "Excuse me while I give a customer a refill."

Damian nursed his coffee until she returned. "Too bad we didn't finish the mystery game Otto made us play. I wouldn't mind knowing how it ends." He took two sips of coffee, giving her time to comment. When she didn't, he said, "I noticed you collecting the booklets from the table Saturday night. Did you take them home with you?"

"No." Not Saturday night anyway. "If you're really curious about how the game ends, ask the police. They searched the yacht thoroughly and might have found the envelope with Otto's solution."

"They have more important things to do than satisfy my curiosity." He put his empty mug down. "I heard you're no stranger to murders. You think that's what happened to Otto, or did he off himself?"

A vulgar and unfeeling comment. "*Off himself*? That's

offensive to anyone touched by a suicide," Val said through clenched teeth.

Damian's eyes widened in surprise. "No offense meant." He reached for his bag and climbed off the bar stool. "If it's not suicide, my money's on the ex or the kid." He slapped a five-dollar bill down on the bar.

Val watched him leave the café. *Cary Grant he ain't,* she thought, echoing Granddad's comment about Louisa. Damian lacked the polish of the characters the Hollywood star played. In fact, he resembled the person Otto had given him to play in the mystery game—a man from a lower-class background who'd married for money. Did he have more than that in common with the *Titanic* passenger he'd played?

Val was convinced he'd come to the café to find out if she had the scripts. Why was he so interested in them, and could he have pushed her into her trunk to get them? She was still pondering those questions two hours later when his wife sat down at the eating bar for lunch.

Louisa's outfit and air of serenity suggested she'd just come from a yoga class. She took her time eating her Cobb salad and drinking her smoothie.

With the café busier than usual, Val had little chance to talk with any of her customers.

Louisa caught her eye as the lunch crowd thinned out. "Cheyenne was on TV this morning, saying Otto would never have committed suicide. He was such an odd duck, I wouldn't be surprised if he killed himself. When he disappeared on the yacht, it occurred to me he might have jumped into the bay."

The older woman sitting next to Louisa spoke up. "I volunteer on a suicide hotline. Hardly anyone commits suicide by drowning. It's an agonizing way to die. Suicidal people look for fast and easy methods."

Louisa nodded. "Like guns. I heard gun suicides are more common than gun murders."

Val wiped the counter. "That doesn't mean Otto committed suicide."

Louisa gave her a sharp look. "So you think he was murdered? Are the police treating his death as a murder?"

Val shrugged. "They haven't said."

On the way home from the café, Val stopped at the Warbecks' house, a nice but ordinary two-story neo-Colonial.

Cheyenne answered the doorbell. "Val, I'm so glad you came by. I was planning to get in touch with you." She opened the door wide and beckoned Val into the hallway with a staircase to the upper floor.

An enthusiastic welcome, considering Cheyenne hadn't even seen the chocolate chip cookies Val had brought. Had she really intended to contact Val, or did she just say that out of politeness? "I stopped by to say how sorry I am for your loss. And I brought you some cookies."

Cheyenne took the tin Val held out. "Aw. Thank you. You are so nice, like everyone else in this town."

"Bayport has lots of friendly people. It's a good place to get your bearings."

"I'd have been happy to live here with Otto. Now, without him, I doubt I'll stay. Come in and sit down." She led the way into the living room and put the cookie tin on the coffee table next to her phone. "I'll get us some iced tea." She bustled through the dining room to the kitchen.

Val nearly tripped on the fringe of a Persian rug as

she crossed the room, which looked like a *Titanic* museum. The decor recalled the opulence of a bygone era—Tiffany lamps, claw-foot chairs and sofas upholstered in velvet and brocade, marble-topped side tables with carved wood bases. A painting over the sofa depicted the majestic ship leaving port. Val glanced at the newspaper front pages framed and displayed on the walls. The *Boston Globe* with the headline "Titanic Sinks, 1500 Die" hung next to the *Evening Sun* reporting "All Titanic Passengers Are Safe." News and false hope, side by side. A curio cabinet held a wood model of the ship and antique silver serving pieces— things that would catch dust and need polishing.

Poor Cheyenne. She was stuck in a house full of century-old objects related to a disaster with a huge death toll. No wonder she wanted to leave.

She came back from the kitchen with two iced teas and put them on the glass-topped coffee table. Val sat down on a pink velvet love seat.

Cheyenne sank into a brocade-covered sofa at right angles to the love seat. "How long have you lived in Bayport?"

"I moved here a little over a year ago, after professional and personal setbacks. Now I feel like it's the home I always wanted and didn't have most of my life."

"You're lucky. I don't know where home for me is yet." The widow sipped her iced tea. "Bethany told me you've looked into some mysterious deaths here and found evidence of what happened. Can you prove that my husband didn't commit suicide?" When Val hesitated, Cheyenne added, "I'll pay you."

"I won't take any money." Val was glad Granddad didn't hear her say that. Money always came with strings attached to the person who was paying. "To prove something didn't happen, you have to find out what did happen."

"That's what I want you to do. Find out who shot Otto." She set her iced tea glass on the table. "Otto had a secret agenda for that dinner party. I don't know if it had anything to do with his death, but I'll share with you what he told me about his guests."

Chapter 12

Cheyenne opened the tin with the cookies. "Some small things disappeared from Otto's *Titanic* collection around the time when he was breaking up with Stacy. He suspected Trey of stealing them, but he couldn't prove it. A few months ago, before we moved here, he saw one of them in the antique shop Homer owns."

Val glanced at the curio shelves full of small things, easy to swipe. "What was it?"

"A silver bud vase with the emblem of the White Star Line. It came from a sister ship, not the *Titanic*. They both had vases like that."

The White Star Line must have ordered those vases by the cartload, but if few existed a hundred years later, a single vase might be worth a lot. "How did Otto know that the one in Homer's shop came from his collection?"

"Otto said the vase had scratches identical to the ones on his vase. Homer asked for proof of ownership. Otto had to search for the paperwork because we were in the process of moving. By the time he went back to the shop, the vase was gone. Homer said the consigner had taken it back. He wouldn't give Otto the name of the person who brought in the vase. He said anonymity was part of the consignment agreement."

Val could understand Homer's reluctance to get in the middle of a dispute about ownership. "I guess there was nothing Otto could do to get the vase back."

"He tried. He thought Homer was keeping it to sell under the table. Otto sent me to the antique shop. I used my maiden name and told Homer I was looking for *Titanic* collectibles for my husband. He showed me all kinds of things, but nothing on Otto's list of stolen items. My husband sent me to the shop twice more. I even asked to see vases from other ocean liners. No luck."

The antique dealer had either acted aboveboard or suspected a trap. "Did Homer have any idea who you were?" Val said.

"I don't think so. When he boarded the yacht on Saturday, he told me I looked like someone he once knew." Cheyenne laughed.

Val sipped her iced tea. "With Otto's suspicions about the stolen vase, it's strange he invited Homer to the dinner party."

"He said he had unfinished business with Homer. When I found out Trey was invited too, I realized what Otto had in mind. He wanted to see if Trey and Homer gave any sign of knowing each other."

Knowing each other wouldn't prove that they conspired to sell stolen items. Val came up with another possible reason for Otto's invitation. He wanted them to squirm during the mystery game while the other guests served as his mouthpiece. Though Val had been distracted during the game, she'd heard insinuations that Trey was a jewel thief and Homer a shady dealer.

Cheyenne's phone played a tune. She picked it up and glanced at the display. "Excuse me. I'll have to get this." She went into the hall.

Val stood up and took a cookie. Better to eat it on her feet rather than risk dropping a tiny bit of chocolate on the pink velvet upholstery. She noticed some framed pictures of Otto and stacks of photos on the dining room table. She couldn't resist a peek at them.

Cheyenne joined her. "I'm trying to decide which pictures of Otto to include in the video at the memorial service. Just by looking at them, I found out things I never knew about him. Look, he played baseball." She picked up a stack of photos and extracted one of a boy about nine or ten, posing with a bat. Then she showed Val some pictures of Otto on his college baseball team—batting, fielding, and posing with his teammates. "We weren't married long enough for me to get to know him." She bit her lip, holding back tears.

Val leafed through the photos, giving Cheyenne time to handle her onslaught of grief.

The college player looked like a younger version of the Otto Val had met, but the child in the photo didn't. His baseball hat was too big for his small head, as were his ears. His teeth protruded. Either he'd changed a lot during puberty or the boy with the bat was someone else, possibly a brother or a friend. There were piles of pictures for Cheyenne to sift through.

When she looked composed, Val said, "Does Otto have relatives who can help you select photos?"

"Not really. His sister died when he was in his twenties, and his parents are dead too. His closest relatives are second cousins in California. They didn't even bother to come to our wedding, but I heard from them today. Ha." Cheyenne's mock laugh sounded as if she was spitting out something bitter. "One of them even had the nerve to ask about Otto's will. I'd just heard from his lawyer that Otto left me everything, except for the *Titanic* stuff, which goes to different museums. I made that perfectly clear to the California clan. Now that they know they'll get nothing, I'd be surprised if they show up for the memorial service."

"Don't rule it out," Val said. "They may become your new best friends."

Cheyenne groaned. "When you grow up cash-strapped like I did, you imagine that having money will solve all your problems. That's not true. You just have different problems. From now on, I won't know whether people like me for myself or for my money. Not a worry I had with Otto or anybody else, until now." She rubbed her temples, as if the prospect of being rich gave her a throbbing headache. Her phone rang again. "Excuse me." She slipped into the kitchen to take the call.

Val shuffled through the photos on the table. A picture of Otto as a child caught her eye. He looked a lot like the boy with the baseball bat, small-faced with prominent teeth and ears. He had a baby girl on his lap. Was she the sister who'd died young?

Cheyenne came back into the dining room. "I've just lost my husband and I get self-serving phone calls from second cousins, people I used to work with, and even total strangers. They start with condolences and end with schemes they want me to invest in or donations they say Otto intended to make. Let's sit down again. I want to try your cookies. I haven't eaten much since Sunday night. What were we talking about?"

"Otto's suspicions about Trey and Homer." Val followed Cheyenne into the living room.

Cheyenne perched on the sofa and bit into a cookie. "Mmm. This is heavenly." She gobbled it up. "I couldn't understand why Otto was so convinced Trey was the thief when Stacy could have stolen the stuff just as easily."

A touch of resentment against wife number one? Maybe everything Cheyenne had said previously had been leading up to an accusation against Stacy. "Did it bother you that Otto invited his former wife to the party?"

"Yes, it bothered me. Especially because he didn't tell me until half an hour before the party started. I couldn't do anything to change his mind then."

Except complain loudly. As Cheyenne reached for another cookie, Val remembered hearing the raised voices of Otto and his wife as they argued on the lower deck, possibly about his former wife. Could he have decided to turn back the clock, divorce his new wife, and try again with Stacy? If so, Cheyenne would have had a reason to kill him before he could do that. She also had a reason to suggest the theft of *Titanic* artifacts as the motive for his murder.

Val decided to push the issue. "Do you think Otto's pursuit of the stolen artifacts had something to do with his death?"

Cheyenne fidgeted. "Stacy and Trey wouldn't want the theft to come out. Draw your own conclusion."

Val preferred probing to accepting Cheyenne's implications. "If Otto didn't have proof that Trey stole the item when the theft occurred, he certainly wouldn't have found it now."

"But people don't think things through when they feel threatened. Trey must have known Otto suspected him after Otto gave him the part of a thief in the mystery game."

Val seized her chance to bring up the reason for her visit. "Speaking of the game, is there a copy of it on Otto's computer?"

"I don't know, and I can't check. The police took his electronic equipment, the computer, the printer, and the cell phone." Cheyenne tilted her head sideways, scrutinizing Val. "Bethany told me you'd collected the booklets from the table Saturday and left them on the yacht. She said you were going to pick them up along with the leftover food. Didn't you find them?"

"All except Homer's. I hoped you could get it from Otto's computer." Val felt she had to justify her interest in the booklets. "I enjoy solving mysteries, as Bethany told you. To solve the one in the game, I need to know what comes out in the last scenes."

"You and Homer. He called me yesterday and asked for the game booklets. I told him they were on the yacht."

Val's heart sped up. Could Homer have been the figure in black lurking on the dock? Though on the far side of sixty, he looked strong, tall, and broad-shouldered. He'd have no trouble shoving a small woman into a trunk. "Did you mention that Bethany and I were going to the yacht for the leftover food and the booklets?"

Cheyenne looked up at the ceiling as if someone up there knew the answer. "Uh-huh. I'd just gotten off the phone with Bethany. She told me you expected to go there later on."

Val warned herself not to jump to conclusions. Homer might have seen them go aboard the yacht, waited until they left, and then followed her all the way home. But would he have assaulted her on the off chance that her bag contained the mystery game booklets? And why would he want them? She could think of one reason—to limit any damage to his reputation if the similarity between his character and the role he played as a crooked dealer came out. He had more to lose than Stacy or Trey if Otto went public with his suspicions about the stolen *Titanic* artifacts. His business would decline if customers couldn't rely on his honesty.

Cheyenne took another cookie. "I expected the *Titanic* mystery game to bomb, but I was really grateful for it that night. It was the cocktail hour that bombed. Stacy lectured Damian, and Louisa lit into her. Trey was rude, and Homer was boring. I was glad we had scripts to follow at the table. Then I didn't have to make conversation with those horrible people. Damian was the only tolerable guest."

"Was that the first time you met him and Louisa?"

"I talked to them briefly at the Protect the Bay Barbecue two weeks ago. Damian and Otto played golf together a few days after that."

"They must have gotten along well for Otto to invite him and his wife to the dinner."

"When he first mentioned the *Titanic* party, I suggested inviting a lawyer from his old firm, Jerry Kindell, and his wife. They'd asked us to dinner when we got engaged and come to our wedding. They couldn't make it, so Otto invited Damian and Louisa instead. He needed another couple for his mystery game to work."

Cheyenne's phone summoned her again.

"Hello . . . Yes." She listened and said, "Funny you should call. Give me a second." She turned to Val. "I'll be right back."

Val watched her leave for the kitchen. Otto's wife had talked freely, but not because Val had brought cookies or expertly coaxed information from her. Cheyenne had revealed what she'd wanted others to know and probably concealed at least as much. Unless she was a very good actress, she hadn't faked her deep unhappiness. She could be grieving even if she'd murdered Otto—grieving for a marriage that didn't work out.

Cheyenne didn't sit down when she returned to the living room. Instead she moved toward the foyer. "Thank you so much for the cookies. It was good to talk to you."

Reluctantly, Val stood up. "Have you told the police what Otto suspected about the stolen *Titanic* artifacts?"

Cheyenne shook her head. "What if he was wrong? I'd hate to denounce anyone to the police without any evidence. If you find some evidence, you could bring it to their attention. It would be more believable if it came from you. You're someone they know."

With Cheyenne moving closer to the front door, Val could no longer ignore the hints to leave. Thanks to the widow, she knew where to go next. "What's the name of Homer's antique shop?"

"Timeless Treasures. More trinkets than treasures in that place. Thank you again for coming by. I'd appreciate anything you can do to put a lid on the idea that Otto committed suicide."

Back in the car Val checked for the shop's address and phone number. Barring an accident on the Chesapeake Bay Bridge, Val had enough time to get to the shop and back before dinner. She called the shop to make sure Homer would be there and then drove toward Annapolis.

Chapter 13

A sixtyish woman with henna hair and foot-long feather earrings smiled from behind the counter at Homer's antique shop. Vintage jewelry hung from her neck and encircled her arms.

"Welcome to Timeless Treasures," she said in a Southern drawl. "We specialize in itty-bitty things. Our shop is full of unique, exquisite pieces small enough to fit in your purse or under your arm. Is there something in particular you're looking for?"

Homer, but he was far from small. Val spotted him with a customer at the other end of the long, narrow shop. "I'll browse a bit." Several thousand items stood between her and Homer.

"You poke around all you like, hon." The woman took a sip from a crystal water glass near the checkout counter. "Smalls are big in the world of antiques these days—tiny collectibles with lots of personality and fascinating histories. People make groupings of little treasures. They're so economical you can replace them frequently and have something new for your friends to admire each time they visit. And they make such nice gifts too."

Val surveyed the room. The smalls rested on shelves and glass cases along the side walls and on tables that stretched like a chain of islands from the front to the back of the shop. The table nearest the checkout counter held brass horse irons, glass ink bottles, crystal salt cellars, china cups, silver candle snuffers, wood bowls, and enamel boxes of myriad sizes and shapes. She knew little about antiques, but she would have expected groupings by function or material. "Do you have the smalls organized by their origin or historical period?"

"Nothing like that. You can focus on a treasure better if it's not surrounded by similar things." The woman joined Val at the table, carrying her glass with her. "We do have some special sections toward the back, one for nautical collectibles—mostly things from ocean liners. Along the far wall, where you see my husband, we have vintage jewelry and *Titanic* treasures."

Startled that the woman was married to Homer, Val thought of the old quip about England and America as countries divided by a common language. The Huxbys were similarly divided, the husband with clipped British tones, the wife with elongated syllables like molasses slowly spreading. "I met Homer for the first time last weekend. I didn't realize he was your husband. I'm Val Deniston."

Homer's wife switched her glass into her left hand and thrust out her right hand to shake Val's. "I'm Emma Jean Huxby. Pleased to make your acquaintance. Are you visiting, or are you local?"

"Local, but not close by. I live forty-five minutes away." Though Val hated to come across as nosy, she couldn't tamp down her curiosity about how the Huxbys had met. Emma Jean had opened a door with her personal question. "I'm guessing from the way you talk that you aren't from this part of Maryland, and Homer isn't either."

"We come from Chattanooga. We've known each other since we were kids."

Val gaped at her. Hard to believe the husband and wife came from the same hemisphere. "Were Homer's parents British?"

"His momma was. She married a GI stationed in England. He brought her back to Tennessee. Homer took to talking like her, not like his daddy and the rest of us." She sipped from her glass. "Homer and I lived in London for five years right after we were married. I never did pick up the accent. Homer didn't just pick it up—he held on tight to it."

Val suppressed a smile. "I took him for a Brit."

"He visits England every year to buy smalls and get a booster shot for his accent." Emma Jean giggled into her glass.

"How did you end up in Maryland?"

"We've got a son in Pennsylvania, a daughter in Virginia, and another one in North Carolina. So we plunked ourselves down in the middle when we retired and started our antiques business." The bell over the shop door jingled as two women came in. Emma Jean put her glass down amid the smalls on the table. "If you have any questions, just holler."

She met the newcomers with the same welcome speech she'd given Val, word for word. Val leaned down to peer at the tiny flowers painted on an enamel pillbox and got a whiff of evergreen and alcohol. The fragrance came from the glass inches from her nose. Emma Jean had been drinking gin, not water.

Val straightened up, simmering inside about the nastiness of Otto's game. If Emma Jean had attended his dinner with her husband as planned, she would have played the role assigned to Bethany, the chaperone with a drinking problem. Val realized for the first time that Otto wasn't just manipulative, he was malicious. He'd intended to embarrass one, or all, of his guests.

Val could understand his frustration at being cheated by Trey and Homer and the urge to take revenge for that. But she couldn't excuse Otto for drawing attention to a woman's weakness. Fortunately, Emma Jean had escaped embarrassment by staying home. But Otto's cruel intentions would have been obvious to her husband. Homer might have felt the urge to kill as he sat at the dinner table, but would he have brought a gun with him?

Val drifted toward the back of the shop, ready to claim Homer's attention as soon as he was free. She stopped at the table devoted to ocean liner memorabilia. On one side of the table were postcards, menus, and brochures, all in cellophane envelopes, from a variety of passenger ships. Most of the memorabilia dated from the first half of the twentieth century. The table also held souvenirs passengers had either bought in a gift shop on board or swiped, like playing cards, ashtrays, and napkin rings. There was an eggcup from the *SS United States*, a silver spoon with the Cunard crest on it, and two bud vases, neither of them the White Star Line vase Otto had told Homer was stolen.

Despite that claim, Homer had accepted Otto's dinner invitation. Val wondered why.

She studied the emblem on the eggcup and tuned in to Homer's sales pitch when she heard him mention the *Titanic* to the young woman he was helping.

"This silver ring is modeled on an original artifact recovered from the *Titanic*," he said. "Openwork designs like this were popular in the Edwardian era. The ring has seventy-nine crystals. Can you read the inscription here?" He handed his customer a magnifying glass.

"It looks like letters and numbers."

"Yes. *L to A 6.9.10.* The numbers are the date: the ninth of June in 1910. The inscription suggests someone with the initial *L* gave the ring to someone with the initial *A*. It was salvaged from the wreckage at the bottom of the sea, protected by a leather purser's bag. Leather is impermeable, and the fish don't eat it. The same bag contained an ID bracelet with the name *Amy* spelled out in diamonds. The *A* in the ring inscription may refer to Amy. Alas, no one knows for sure who she was."

Nicely done, Val thought. His customer tried on the ring. He'd told her up front that the ring was a replica, but from then on he'd talked only about the real artifact. The history of the original embellished the copy of it.

"I love it! Would you please put it aside for me?" his customer said. "I'm going to ask my husband to buy it for my birthday."

"Talk to Emma Jean at the counter up front. She'll explain our policies on holding merchandise." He locked the ring away in the jewelry display.

Val put down the eggcup as the tall, thickset man

wearing a red plaid bow tie approached her. "Hello, Homer. We meet again. I'm Val, the caterer on Otto's yacht."

He looked at her over his reading glasses, which rested halfway down his nose. "I remember your excellent dinner, sadly cut short. Such a tragedy. And now, we hear a gun was involved. Do you know that a few *Titanic* survivors reported hearing gunshots as the lifeboats were deployed? Rather more realism than any of us bargained for Saturday night." Homer tucked his reading glasses into his shirt pocket. "I'm delighted you stopped in. I have something to discuss with you. But first, have you found any treasures that interest you?"

"Nothing on this table caught my eye." She pointed to the ocean liner souvenirs. "But I enjoyed your description of the ring. I couldn't help overhearing the fascinating story behind it."

"Unlike most antique purveyors, I tell the history behind the object, making it more meaningful. So often the story sells the item. Come with me and I'll show you our vintage jewelry collection." He led her to a wall decorated with dangling necklaces and bracelets. "Here you have high-quality costume jewelry. More valuable pieces are in the glass cases."

"Do you have any real *Titanic* artifacts?"

He laughed. "Real artifacts go for a fortune. Low supply, high demand. *Titanic* museums in Southampton, Belfast, Halifax, and several states in this country want them, not to mention private collectors. The Amy bracelet you heard me describe was part of a jewelry collection that sold for two hundred million. A letter written on the *Titanic*, saved in the jacket a survivor wore, went for almost two hundred thousand dollars. I don't have anything of that caliber, but I do have some White Star Line decorative objects, as well as jewelry and decorative items from the same era." He pointed to a glass case along the wall. A sign on top read *Titanic*-Era Collectibles. "If you see anything in here that catches your fancy, I'll unlock the case and you can look more closely at it."

Val scanned the case for the bud vase that Otto had believed was his. Nothing like that was in it. "Is this the sort of thing Otto collected, or did he have genuine artifacts?"

"More the former than the latter, I suspect, though I'm not familiar with his collection." Homer took a key from his pocket but tucked it back in after Val moved away from the glass case. "When I offered my condolences to Otto's widow yesterday, I asked about the booklets from the mystery game. She said you were to fetch them from the yacht. If you've done so, I'd very much like to have them." He paused and then added, "Happy to pick them up from . . . wherever you call home."

Wherever you call home. Was that to convince her he couldn't have pushed her into the trunk because he didn't know where she lived? "Your booklet wasn't with the others on the yacht. I assume you took it with you. Do you mind if I borrow it for a few days?"

"What are you going to do with the booklets in the next few days?"

"Satisfy my curiosity about how Otto's game was supposed to end. What are *you* going to do with them?" Val suspected he planned to "lose" them, the sooner the better.

"Throw *Titanic* dinners, much like Otto's, but on

land. People pay to attend mystery dinners. Mine would have the added attraction of a *Titanic* theme. I'll move from table to table, share stories about the *Titanic* passengers, and showcase my collectibles to entice people to the shop."

His marketing scheme impressed Val. He'd charge for the dinner and use it to drum up customers—but he didn't need Otto's scripts to do that. "You can download a mystery game much like Otto's. I'll send you a link for the website where you'll find the game that I believe he based his on."

Homer flicked his wrist. "I've played that game in the UK. Twice. I want to offer a unique experience."

Val pounced on his words. "Unique because Otto customized it for the guests he invited?"

The antique dealer's gray eyes hardened into stones. "Unique because no one else has a copy, and because there's a real mystery associated with the fictional mystery. What happened to the girl on the *Titanic*, and what happened the first time the game was played?"

"You mean the dinner on a yacht, a storm on the bay, and a tragic death." Probably a murder. "That's the story you're going to tell your guests?" Nothing like exploiting someone else's misfortune.

"Precisely. The connection of the mystery game to a recent death would make the dinner more piquant, don't you think? Past and present coming together. We will, of course, have a moment of silence for Otto." Homer indulged in a split-second of silence. "I envision holding these dinners several times a year, if possible with multiple tables." He smiled at her like a kindly uncle bestowing an unexpected gift. "Perhaps you'd like to cater the dinners?"

Otto's proposed dinner had tempted Val. This one

didn't. She opened her mouth to decline, but changed her mind. As someone who could help him, she had a bargaining chip she could use to extract information. "We'd have to iron out the details. By the way, how did you meet Otto?"

"He visited the shop a few months ago. We found out we shared an interest in the *Titanic*."

"And he became a regular customer?"

"No. He only came here a couple of times."

But Cheyenne had visited the shop more often. Which of them had noticed Emma Jean's tippling? "Were you surprised when Otto invited you to the dinner on the yacht?"

"Frankly, yes. He invited me under false pretenses, as I discovered. He led me to believe the dinner would be a gathering of *Titanic* enthusiasts who might be interested in my antiques. That proved not to be true. He also hinted that he planned to sell off some of the less expensive items in his collection and would give me first shot at them. Obviously, *he* can't do that now, but perhaps his widow will."

Not if she knew Homer would use the story of Otto's death as dinner party entertainment.

The shop door had rung three times while Val was talking to Homer, and a couple of customers were now heading toward them. "I don't want to take up any more of your time, Homer." Cut to the chase. "Do you have your booklet with you?"

"No, I don't, but let's talk again."

Val left Timeless Treasures without the one thing she'd come for, but the trip hadn't been a waste. She'd been mistaken about Homer's reasons for wanting the scripts. He wasn't going to destroy the booklets with their hints that he was dishonest and his wife drank to excess. Rather, he'd hatched a scheme for making money from Otto's game—an idea so weird that it had to be the truth.

Talking with Cheyenne, Emma Jean, and Homer had given Val insights into Otto and the mystery game that might explain his death. He'd assigned at least three guests roles intended to make them uneasy—the possible thief Trey, the possible fence Homer, and the definite imbiber Emma Jean. Did the parts Otto assigned the others at the table follow the same pattern? To answer that, Val would have to study not just the scripts but also the people who'd played the roles.

Chapter 14

On her way home from Homer's antique shop, Val stopped off at the Bayport police station. Otto's business card with the message on the back had been burning a hole in her pocket all day. If the chief wasn't in the building, she'd leave the card at the reception desk with a note of explanation.

She was glad the chief was in his office and willing to see her. She sat across the desk from him, in a hard metal chair designed to discourage long visits.

He took a sheet of paper from a folder on his desk. "I was gone all day and just saw the report that someone assaulted you last night. The officer described it as a purse-snatching with minor injuries to the victim."

She rubbed the bruise on the back of her right leg. Tender to the touch, but not otherwise painful. "I agree about the minor injuries, though being stuffed in my car's trunk freaked me out. I don't think the thief was after cash."

"What then?"

"The booklets for the role-playing mystery game

Otto created for his guests. I picked them up from the yacht."

The chief rested his folded arms on the desk in an I'm-listening pose. "Why would anyone want them?"

"Otto modified a *Titanic* mystery game that he'd downloaded. He customized the plot and the roles, using the game to accuse his guests of crimes and failings he suspected they had in reality. Those guests might not want their faults to become public."

Val recounted what she'd learned from her visit with Cheyenne and the trip to the antique shop. The chief took notes as she talked.

He twirled his pen when she finished. "Otto suspected Trey of stealing and Homer of fencing stolen items. He had no proof, so he taunted them through his mystery game?"

"Yes, and he intended to humiliate Homer's wife. She's fond of alcohol, like the character she was supposed to play in the game. Otto might have ferreted out the other guests' secrets and planned to expose them. Maybe one of them put an end to his game and him." She could tell she hadn't yet convinced the chief that the game had been a factor in Otto's death. "I found evidence on the yacht that Otto had set up a private meeting with one guest in the middle of dinner. Maybe they had a confrontation."

The chief sat up straighter in his chair. "What evidence?"

She turned her jacket upside down over his desk and shook it until Otto's business card fell out of the pocket. "This card dropped out of one of the booklets. I don't know which one."

The chief leaned over the note. "*Meet me, swim*

platform 8:45. Hmm. We'll check if this is Otto's writing and if there are any fingerprints on the card."

"Bethany and I handled it before we knew it had a note on the back. We may have smudged any prints that were on it."

The chief grunted. "Even so, the note may be useful. Exactly what's in those booklets?"

"The goal was to identify the person responsible for a young woman's death. Each guest got a booklet containing lines to speak, questions to ask, and answers to give. To make it easier to see the big picture, Granddad, Bethany, Gunnar, and I are going to play all the parts tonight. We'll do it while we eat the leftovers from Otto's *Titanic* dinner. You want to join us at seven?"

"I'm not going to play a mystery game, but dinner sounds good. I'll come if I don't get bogged down with paperwork." He pointed to a stack of folders on his desk. "I'll call you either way."

"If you come, you may be able to figure out who Otto's culprit was. He put his solution in an envelope and hid it somewhere on the yacht. Did the officers who searched it find the envelope?"

He shook his head. "They were looking for evidence of a crime, not for a game piece."

"Homer's script wasn't with the others. He took it with him on Saturday night. I went to his shop to get it, but he didn't have it there." Or so he'd said. She debated a moment before hinting at her suspicion that Homer had pushed her into the trunk. "I also found out Cheyenne told him that I was going to pick up the booklets yesterday evening. Bethany saw someone lurking near the yacht while we were there."

He leaned forward. "Are you saying he followed you

from the marina and pushed you into the trunk to get the scripts?"

"Possibly." Another scenario popped into her head. "Or he might have told Trey I was going to get them." It made more sense that Trey would hang around the Bayport marina than Homer, who lived in Annapolis.

The chief thought for a moment and shook his head. "You're jumping to conclusions again, Val. Most people would assume there are other copies of this game. They wouldn't risk an assault charge to suppress one set of them." He picked up the paper in front of him and put it in a folder. "We'll stick with what the report says for now—a purse snatcher. I'm looking forward to dinner tonight."

A clear dismissal of her, but she hoped not of her information. "See you later, Chief."

Val expected Granddad to be home, but his car wasn't parked on the street when she pulled into the driveway. Usually by this time of the evening, if dinner wasn't ready, he was popping open a beer and foraging for a snack.

As she climbed out of the car, she saw her neighbor Harvey fertilizing his lawn. He'd retired a year ago and now lavished time on the lawn and landscape he'd previously neglected. She greeted him and asked if he'd seen Granddad.

"Not for a couple of hours." Harvey leaned toward her as if telling her a secret. "A woman visited him this afternoon and stayed a good while. Ten minutes after she left, he drove off. Haven't seen him since."

Val guessed Granddad's visitor was a woman he knew

from church or from the retirement village where some of his friends lived. "What did she look like?"

"Small like you, with short, brownish hair. Fifteen or so years older than you. Your grandfather's quite a silver fox." Harvey sounded as if he wouldn't mind being a silver fox himself. He went back to fertilizing the lawn.

Val couldn't think of any women Granddad knew well who fit that description. But someone at the *Titanic* dinner did—the poultry queen-in-waiting, Louisa Brown.

Once inside the house, Val called Granddad's cell phone and heard it ring in the sitting room. Now she knew why he hadn't responded to her earlier voice mail.

She made tent place cards with the names of Otto's guests written on both sides and positioned the cards to duplicate the seating arrangement on the yacht. The setup might help her, Bethany, and Granddad to remember what had gone on. It would also help the chief and Gunnar visualize the dinner. Then she set the table for tonight's dinner.

The front door squeaked open. "Granddad?" she called out.

"Be right with you," he said from the hall.

She went into the kitchen and surveyed the *Titanic* dinner leftovers in the fridge. Plenty of food for five. Otto's guests had consumed barely half of the roast beef. Understandable. By the time they got around to eating it, they'd gone through four courses, a squall, and a man overboard. This evening she'd roast potatoes to serve with the beef, along with the asparagus vinaigrette, a course that never made it to the table Saturday night. The Waldorf pudding, untouched on

Saturday night, would suffice for dessert this evening. Tonight's dinner wouldn't be the sumptuous meal Otto had planned, but at least she and Granddad would be sitting at the table, instead of plating and delivering multiple courses.

When he joined her in the kitchen, she noticed he was walking stiffly. "I was starting to wonder where you were. What have you been doing?"

"Sitting too long in the car." He opened the fridge. "I need a beer."

"Were you stuck in traffic?"

"Nope." He took a beer from the fridge, opened it, and guzzled some.

She waited for him to say more about sitting in the car, and when he didn't, she broached a different subject. "Why did Louisa Brown come here today?"

He gave her a sharp look. "How do you know she did?"

Because you would have denied it if she hadn't. "Harvey described the woman who visited you."

Granddad rolled his eyes. "Since he retired, nobody on this street has any privacy."

Val turned on the oven and took out the potato peeler. "What did Louisa want?"

"My advice. She asked me which clubs and volunteer groups to join so she could become part of the community. She also said the house smelled delicious. I'd just finished baking those little muffins that taste like pecan pie."

"Why did you bake today, Granddad?" He usually cooked only when the Monday deadline for his recipe column approached.

"I wanted to give my condolences to Cheyenne, so I made the muffins to take to her. I offered some to

Louisa. She didn't stay put while I was in the kitchen getting them. When I went back to the sitting room, I saw her come out of the study. She said she was admiring the Victorian-era woodwork."

Val stopped peeling a potato. "She was snooping. Was there anything private on the computer screen or the desk?"

"The password screen was up, and the desk was covered with the recipes and notes for the column I submitted yesterday."

So Louisa had seen nothing of any importance. "Did she gobble up the muffins the way she did s'mores on the yacht?"

"I only gave her three. She nibbled them while we talked about life in Bayport." He took a bag of pretzels from the pantry. "She said she'd heard I was thick with the police chief."

"Huh. I'll bet she wanted to know about the investigation into Otto's death." When he nodded, Val recounted her conversation with Louisa at the café. "When I rejected her theory that Otto killed himself, she asked how the police were handling the case, as if she expected me to have inside knowledge. What did you say to her?"

"I asked what exactly she wanted to know about the investigation. After hemming and hawing, she came out with her question—*Do the police think Otto committed suicide?*" Granddad imitated Louisa's high-pitched voice. "I told her they hadn't ruled out murder. She was a little jumpy when she first came in, and that news made her jumpier. I offered her a drink. Wine, brandy, or liqueur. Didn't think she was the beer type."

Val pretended to be shocked. "Granddad! You entertained a younger woman and plied her with liquor?"

He grinned. "I plied her with *liqueur*. She asked if the local police knew what they were doing. She hoped they were looking closely at Otto's wife, his ex-wife, and her son, because people are usually murdered by family members. She hinted she'd like a refill on the liqueur. I wasn't gonna give her another drink before she got behind the wheel, so I told her I had an appointment."

"I'd have given her a refill and offered to drive her home. You might have found out why she was so nervous."

"I did. She was almost out the door when she spit it out. She said, *Please tell me if you find out my husband's a suspect.*"

"What!" Val nearly sliced off a layer of skin with the potato peeler. "Why would she say that?"

"She claimed she wanted to know if she needed to get him a good lawyer. She left, still a nervous wreck."

"Weird." Val thought about her brief chats with the Browns in the café today. "This morning Damian came into the café, relaxed, not like a man worried he'd be a murder suspect. And when she came in a couple of hours later, she wasn't nervous. Maybe she found out something since then that made her believe her husband could—or should—be a suspect."

"I can guess what she found out." Granddad smiled smugly and took a long drink of his beer. "After she left, I drove to Cheyenne's house with my muffins and spotted Louisa's husband on the doorstep. Cheyenne let him in. I parked at the end of the street and waited for him to leave so I could talk to the widow alone. Then a shiny black Mercedes crept past the house. Same car Louisa drove when she came here. I didn't know if she was gonna park and join him in giving condolences or if she was spying on him. I hunched down in the seat and put on my sunglasses and baseball cap. Louisa never got out of the car. She stayed for twenty minutes. Then she drove away without even glancing at me."

"She was spying." Val cut a potato in small cubes. "She snooped here. She spied there." Did Louisa always behave like that, or was today special?

"It wasn't like she followed him there. She didn't show up until a good ten minutes after he did."

"That means she had a reason to think he might be with Cheyenne." Val remembered Otto's wife and Louisa's husband sitting together for much of the cocktail hour. The part of their conversation she'd overheard hadn't sounded like flirting, but she hadn't listened long. As the hostess, Cheyenne should have been circulating among the guests instead of entertaining only Damian. Their concentration on each other might have aroused his wife's suspicions. "Louisa may assume Damian and Cheyenne are having an affair, but she could be wrong."

"Nah. I took the muffins and knocked on Cheyenne's door. She didn't answer, so I walked around the house and looked in the windows."

Val put her hands on her hips. "Suppose someone in the neighborhood saw you peeking in windows?"

He shrugged. "An old guy with muffins can get away with a lot. Cheyenne and Damian weren't in the living room or the dining room. The blinds were shut where I figured the kitchen was. So what's left? The upstairs bedrooms."

Val could have argued that an upstairs room is often used as a study, but Granddad would call her naive to imagine Cheyenne and Damian huddled over a computer. Would Cheyenne have entertained Damian in the kitchen? Unlikely. She hadn't invited Val to come along with her to the kitchen. "Okay, those two *might* be having an affair. It doesn't follow that he killed her husband. The Browns and the Warbecks met two weeks ago. Hard to believe Damian would fall so hard and fast for Cheyenne that he'd murder for her."

"The couples just met. Maybe Damian and Cheyenne knew each other longer and plotted the whole thing. Her marriage to a rich man. The dinner party on the yacht. The murder." Granddad ticked off each element of the plot on his fingers.

Val tried to superimpose his scenario on her memory of the cocktail hour on the deck. It didn't fit. "If they conspired against Otto, they would have concealed their attraction to each other on the yacht. Instead, they enjoyed each other's company. And now, three days after the murder, they're having a tryst, according to you. Murder conspirators would have stayed away from each other so they don't arouse the kind of suspicions you and Louisa have about them."

"Hmm." Granddad filled a small bowl with pretzels. "The way I see it, Cheyenne lured him to the house because she's setting him up to take the fall. She seduced him into killing her husband, and now that she's a rich widow, she doesn't need him anymore. She'll claim Damian acted on his own."

"You stole that plot from a film noir." His video collection included a lot of movies from the 1940s and 1950s. The phone in the front hall rang. "Do you want me to answer it, or should we let it ring?"

Granddad was already halfway across the kitchen.

"I'll answer it. I gotta keep moving to shake out the stiffness."

She spread out the potato cubes in a roasting pan. Could he be right about Cheyenne orchestrating the *Titanic* dinner? Val had taken it for granted that Otto had masterminded the evening because he'd come across as controlling. But maybe his wife managed him in a subtle way, pulling his strings behind the scenes so he'd dance to her tune. After all, she'd prevailed on him to serve s'mores at a formal dinner. True, Otto had balked at the idea at first and only agreed after Val seconded it. But his wife might have wheedled him into it even without Val's support.

Had Cheyenne also cajoled him into inviting the Browns? This morning she'd mentioned another couple she'd suggested Otto invite and her surprise that the Browns had come instead. She could say anything now, because Otto wasn't around to contradict her.

Granddad returned to the kitchen. "That was someone calling about you catering a dinner party. I wrote down the name and number. Figured you were too busy with this dinner to talk now."

"Thanks." Val took a pretzel. "When I visited Cheyenne today, her grief over Otto looked real. I don't see her as a femme fatale or Damian as a patsy, but maybe he acted on his own. He hoped to marry a rich young widow to replace his older wife, who holds the purse strings and a prenup."

Granddad took the pretzel bowl and his beer to the breakfast table and sat down. "What's in the prenup? Divorce me and you get nothing?"

Val recalled what Chatty had heard about the Browns'

prenup. "Yes, and it goes beyond that. Damian gets nothing even if Louisa wants a divorce and he doesn't."

"I'll bet he inherits if she dies." Granddad snapped his fingers. "It's obvious who the next murder victim will be."

Chapter 15

"The next murder victim?" Val repeated Granddad's words. "You mean Louisa?"

"Uh-huh. I should have said it's obvious to *her* she'll be the next victim. Here's what I think is going through her mind. She assumes Damian's having an affair with Cheyenne. She suspects he killed Otto to marry the rich widow. Louisa's afraid he'll want her money too and bump her off. That explains her nervousness today."

Val put the potatoes in the oven. "If she feared for her life, she'd go to the police. She's not stupid."

"She doesn't know for sure that her husband killed Otto. She wants to find out if the police have evidence of that. But if he didn't do it, she doesn't want to give the police a reason to suspect him. That's why she asked me to find out if there's any evidence against him."

"I assume you'll tell the police what she said. You may get the chance tonight. I invited Chief Yardley to join us for dinner. What did you do after you peeked in Cheyenne's windows?"

"Went back to the car and waited for Damian to leave. He didn't come out, at least while I was there. I drove away when my legs stiffened up." The doorbell rang. "I'll get it. It might be the chief."

"Or Bethany. Don't tell her your suspicions about Cheyenne. The two of them have bonded."

Val took the asparagus she'd made for the *Titanic* dinner from the refrigerator and ate a stalk. Still good. It would taste better at room temperature. She arranged the stalks on a platter.

Granddad returned with Bethany. She sauntered into the kitchen wearing a red cardigan, a pink-and-yellow dress, black leggings, and purple athletic shoes—a far cry from the black outfit she'd worn at the last *Titanic* dinner.

She plunked a baguette on the counter. "I grabbed this right before the bakery closed."

"Thank you. We can have it with the pâté before dinner and the cheese after dinner."

Granddad picked up the corkscrew. "How about some wine, Bethany? Red or white?"

"White, please." Bethany turned to Val. "I called Cheyenne to find out how she was doing. She told me you visited her today. How did she seem to you?"

"She's keeping busy gathering photos for Otto's memorial service and defending him against rumors of suicide."

"That's better than being immobilized by his death," Bethany said.

"She looked sad, but she didn't talk about their life together or what she loved about him." Val wondered what besides money had attracted Cheyenne to him.

"Did she open up to you when you were with her on Sunday?"

Bethany took the wineglass Granddad handed her. "She told me she was married once before. She met the guy in college. They were crazy in love and rushed off to Vegas to get married. It lasted less than two years. She divorced him after he cheated on her. She didn't say so, but I think Otto appealed to her because he was completely different from the first hubby."

A familiar story to Val. She'd found Gunnar attractive initially because he was so unlike her longtime fiancé, the handsome, sweet-talking Tony. Fortunately, she'd found out *before* the wedding that Tony was cheating on her. "From what she told me, she's thinking about who might have killed Otto."

"That doesn't surprise me." Granddad downed his beer. "Who is she fingering?"

"Before I tell you her theory, I have a question. Did either of you notice how Homer and Trey acted when they saw each other on the yacht? Like they'd just met, or like they already knew each other?"

Granddad shook his head. "Didn't pay attention. Too busy serving drinks."

Bethany sipped her wine. "I was watching. Trey looked startled. Homer said something stilted, like *Pleased to make your acquaintance.* Then he introduced himself and held out his hand. For a moment Trey just stared at him, and then he pumped Homer's hand." She demonstrated a vigorous handshake. "Why are you asking?"

"According to Cheyenne, Otto suspected Trey of stealing *Titanic* memorabilia and Homer of fencing it." Val summarized what she'd seen at Homer's antique shop, including Emma Jean's glass of gin.

Bethany looked shocked. "So my role as an alcoholic was based on her? I'm so glad she didn't come to the dinner, but even without her there, Homer must have been furious. He had a reason to kill Otto."

"But not a reason to put a gun in his tux. He didn't know when he came aboard that Otto was going to pick on Emma Jean."

Val's phone chimed. Chief Yardley was on the line, saying he was leaving his office and would join them shortly. She relayed his message to Granddad and Bethany.

Granddad tossed his empty beer bottle in the recycle bin. "I'll go wait for him on the front porch."

Val nodded her approval, certain that before they came inside, the chief would hear about Louisa's visit here and her husband's visit to Cheyenne's house.

Val called Gunnar, who said he was on Route 50 near the turnoff for Bayport. He'd be at the house in fifteen minutes.

"Perfect. Dinner will be ready."

Granddad and the chief were still talking on the porch when Gunnar arrived. He strode into the kitchen and greeted Val and Bethany.

Val hugged him. "Thanks for coming." He looked far more cheerful than when she'd last seen him. "You had a good day in Washington?"

He nodded. "I looked into some acting programs there. I liked what the conservatory had to offer."

Val was taken aback. He hadn't mentioned he planned to study acting in Washington. He must have intended to tell her last night, but she'd left him to pick up the food on the yacht before he'd gotten around to it. "How long is the program?"

He spread pâté on a slice of French bread. "Almost two thousand hours of training over sixteen months."

Val gaped at him. More than a year. "That's intensive."

"Close to thirty hours a week. And that's just the basic program. They have an advanced one too. I'll see how the first one goes before I enroll in that."

So he'd committed to the basic program? Thirty hours a week plus an eighty-mile commute plus his accounting work wouldn't leave him much free time. Val tried to look enthusiastic. "That's exciting, Gunnar. Does the program start in the fall?" That would give him months to change his mind.

"I still have to audition. If I get through it, I'll start classes in May."

Only a few weeks from now. So much for Val's hope of seeing more of him now that tax season was over. "You'll do great in the audition."

"You can practice your acting tonight," Bethany said.

Val poured him a glass of red wine and explained the plan for the evening.

"You want me to play two different men who are each assuming a role in a mystery game?" When she nodded, he continued, "I need more information. How do the men feel about the other people at the table? What motivates them and the characters they're playing?"

Val groaned inwardly. He apparently wanted to prepare for tonight's game as he would for the stage. "We can give you some info, but basically all you have to do is read the lines in these scripts." She gave him two booklets—Damian's and Trey's.

He flipped through them while she took the potatoes from the oven. She looked up to see a pained expression on his face, as if he'd just noticed a worm in his half-eaten salad. "What's wrong, Gunnar?"

"Nobody talks like this. Who wrote this dialogue?"

Bethany giggled. "Definitely not Shakespeare."

Val transferred the potatoes to a serving dish. "Go for campy. That's what Bethany did with her role on Saturday night."

"Hmm. You want me to be a ham." He didn't look happy about the assignment. "What are the two men really like, apart from their roles?"

Val wished she knew. "I can only tell you how they behaved on the yacht. Middle-aged Damian was suave. Think Cary Grant or George Clooney. Young Trey was hostile to his former stepfather, Otto, and critical of the game."

"So I should say his lines with barely concealed antagonism?"

Val rolled her eyes. "You're overthinking this, Gunnar."

He scowled. "I don't say that when you add pinches of a dozen spices to a dish."

His comment shocked Val. She'd had no idea he didn't value her culinary experiments. Her ex-fiancé, for all his faults, had at least appreciated her cooking.

Bethany watched them warily. "To answer your question, Gunnar, the chip on Trey's shoulder stayed there throughout the dinner."

"How did Damian behave at the table?"

"Very cool," Val said. "He looked faintly amused by the game."

Bethany added, "His wife was not amused. She's

rather high-strung. When someone hinted that Damian pushed drugs on young women, she looked ready to erupt, even though it was just a line from the script."

"How did Stacy react?" Val said. "From the galley I couldn't see her face well."

Bethany sat down at the breakfast table. "Stacy was preoccupied. Otto had to remind her to say her lines during the scenes, and she didn't put much feeling into them."

Val heard Granddad and the chief coming inside. "Let's get the food on the table." And raise the curtain on *The Titanic Mystery* by Otto Warbeck.

Chapter 16

With everyone gathered in the dining room, Val assigned seats. "Granddad will be at the head of the table, like Otto was on the yacht, and read his lines." She consulted her seating chart.

"Bethany will sit opposite him in the hostess seat, playing Cheyenne's part and the chaperone's. Chief, please sit to her right, where Homer was. Since we don't have his booklet, you don't have any lines to say."

He took a small spiral notebook from his pocket. "I'll figure out which of you is guilty."

Val pointed to the chair on Granddad's left. "Gunnar will sit where Damian sat to play his part and Trey's. I'll sit across from Gunnar and play Louisa and Stacy. You're all *Titanic* passengers trying to determine who's responsible for what happened to a young woman on the ship."

Bethany plopped into the hostess's chair. "In each scene, everyone asks a question and gives an answer. One of us has a response to Homer's question, so we should be able to figure out what he asked. One of us has a question for him, and I'll try to remember his response."

Val took her seat on Granddad's right. "That will work for the first two scenes. For the last two, we'll have to guess at his responses. Granddad, as the captain, you get to read the first lines. You can skip the part where he welcomes everyone to the captain's table and get to the meat of the story."

Granddad finished piling slices of beef on his plate, passed the platter to Val, and adjusted his bifocals. "I'm sorry to tell you that Annie Milner, a nineteen-year-old, disappeared from the ship last night. After a thorough search, we've concluded that she must have gone overboard. I've invited all of you to my table tonight because I understand you each spent time with her in the last few days. Perhaps one of you can shed light on what happened to her." He peered over the top of his glasses at Val. "Mrs. Brown, I've noticed you taking pills. I hope the motion of the ship isn't bothering you."

Val picked up Louisa Brown's script and tried to imitate her high-pitched voice. "I take pills for anxiety. We tempt fate if we believe any ship is unsinkable. I can't rid myself of the fear that this ship is doomed."

"Clumsy foreshadowing," Gunnar mumbled.

Val ignored him, glanced at her script, and saw that she had to ask a question as Louisa and answer it as Stacy. "I understand you're a widow, Lady Stacy. My condolences on your loss and on the aftermath of it. I read in the London papers that Lord Stacy amassed huge debts and gambled away the fortune you brought to the marriage."

Gunnar groaned. "Such subtle dialogue."

Val glared at him. She switched to a lower-pitched voice and spoke slowly to answer the question as Stacy. "I cannot deny it, but I have sufficient funds, or I wouldn't be in first class." With her job finished for the first scene, Val served herself potatoes and asparagus.

Bethany spoke up. "As Annie's chaperone, I was concerned when I noticed certain people in first class who didn't belong here." She pointed at Gunnar. "I saw that you, Mr. Trey Turnstone, boarded the ship as a third-class passenger. How is it you're eating in the first-class dining room?"

Gunnar put on a forced smile. "Yes, Madame Chaperone, my ticket is for third class. The captain invited me to his table because he was grateful to me for helping Annie down from the ship's railing when she climbed there on our first night at sea. Captain, is the purpose of our gathering tonight to assign blame for what happened to Annie?"

Granddad checked his script. "The goal is to find out the truth about Annie's disappearance. This will be my last voyage as captain. If we discover someone is responsible for her death, I'll devote the rest of my life to making sure that person pays for it."

The questions and answers continued in similar fashion through the first scene. But the "questions" in the next two scenes resembled witness statements and accusations, some of which Val remembered overhearing while she worked in the galley Saturday night. The chaperone drank to excess. The captain neglected his other duties while paying extraordinary attention to young Annie. Cheyenne, as a married woman traveling solo, had entertained another woman's husband in her cabin—Damian.

Val exchanged a look with her grandfather when that tidbit came up. He must be wondering, as she was, whether Otto could have suspected an affair between his wife and Damian.

The revelations continued. Annie spent one evening alone with Damian and another evening with Trey, who took great interest in her jewelry. The insomniac Louisa slinked around the decks at night and was overheard telling Annie to stay away from Damian or she'd be sorry. That information came from Stacy, whose eavesdropping suggested she might be a blackmailer. Homer, often seen with Trey, was accused of trying to sell a diamond brooch that a woman on the ship had reported stolen.

Val sipped her wine, thinking about Otto's assignment of parts. He'd created the roles of thief for Trey, fence for Homer, and heavy drinker for Homer's wife, based on his suspicions about them. Did suspicions also explain why he'd given his ex-wife the role of blackmailer, Cheyenne the role of a cheating wife, Damian the role of philanderer, and Louisa the role of jealous wife? Val reminded herself that Otto had written the mystery game, possibly expecting a different couple at the dinner, the Kindells, not Damian and Louisa Brown.

Val called for a break before the last scene. She

plated the Waldorf pudding while Bethany collected the dinner dishes from the table and Gunnar poured the coffee.

They went through the last scene of the game over dessert and coffee. Instead of questions and answers, the script consisted of pieces of "evidence" tucked into each booklet. A complaint from an unnamed passenger that Damian tried to induce her to use cocaine. Reports from cabin stewards of finding stolen jewelry in Trey's luggage and cocaine in Damian and Louisa's bathroom. A letter proving Annie was the captain's niece. Eyewitness statements giving Homer and Stacy alibis for the time when Annie disappeared.

Stacy's booklet contained proof she was a Pinkerton detective on the trail of international jewel thieves and a statement that she'd overheard Annie tell Trey to leave her alone. Annie then headed toward the bow of the ship.

Val put her booklet facedown. "Was someone waiting there for her, or was she followed? Did she fall from the same railing where she sat the first night at sea, or was she pushed?"

Granddad read from his booklet. "As the captain, I have a brief statement to make. Now that we've reviewed the evidence and clues, it's up to us to decide who's responsible for Annie's death. I'd like to hear what each of you has to say." He closed the booklet. "Notice there's no mention of murder, but you can't rule it out. Anyone want to guess what happened to her and who's responsible?"

When no one volunteered, the chief said. "I'll share my brief notes. Maybe it will become clearer who the culprit is as I do that. Speak up if you think you know who's to blame. I'll start with the chaperone. Retired governess. Drank a lot. Fell asleep early every night, allowing Annie to slip away."

"Can't blame her," Granddad said. "Even if she'd stayed awake longer, Annie would have outlasted her and snuck out for some fun later."

"Any other comments?" The chief looked around. "No. Then I'll move on to the young wife traveling alone, Cheyenne's role. It came out in scene three that Annie called her a seducer and threatened to telegraph her husband if she didn't stay away from Damian."

"I'll bet Cheyenne pushed Annie overboard," Granddad said. "She was jealous of her and afraid Annie would carry through on her threat."

His comment didn't surprise Val. In his eyes Cheyenne was guilty of murder, both in the mystery game and in real life. "Who's next on your list, Chief?"

"The two with airtight alibis—Stacy and Homer. We know they're not guilty."

Not guilty in the game, Val thought, but possibly in reality.

The chief flipped a page in his notebook. "Trey, suspected jewel thief. Tagged after Annie until Damian charmed her. Accosted her the night she disappeared. She told him to get lost. Her emerald necklace got lost too."

Bethany piped up. "Trey's responsible. He resented how Annie treated him and wanted her necklace. She climbed up on the railing again. This time he saved her necklace, but not her."

"Anyone else agree?" Chief Yardley asked. When no one spoke up, he said. "Now for the captain. Reputation as a ladies' man. Spent many hours with Annie, his niece who'd been put up for adoption after birth. Blames himself for not assigning a crew member to keep her safe."

"He's taking partial blame," Granddad said. "But that doesn't mean someone else isn't more to blame. Otto wouldn't make himself the guilty one in his own game."

The chief smiled. "But he'd be the least likely person. That's the usual culprit in a mystery." He turned to the next page in his notes. "Finally, we come to the married couple with cocaine in their cabin, Louisa and Damian. He hung out with Cheyenne at first. Switched his attentions to Annie. His wife threatened to ruin Annie's reputation. Annie responded that Louisa was too ugly to attract any man."

"Annie was a firebrand," Granddad said. "Headstrong. Did what she wanted and feared no one. That turned out to be a fatal mistake."

Was there a real Annie? If Val had learned anything by this exercise, it was that she needed to know more about the victim.

Gunnar spoke up. "Damian encouraged women to take cocaine, possibly so they'd submit to his sexual advances. If he tried that with Annie, she might have threatened to report him to the police, giving him a reason to get rid of her."

The chief shook his head. "He had nothing to fear. The first laws against distribution of narcotics weren't enacted until 1914. That's two years after the *Titanic* sank."

Gunnar shrugged. "So maybe he coaxed Annie into taking drugs. Under the influence of them, she fell or threw herself overboard. Either way, he's responsible."

The chief sat back in his chair and laced his fingers behind his head. "We don't have a consensus here. One vote each for the cheating wife, the young thief, and the womanizing drug pusher. What's your solution, Val?"

"Those three had reasons to want Annie dead, but there's no evidence anyone killed her. Though it's probably not what Otto had in mind, I'd blame the chaperone and the captain. They're morally responsible for Annie's death. She'd done something foolish by sitting on the rail the first night at sea. Someone should have watched her at all times after that." Val looked at the chief. "Your turn."

"You're right. No evidence of a crime. Accident and suicide are also possibilities. When Annie climbed on the railing the first night, she might have intended to jump, like the girl in the *Titanic* movie. A young man coaxed her down from the railing once, but she could have tried again when no one was around to talk her out of it. In the absence of a witness who saw her jump, her death would go down as an accident."

Val finished the last bite of her pudding. "That would happen in the real world, but not in Otto's fantasy *Titanic* mystery. We haven't found the envelope that contains the name of his culprit. But it's clear where he was going with this game. He stuck the knife into everyone at the table, but he stuck it farthest into Damian."

"The drug pusher and sexual predator," the chief said. "He's the worst of the bunch *in the game.*" He paused before his last few words and looked pointedly at Val.

Val interpreted his look as a warning not to leap

from game to life. She agreed with him, at least about Damian. "Otto created characters who were dishonest, jealous, irresponsible, and unfaithful. He matched each fault with the guest most likely to have it. But Damian the man doesn't necessarily have the faults of Damian the character. I heard he and Louisa were last-minute substitutes for another couple, who might have been the models for the mystery game characters."

Granddad raised a skeptical eyebrow. "Who told you about this other couple? Cheyenne?"

Val guessed what he was thinking: Cheyenne could have invented the other couple to obscure the fact that she had manipulated Otto into inviting Damian to the dinner. Come to think of it, Cheyenne could have also invented the story of the *Titanic* artifacts to suggest Trey and Homer had motives for silencing Otto.

Chief Yardley put his notebook in his pocket. "There's no proof Otto's guests committed crimes like the ones in his script. Even if they did, you can't assume his death was related to the game." The chief caught Val's eye. "Nothing in the scripts was worth assaulting you to get them."

Though she agreed the game might prove a dead end, she refused to blame a random purse snatcher for her ordeal in the trunk. "That's an easy conclusion now that we've gone through the game. Otto's guests didn't know what kind of damning information would come to light in the last two scenes or in his solution. Maybe that information wasn't worth killing for, but it might be worth keeping it from the press and the police."

"Fair enough." The chief stood up. "I'll take the scripts

with me and send an officer to patrol this street tonight in case someone tries again to grab them. Thank you. This was more entertaining than most criminal investigations. And the food was way better than what I usually eat when I'm on a case."

Granddad walked him to the front door.

Bethany sighed. "I'm disappointed. I was sure we'd find out Annie was murdered. These mystery games are always about murder."

Gunnar pushed back his chair and picked up his plate and Granddad's.

Val stood up. "Stop collecting the plates from the table, Gunnar. Granddad and I will clean up. You've had a long day." Maybe that explained why he'd been so crabby tonight.

She thanked him and Bethany for coming and saw them out. Gunnar reminded her that she was having dinner at his place tomorrow.

She and Granddad cleared the table. While she loaded the dishwasher, he put away the leftovers from the leftovers.

"You know what the setup with the yacht and the mystery game reminded me of?" he said. "The plot of *And Then There Were None*. A man invites a bunch of people with nothing in common to an island. A taped voice announces they're all guilty of something. Totally cut off from the rest of the world, they pay for their crimes one by one."

The comparison struck a chord with Val. "Otto's yacht was a floating island. For a while, we all wondered if we'd make it back to shore. Fortunately, we did. The accuser was the only person who died."

"So far." Granddad checked to make sure the back door was locked. "So far."

Chapter 17

Val closed the dishwasher and turned to face her grandfather. "You're expecting some more murders?"

"S'more murders. That would make a good book title." He sat down at the breakfast table. "Louisa could be in danger from her husband or from Cheyenne. Maybe she and Damian exchanged murders, like in that Hitchcock movie. He'd kill her husband and she'd kill his wife. Those two would have a lot more money to play with if Louisa was dead."

The femme fatale plot with a twist. Val wiped down the kitchen counter. "If you told the chief that, I'll bet he said, *You're jumping to a conclusion.*" Val had heard that line often enough from him.

"Yes, but I figured he'd change his mind after seeing that Otto cast Damian and Cheyenne as cheating spouses and Louisa as a jealous rich woman. Then you muddied the waters by bringing up that other pair who were supposed to be invited."

"I thought the chief should know. He can decide if they're relevant." Val started the dishwasher. "The police would take a long, hard look at Damian and

Cheyenne if both their spouses died suddenly and left them fortunes." Val could tell by Granddad's silence that he wasn't going to argue the point.

He sat down at the breakfast table. "You got a better theory on who shot him?"

"Not yet, but I know what I'm missing—the truth about the victim. It's always about the victim."

"You mean Otto?"

"No, Annie, the game's victim. He modeled the other characters in his game on real people. Who was the model for the young woman who fell overboard?" When Granddad shrugged, she said, "I've got one candidate. Cheyenne told me Otto had a younger sister who died when he was in his twenties. I'd like to know how she died."

Granddad stroked his chin. "Otto was closing in on sixty. That means his sister died thirty or more years ago . . . in the dark ages before every little thing got posted on the Internet. You won't find out much about her online unless her death was unusual."

"I won't dig up *anything* without knowing her name and when she died." Granddad might be able to help with that. Val sat down across from him. "You didn't get a chance to visit with Cheyenne today. You can try again tomorrow and do some snooping at her house." Assuming he could face the widow without betraying that he suspected her of adultery and conspiracy to murder.

His eyes lit up. "What kind of snooping?"

"Her dining table is covered with photos of Otto when he was younger. I saw one of him with his sister when she was a baby. There must be other pictures of her. Turn them over to see if there's a date or her name on the back."

"I could try pumping Cheyenne for information, but she wasn't even alive thirty years ago. Wife number one might know more about his sister."

Val gave him a thumbs-up. "I'll visit Stacy tomorrow. I want to talk to her anyway. In the game she morphed from a possible blackmailer into a Pinkerton detective. Did those roles have anything to do with the woman she really is? Why did Otto invite her?"

Granddad shrugged. "She came off smelling sweet. Maybe Otto wanted to patch things up with her, especially if he suspected his new wife of cheating. Do you know where Stacy lives?"

Val nodded. "She's staying with Trey in the place where he's house-sitting. The address she gave the Coast Guard officer was 312 Belleview Avenue. Louisa and Damian are at 301 Belleview Avenue."

"The corner house. Ritzy neighborhood. The even-numbered houses backing to the river are the prized ones. The houses on the other side are newer and on smaller lots."

The Browns had bought a house on the most expensive street in town, but they lived on the wrong side of it. That might explain why Louisa's prominent neighbors were less friendly than she'd hoped.

At three o'clock on Wednesday, Val walked along Belleview Avenue. The two-story frame house where Trey was staying had one-story additions on both sides and a covered porch across the front.

She climbed up two steps to the porch and rang the bell, setting off loud barking.

Trey opened the door. His jeans had holes. He hadn't shaved in days, probably since Saturday night, when he'd looked neat in a tuxedo and ponytail. Now his hair was loose and needed combing.

He held a chocolate Labrador retriever by the collar. The dog, tail wagging furiously, was apparently happy to see Val, but Trey eyed her as if she were selling magazine subscriptions. "H'lo."

"Hi, Trey. I was hoping to talk to your mother."

"She's gone to the supermarket." He glanced at Val's plastic-wrapped plate of macaroons and oatmeal cookies. "If you'd like to come in and wait, she should be back soon."

Cookies opened doors.

"Thank you." Val went inside. "Cute dog. Yours?"

Trey shook his head. "I'm the house sitter and the dog sitter."

Val patted the dog on the head with one hand, and held the cookie plate aloft with the other. "Is there someplace I can set the cookies down so the dog won't eat them?"

Trey led her into a spacious kitchen, probably an addition to the back of the house. He pointed to the table by the bay window. "You can put the cookies there. Gretel knows the table is off-limits for her." He gave Gretel two dog treats.

Val crossed the state-of-the-art kitchen to the eating area. The gleaming pots and pans hanging above the granite counter looked as if no one had ever used them on the stove. But the counter had crumbs on it. The sink contained a dirty dish, a greasy frying pan, and a carafe half-filled with coffee. If she needed a house sitter, she wouldn't hire Trey.

Val turned away from the unappetizing sight and looked out the bay window. The river sparkled in the sunshine. "Nice view."

Trey watched her take the plastic wrap off the plate of cookies. "Would you like something to drink?"

"Water, please."

He brought a glass of water and a glass of milk to the table. At Val's suggestion, he sat down and helped himself to the cookies.

"My condolences on the death of your stepfather," she said.

Trey finished chewing a macaroon before responding. "Ex-stepfather. He hasn't been part of my life for the last six years, so I won't miss him."

Val assumed he was exaggerating. "He asked you to a special dinner, and you went."

"First time I'd heard from him in years. I wouldn't have gone except he promised to make a big donation to the Protect the Bay Fund. I guess I can ask his widow for it. Not right away, of course. I'll wait a while before I approach her, but I won't let it go. I'm shameless when it comes to that cause." He gave her a boyish smile.

Val felt herself warming to him. Why had he acted like such a jerk on the boat? "I couldn't help noticing that you weren't happy at Otto's dinner."

"Otto invited me to the party and demanded I wear a tux he rented for me. He did not order me to be happy. My happiness was never his priority." Trey gulped some milk. "When my mother was married to him, we spent vacations and every weekend on his sailboat, unless it rained. He belittled me because I got seasick and insisted that more time on the water would cure me."

Val winced. "Not fun."

"No. For years, starting when I was eight, family time meant upchucking. When I turned thirteen, I refused to get on his boat again. Otto and Mom argued about it. I went from being the boy who ruined vacations to the one who caused strife in the family."

Prone to seasickness, yet he'd shown no sign of it when the yacht was heaving and rolling. "You handled the rough water well on Saturday night."

"I had a scopolamine patch here." He touched behind his ear, as she'd seen him do on the yacht. "I tried the patch a few years ago. Going on boats isn't a big problem anymore." He refilled his milk glass and returned to the table. "Otto and I had our differences. That doesn't mean I wanted him dead, but I *was* glad to hear about the bullet wound."

Huh? "Why?"

"Because no one can blame his death on the pilot. Before Otto's body turned up with a bullet hole, people thought he fell overboard in the squall. The Coast Guard seemed to fault Jerome for not controlling the yacht."

Val wondered why Trey cared. If he'd drugged Jerome, he might feel guilty about the pilot being blamed for Otto's death. Could she nudge him into admitting what he'd done? "Jerome is still in hot water. Even if he isn't blamed for Otto's death, the rumor that he was on drugs will hang over him. He'll have trouble getting a piloting job."

Trey raked his hair and looked out the window but said nothing.

Not ready to confess? Val decided to apply a bit more pressure. "I heard a theory that Otto might have discovered Jerome under the influence of drugs, and Jerome killed him to silence him."

Trey hit the table with his fist like a judge with a

gavel. "No way. When I went up to the bridge, he was barely conscious. He was in no condition to shoot straight."

"Because he was under the influence of drugs, which won't count in his favor. How soon after Otto went outside did you go up to the bridge?"

"A minute or so later. First I stopped at the head and then went up to the bridge."

He'd had enough time to shoot Otto and push him overboard. Val made eye contact with Trey. "Did you see Otto on the deck?"

Trey returned her steady look. "I didn't see him. I didn't kill him. And I don't believe Jerome did either." The dog barked and shot out of the room. "My mother's back. I'll help her with the groceries."

Trey left and returned in half a minute with two canvas bags of groceries. "I'm going to take Gretel for a walk. Mom will be right in." As he left the room, his mother entered with another canvas bag.

Val stood up. "Hi, Stacy. I hope you don't mind my dropping in."

"Not at all." Stacy filled an electric kettle with water. "I'm going to make myself tea. Would you like a cup?" She put her grocery bag on the counter near the built-in fridge.

"I'd love one." As Val watched her move yogurt and tofu from the bag to the refrigerator, she was struck by wife one's resemblance to wife two—both tall and lean, both with long, blondish-brown hair. In twenty years, Cheyenne would resemble Stacy, with smile lines and a hint of crow's feet. "Do you often stay where Trey is house-sitting?"

"No. I'd planned to spend only Saturday night here

so I wouldn't have to drive home after Otto's dinner party. But after what happened, Trey needed support, though he'd never admit it." Stacy took lettuce from her grocery bag. "For eight years, more than a third of Trey's life, Otto was his father. Like most young men, Trey keeps his emotions bottled up. But it will hit him soon that the only father he ever knew is gone."

Trey's mother was probably right about his delayed reaction. "It's great that your job allows you to take time off to be with him."

"I'm writing a book while I'm on sabbatical from teaching at the University of Maryland. I picked up some clothes, my computer, and my notes so I could work from here. And Trey doesn't mind having someone around to cook for him." She grimaced at the sink with the dirty dishes. "Or to clean up when he cooks for himself."

"My grandfather feels the same way about me. What's your book about?"

"Teaching science to young children. I give lectures on that subject and decided to rework the material into a book." Stacy poured boiling water into a teapot. "But you didn't come here with your cookies to talk about that."

Val had planned to work up to the subject of Otto, but a direct approach might work better with the no-nonsense Stacy. "I hoped you could tell me how Otto's sister died."

"Why are you asking?"

"Otto's mystery game intrigued me. I found a *Titanic* dinner mystery online that probably inspired his. He changed the characters so that they resembled his guests in age and marital status. That made sense, but he also changed the victim from a *Titanic* crew member to a female passenger. When I heard he had a sister who died young, I wondered if she might have been the model for Annie."

Stacy studied Val as if trying to read her mind. "Good guess. Otto's half sister, Andrea, was a sophomore in college when she died. She went to a party at an off-campus apartment. The students were drinking, some of them doing drugs. There was an accident that killed Andrea."

Val shuddered. How awful to send a child to college and lose her forever. "Her family must have been devastated. Was it a car accident?"

Stacy took cups to the table and gazed at the river through the bay window. "The party Andrea attended spilled over onto the balcony. She sat on the railing, lost her balance, and fell to her death."

"Wow!" Val hadn't expected such an obvious similarity between Otto's sister and the victim in his mystery. "Andrea and Annie both fell off a railing."

"Yes, but Annie fell into imaginary water, and Andrea hit real concrete." Stacy turned away from the window. "Andrea was ten years younger than Otto. He felt protective of her. He blamed himself for not being a bigger part of her life, talking to her on the phone more often, visiting her at college. I doubt any of that could have prevented her death."

Val wondered if the railing was the only similarity between Andrea's and Annie's deaths. "Did Otto ever suggest someone might have been responsible for his sister's *accident*?" As his script suggested about Annie.

Stacy brought the tea to the table and sat down. "What happened to Andrea isn't unusual on campuses. A student falls down the stairs while under the influence, or dies of alcohol poisoning, or ODs on drugs.

It's hard for a grieving family to accept the senseless death of someone so young."

Not an answer to the question Val had asked, but she took Stacy's evasive response as a *yes*. She sat down across from Stacy. "Where did Andrea go to school?"

"Virginia Tech. Five hours away from Washington, D.C., where Otto was working long hours."

"How old was she when she died?"

Stacy poured tea into the cups. "Nineteen."

"Could something have happened recently that made Otto think about her death after such a long time?"

"Her death haunted him for the rest of his life. When I met him, fifteen years later, one of the first personal things he told me was about Andrea's death."

Val stirred sugar into her tea and switched to a less grim topic of conversation. "Where did you meet Otto?"

"I was on *Antiques Roadshow*. He saw the show and tracked me down because he wanted to buy what I'd gotten appraised on the show. Can you guess what?"

"Something to do with the *Titanic*?"

Stacy nodded. "My great-grandmother was a *Titanic* survivor. She was in third class, coming to visit her older sister, who'd traveled to America a few years earlier and married an American. After Great-Granny survived the *Titanic*, she wouldn't get on another boat . . . ever."

Val reached for a macaroon. "Understandable."

"She wrote a letter to her younger sister back in Europe to explain why she was never crossing the ocean again. The letter was filled with details about the night the ship sank. When the younger sister came here for a visit after the first World War, she gave the letter back to Great-Granny."

"That sounds like something you'd want to keep, to show *your* grandchildren. Do you still have the letter, or did you sell it?"

Stacy went motionless with the cup of tea halfway to her mouth. "I sold it."

Val waited for her to say more, but Stacy just sipped her tea. Time for another guess. "Did you sell the letter to Otto?"

"In a way. When I told Otto I wanted a divorce, he said he'd like to keep the letter. I refused, of course. I planned to sell the letter to pay for Trey's college education. Otto offered to do that if I gave up the letter. So I did. Trey graduated last year from an excellent and expensive liberal arts college, and Otto paid for all of it."

"It must have bothered you to lose a piece of your family history." It would have bothered Val.

"Yes, but I nearly got it back. Now that Otto's dead, I've lost my chance. When I turned down his invitation to dinner on the yacht, he said, *What would it take to get you to say yes?* I told him my great-grandmother's letter. I thought he'd laugh at me, but he agreed. That's why I went to his dinner."

Val's jaw slackened with surprise. Otto's biggest bribe yet. "He must have wanted you there badly. Do you know why?"

Stacy plucked a macaroon from the cookie plate and chewed two bites thoroughly before responding. "I can guess. He'd recently acquired a luxury yacht and a beautiful young wife. He hoped I'd be jealous."

Even for Stacy, who deliberated before saying anything, the delay before answering Val's question had been exceptionally long. Sign of a lie? As a scientist and educator, she gathered facts, analyzed them, and taught her students to do the same. She probably didn't make things up as a rule, so she had to think about it beforehand. Val couldn't imagine what Stacy was hiding. "What do you think happened to Otto?"

"I thought you'd never ask," Stacy said. "He committed suicide. He took care of his father, who had early-onset Alzheimer's. Otto told me he'd kill himself if he found out he had the same disease. He must have gotten tested and discovered he had signs of it. That would explain his early retirement. He took matters into his own hands while he still could."

"Did you tell the police that?"

"There's no point unless the autopsy shows that he had the disease. I'll wait for that."

Did Otto tip off Stacy about his plans, or was she only guessing? "You left the saloon shortly after Otto went out on deck. Did he tell you then that he was going to kill himself?"

"No." Stacy looked at Val over the top of her cup. "You were in the room when I said I didn't see him."

True, but she could have simply answered Val's question by saying, *I didn't see him.* Instead, she'd chosen her words carefully. "If he intended to commit suicide, why did he go to the trouble of creating a mystery game for his guests to play?"

"It diverted our attention. When he left the table, he told us to read our scripts for the next scene, his way of making sure he'd be alone outside and no one would stop him from killing himself. That's the practical reason, but I think Otto had another reason."

"What was it?"

Stacy poured more tea into her cup. "You've been asking me a lot of questions. Now I've got one for you.

If you knew exactly when you would die, how would you spend your last hours on this earth?"

Val hesitated, as her hostess had several times, to give herself time to think. She pointed to the plate of sweets on the table. "I'd bake a batch of cookies, probably chocolate chip, and invite my family and friends to share them with me." She envisioned the gathering. After only a year here, she had more friends to invite from Bayport than from New York, where she'd spent ten years. "On my final day, I'd do the same thing I enjoyed throughout my life. I'm guessing most people would."

"I believe Otto did exactly that. He loved being on the water and he was crazy about the *Titanic*. He enjoyed entertaining eclectic groups of people for dinner, a mix of old friends and new ones. Otto often planned some kind of game, a scavenger hunt or trivia over cocktails." Stacy stirred her tea. "On Saturday night he indulged all his passions at once. The yacht, the *Titanic* dinner, the guests, the game. He wrapped them all into a grand finale and then left this world with a bang, not a whimper."

Her explanation for the dinner, the yacht, and the game made sense, but the suicide conclusion didn't necessarily follow. Val had seen another of Otto's passions play out on Saturday night—a desire to expose the wrongs of others. "Otto put several people on the spot during his mystery game. Did he always entertain guests by making them uncomfortable?"

Stacy flicked her wrist. "They were all playing their roles to the hilt."

Her phone played a tune from the counter where she'd left it. "Excuse me." Stacy got up and answered it. "What's up, Trey? . . . Okay. I'll be right there." She hung up and turned to Val. "Trey heard a loud bang. He thought it might be a gunshot. It came from the house on the corner."

Damian and Louisa's place? Val and Stacy dashed outside.

Chapter 18

Val ran as fast as she could to keep up with the longer-legged Stacy. They reached the house on the corner at the same time and rushed up the driveway. Trey stood on the doorstep of the brick two-story house, a lanky, gray-haired man beside him. Gretel sniffed around the door.

The older man grasped the doorknob and pushed the door open. "Hello? Anybody home?"

Wailing came from inside.

Gretel broke free, zipped into the house, and disappeared to the left.

"Gretel!" Trey roared. He went in after the dog.

The tall man, Stacy, and Val followed. A door in the foyer was open. Barking and moaning came from beyond it. Val rushed into the garage.

To the right of the doorway, Val saw the legs of a man who was lying faceup on the concrete floor. Her view of the man's torso and face were blocked by Louisa, who was bending over him.

"Damian!" she cried. "Talk to me. Damian!"

The older man slipped between her and the black

Mercedes in the garage, bent down, and picked up Damian's wrist, apparently checking for a pulse. He turned to Trey. "Get the dog out of here and call 911. I'm a doctor."

Trey picked up the leash and tugged the dog back to the foyer.

Louisa looked up. "Please save him. Oh, God. Damian." Tears streamed down her cheeks.

Val spotted a small revolver on the floor near Damian. Had he shot himself?

Stacy said, "I'm certified in CPR. Can I help, Doctor?"

"Okay, you stay." He looked at Val. "*You* take *her* out of here." He pointed to Louisa.

As Stacy coaxed Louisa away from Damian, Val glimpsed his blood-soaked shirt. She put her arm around Louisa's shoulder and hurried her into the foyer.

Trey stood there, wide-eyed and pale, holding Gretel's leash tightly and fumbling with his phone.

Val pointed to the front door. "Make that call outside."

"Okay." He left with the dog.

Val started to take Louisa to the living room, but then noticed the kitchen at the end of the hall. A better place, farther from the garage. She led Louisa there and sat her down at a tiled table in the corner.

Unlike the last kitchen Val had visited, this one was sparkling clean. Nothing in the sink. No fingerprints on the stainless steel appliances. It would have looked sterile except for its country kitchen touches. Ceramic hens and chicks sat on the windowsill. The curtains featured roosters. Even Louisa's old-fashioned cobbler apron had chickens on it.

Val reached up for one of the glasses hanging upside

down from an under-cabinet rack. She filled the glass with water and brought it to Louisa, who stared out the window with vacant eyes. "Take a sip, Louisa."

Louisa didn't move. She could probably use something stronger—brandy, whiskey, or even wine. With stemmed glasses so near, could wine be far away?

Val checked the refrigerator. No luck. She went over to the breakfront. Its shelves held family photos, a few cookbooks, and poultry-themed items—salt and pepper shakers shaped like chickens, a teapot and a sugar bowl with rooster-head tops. Val opened the doors to the cabinet and found assorted glasses and some hard stuff to pour in them. Bypassing the scotch and gin, she selected a bottle of apple brandy. She filled a snifter with it and took it to the table.

Louisa gulped the brandy. Her eyes watered. "Damian?" She started to stand up.

Val held on to her arm. "Sit down. The doctor is with him." She gave Louisa time for a few more sips of the apple brandy and then said, "What happened in the garage?"

"I found a gun in Damian's car. He came into the garage and said to put it down. He wouldn't tell me why he had it. He demanded I give it to him. I told him to stay back, but he didn't." She verged on hysteria. "I thought if he took it, he'd shoot me."

Val still didn't understand how he'd ended up with a bullet hole in him. "Did he try to take the gun away from you?"

Louisa nodded. "He grabbed it. I wouldn't let go. Then it went off and he fell." She covered her face and sobbed.

What could Val say to calm her down? She put her

hand on Louisa's shoulder. "Doctors perform miracles these days. Damian may be just fine."

Louisa looked up. "God, I hope you're right." She pulled a tissue from the patch pocket of her apron and blotted her tears.

Once the EMTs and the police arrived, Val would lose her chance to explore the gaps in Louisa's story. Val poured more tongue-loosener into Louisa's glass and said, "Why did you think Damian would shoot you?"

"I'll show you." Louisa stood up, held on to the back of her chair to steady herself, and then turned toward the breakfront. She pulled a slim cookbook off the shelf, *Microwave Dinners for Two*, and removed a business envelope tucked inside the book. "This came in yesterday's mail. I hid it where he'd never look."

She brought the envelope to the table. It had no return address, just a printed mailing label with her name and address. She took a sheet of paper from the envelope, unfolded it, and put it on the table.

Val read the single line of printed, italicized text at the top of the page: *Your husband shot Otto. Find his gun before he uses it on you.*

Huh? Val could easily believe Damian shot Otto, but not that he'd have kept the gun. Who could have seen him shoot Otto? Trey, Jerome, and possibly Stacy were outside at the same time as Damian. They had no reason to hold back what they'd witnessed. Therefore, the letter writer was lying either to implicate an innocent man or to play a nasty trick. A trick that had turned deadly because Louisa was primed to believe her husband wanted to get rid of her.

Louisa sniffed. "Now you see why I wouldn't let Damian have the gun. I was afraid he'd shoot me, throw me in the trunk, and dump my body where no one would find me."

Val watched Louisa wrap her arms around herself as if an icy wind had just hit her. Why had a trunk popped into her mind? Because that's where hit men stowed bodies, or because she knew what had happened to Val? "Don't touch the letter or the envelope again, Louisa. The police might be able to get finger-prints from it."

Louisa dropped the envelope on the table. "I didn't call them yesterday because I thought it was a sick joke. I turned the house upside down and didn't find a gun. Today I got a chance to search Damian's car, when I thought he was in the shower. I found the gun under the passenger's seat." She clutched her head. "What will I tell my children?"

"Are they nearby?" When Louisa shook her head, Val continued, "Is there someone you can call to stay with you until your children get here?"

"My parents are on a trip to Hawaii, but my aunt isn't far away. She'll come over."

Val picked up sirens in the distance. "The ambulance is almost here."

"At last!" Louisa stood up. "I'll splash water on my face and go to the door."

She went into the powder room off the hall near the kitchen.

Val hurried past it toward the foyer.

Stacy emerged from the door that led to the garage, saw Val, and shook her head. "The doctor tried his best. He's their neighbor, a retired surgeon, so he knew what to do. I'm going to sit down." She went into the living room, looking rattled.

Val opened the front door. Trey was on the sidewalk, holding Gretel's leash as she sniffed around the shrubs planted near the street. Val told him what Stacy had said.

He shook his head. "I didn't think Damian would make it. He looked bad."

"Quick question for you. When is the mail delivered on this street?"

"Between two and three. Why?"

"Just curious."

The timing of the mail delivery explained why Louisa, so calm when she'd eaten lunch at the café yesterday, had turned nervous by the time she visited Granddad late in the afternoon. In between, she'd gone home and read her mail. No wonder she'd asked Granddad to find out if the police suspected Damian of Otto's murder.

Val went back inside the house as the siren became deafening. Louisa emerged from the powder room, her eyes still red-rimmed from crying. She'd combed her hair, though, and shed her apron. "I'll go meet the ambulance."

On the way out, her head turned toward the closed door to the garage.

Val paused outside the living room. Stacy stood in front of the sofa at the far end of the room, her back to the foyer. Damian and Louisa's wedding portrait hung on the wall over the sofa. Even from across the room, Val could see the picture well enough to confirm what Chatty had told her two days ago—that Louisa looked more attractive in middle age than she had when younger, and that Damian looked the same except for a few gray hairs.

As Val crossed the room for a better look at the portrait, Stacy aimed her phone at it. Was she snapping a picture of it?

Stacy turned, nodded to Val, and walked past her without a word.

Val trailed her into the hall. "Wait a minute, Stacy. Did you just—?"

Stacy slipped out the front door seconds before the EMTs rushed in.

Val pointed them toward the door to the garage and stopped Louisa from following them. "You can't do anything in there." Val led her to an armchair in the living room. Louisa sat there, staring at her wedding portrait.

The chief came into the house and beckoned to Val.

She pointed to Louisa in the living room. "She may be in shock. I gave her brandy."

He turned to the young officer who'd followed him into the house. "Stay with the woman in the living room, Wade, and get the EMTs to check her over when they're finished in there." He pointed to the garage. "I need a quick rundown of what happened here, Val. Where can we talk?"

"In the kitchen." She gave him a two-minute summary.

He then called for a crime scene unit, went to the living room to talk to Louisa, and sent Officer Wade to the kitchen to take down Val's statement. The young officer wrote notes as Val did a brain dump of every detail she could remember since walking into the Browns' house. When she was finished, the chief came in and told her to leave by the kitchen door to avoid being seen by the neighbors. He cautioned her to say nothing about the incident to the media beyond what the police made public.

On the way home, she thought about how much had changed in the last two hours. When she'd arrived to talk to Stacy, Damian had been at the top of her suspect list. But the anonymous note pointing to him as the murderer made her less sure of his guilt. It raised more questions than it answered. Who'd sent the note? Who had a vested interest in seeing Damian blamed for Otto's death?

As usual, Granddad would have his own take on the anonymous note and the shooting. Would he pull at the same loose threads that bothered her?

Back home she found him in the kitchen sharpening his fish knife.

"I only caught one small croaker today." He scraped the knife along the whetstone. "Not enough for both of us for dinner, but we can have it as an appetizer."

"You can eat the whole thing. I'm having dinner with Gunnar." She glanced at her watch. Forty-five minutes until Gunnar expected her—enough time to bring Granddad up to date. "I've just come from the Browns' house. Damian's dead. Louisa shot him."

Granddad stopped scraping the blade on the stone. "I told you there'd be trouble between those two."

"But you never expected Damian to be the victim."

"I sure didn't. How did it go down?"

As he sharpened the knife, Val summarized what she'd seen and heard at the Browns' house. He stopped scraping when she told him about the anonymous letter. "The chief doesn't want any information leaking about the letter or what happened at the house."

"I'll keep it under my hat." He flipped over the

knife and scraped the other side of the blade against the stone. "The police will look for fingerprints on the letter."

"They probably won't find any except Louisa's. With all the *CSI* shows on TV, people know enough to wear gloves when doing something underhanded. If the sender saw Damian shoot Otto, why not tell the police instead of writing the letter?"

"The usual reason folks keep stuff like that from the police is for blackmail, but that wasn't a blackmail note."

"Exactly, so the letter writer didn't see Damian shoot Otto. Of course, Damian might have shot Otto without anyone seeing him. Or someone else murdered Otto and wanted the police to focus their investigation on Damian."

Granddad turned on the faucet and rinsed the knife he'd just sharpened. "The murderer could have done that with an anonymous tip to the police hotline. There must have been a reason to route it through Louisa."

"Possibly to cause trouble between her and Damian. They're tied to the poultry business, which Trey and his mother detest."

Granddad frowned as he inspected the blade he'd just sharpened. "Could one of them have killed Otto?"

"Trey had the opportunity and a motive. He was out of the saloon a long time and had a big grudge against Otto." As she removed clean plates from the dishwasher, she told Granddad about Trey's seasickness and Otto's demand that he spend more time on the water to get over it.

Granddad scraped the knife against the whetstone,

using short strokes. "That's a rotten thing Otto did, but it was years ago. Besides, if Trey killed him for that reason, he wouldn't have told you his motive."

"He had to explain his rudeness on the boat. He and Stacy made sure I knew they had reasons to want Otto alive." Val told Granddad about Otto's promise to donate to the bay fund and to return Stacy's *Titanic* letter.

"Do they have proof Otto planned to do that?"

"They didn't show me any, or even say they had it." Val transferred the clean dishes from the counter to the cabinet. "Stacy's main goal is protecting Trey. She insisted that Otto wasn't murdered but committed suicide. She may be pushing suicide because she's afraid Trey will be charged with murder."

Granddad rinsed and dried the knife again. "I think you're barking up the wrong tree about the note. How would Stacy or Trey or anyone else know Damian had a gun?"

He'd picked on the loose thread that had been bothering Val too. "The person who wrote the anonymous letter could have guessed there was a gun in the Browns' house. In other words, it was a shot in the dark."

Granddad groaned. "I don't like your pun or your explanation. Damian could have told the woman he had an affair with that he owned a gun."

"Unusual pillow talk."

"Not if she wants you to kill her husband."

Val closed the now empty dishwasher. No matter what information came to light, Granddad would find a way to blame Otto's death on Cheyenne. "If Cheyenne convinced Damian to kill Otto, why would she send an anonymous letter saying he'd done it? Once the police turned up the heat on him, he could implicate her in the murder."

For a change, Granddad didn't come back immediately with a counterargument. He rinsed and dried the knife again, looked closely at it, and nodded. "You're right. That leaves one other person who could have written that letter. Someone who knew Damian had a gun or who could plant one if he didn't."

Val stared at him, astounded. "You mean Louisa?"

Granddad nodded. "I'll bet you're right about the fingerprints on that anonymous letter. They'll all belong to her. That's 'cause she sent it to herself."

Chapter 19

Val couldn't think of any reason to reject Granddad's idea about the anonymous note, nor any reason to accept it. "Explain why Louisa would send herself that letter."

"Jealousy. She knew her husband was spending time with Cheyenne and suspected he'd leave her for a younger woman. So she concocts a scheme to make sure he doesn't. Step one, she sends herself a letter warning that her husband's going to kill her. Step two, she comes to see me yesterday and plants the idea that Damian murdered Otto." Granddad ticked off the steps on his fingers. "Step three, she lures Damian into the garage, shoots him, and then claims she did it by accident or in self-defense."

Had Granddad lifted that idea from an old movie? Val had trouble imagining Louisa planning and executing such a devious plot. "You're saying Louisa committed premeditated murder?"

"Why not? The gun could have been in the house a long time, or she may have just bought it. You have only her word that it was under the passenger seat. There were no witnesses in the garage when Damian was shot."

"True, but her version of what happened in the garage matches her personality more than your version. Based on how she lashed out at Stacy on the yacht, I'd say Louisa is easily agitated and acts on impulse. She's not a planner."

"She lashed out because chicken farming is a hot-button issue with her." Granddad sliced through the fish. "That doesn't mean she can't be cold and calculating about other things. She acted nervous here yesterday, and she probably freaked out after she shot Damian. She could have faked it both times."

"Fortunately, the police don't have to rely on our amateur psychology to decide the case. They'll use science to figure out if she killed him on purpose, by accident, or in self-defense. Their experts will analyze the scene, Damian's wound, and the anonymous letter. The police will trace the gun and question Louisa repeatedly. I have more confidence they'll get to the truth about Damian's death than about Otto's."

"Can you make a case against her as Otto's murderer?"

Val shook her head. "She had no reason to kill him or to take a gun to his dinner party. Everyone went out on deck after he left the saloon except her. She went to the guest head downstairs. You *can* get outside from that deck if you go through the engine room and the storage room, but how would she know that?"

Granddad looked up from filleting the fish. "Cheyenne gave her and Damian a tour of the lower deck."

"Yes, but when she showed me the lower deck, she didn't point out the door to the engine room. I found out about it only because she and I were looking everywhere for Otto and I asked what was behind the door." Val glanced at her watch. "I've got to leave for Gunnar's house."

"Wait. Don't you want to know what I found out at Cheyenne's? I looked at the photos on the table. There weren't any dates or names on the back of them, but I got her to talk a little about the girl in the photos with Otto. She was his half sister, Andrea. Otto's father divorced his mother, and she remarried."

Darn. That meant Andrea had a different last name. Hard to find out anything about her death without knowing her name. "Good job, Granddad."

"Cheyenne told me she's going through the papers on Otto's desk and paying off bills. She wants you to send her an invoice for the remainder of the catering bill."

"I'll hand-carry the invoice to her tomorrow. I'd like to see how she's reacting to Damian's death. I also want to talk to Stacy again. She did something weird at the Browns' house. When she thought no one was looking, she took a photo of Damian and Louisa's wedding portrait."

Granddad stroked his chin. "Stacy looks about the same age as the Browns. Maybe they knew each other years ago."

"That occurred to me too." And Granddad could check into it. "Would you like to practice the skills you learned in your online investigator course?"

Granddad's eyes lit up. "Sure. You want me to spy on somebody, like I did on Cheyenne?"

The mundane task Val had in mind would disappoint him. "Nothing so exciting. Go online and see what you can dig up about Stacy, Damian, Louisa, Cheyenne, and Otto. Find out where they all grew up and went to school. Look for any connections among them. Check where they lived and worked, if you have time."

"You mean, if I don't fall asleep first," he grumbled.

She smiled. "Pessimist. You *might* discover something exciting that cracks the case wide open. I'll see you later, Granddad."

Val went to her room, changed her clothes, and then drove to Gunnar's house.

When she arrived, he greeted her with literal open arms. "We meet again."

She felt warm in his embrace. "This time let's do it right." She stood on tiptoe and gave him a long kiss. Maybe they could ignore the red flags that had popped up between them in the last few days.

It was nearly eight o'clock when Gunnar set out a cold feast for their dinner. "Call it tapas or a hearty antipasto or just a mishmash."

Val surveyed the table. A platter with jumbo shrimp, smoked salmon, and thinly sliced prosciutto. Marinated artichokes and eggplant caponata. A selection of cheese that included Brie and Asiago. A salad of baby tomatoes, cucumber, Greek olives, and feta. And crusty bread.

The setup looked familiar to Val. "We had a picnic dinner like this last summer. We ate in the backyard of the B and B where you were staying." That was just before he moved into this house. Now they were having the same meal before he moved out of the house.

"I remember it. You were trying to solve a murder, and now you're doing it again." Gunnar poured wine for both of them. "Anything new on the *Titanic* collector's death?"

"A related death." Val told him about the anonymous letter Louisa received and her shooting of Damian.

Gunnar gaped at her. "Didn't see that coming. I feel sorry for her and her family." He filled his plate with prosciutto, cheese, and marinated artichokes. "Now that Otto's murder is solved, you can forget about it and think about other things."

Solved? Not yet. "I don't think the anonymous letter or Louisa's suspicions about her husband amount to proof that he killed Otto." Val put shrimp and salmon on her plate. "Granddad is convinced Cheyenne did it or lured Damian into doing it for her. He's hung up on a love triangle as the motive for the murder."

"And you're hung up on the mystery game as the motive. His hang-up is easier to explain than yours. Has he been watching the classic movie station on cable TV?"

"He always does. Why?"

"The station is having a Femme Fatale Festival this month. He's looking at the world through the filter of that plot."

Val understood. Just a few months ago, she'd viewed the motives and suspects in a murder through the lens of Edgar Allan Poe's stories. His writing at least had more variety than femme fatale movie plots. "Enough about murder for tonight. Do you have any leads on a place to rent?"

"No." He concentrated on his plate.

She took his one-syllable response as a sign he'd rather not talk about his house hunt. So she asked about the acting conservatory. As he described the program, which encompassed both classes and productions, she realized it was even more intensive than she'd expected.

"It sounds like a great program," she said, "and a full-time commitment." For sixteen months, or even longer if he decided to enroll in the advanced courses.

"I'll find time for other things, but I can't pass this up."

Would she be one of those *other things*? She forced herself to say something positive. "Washington's not that far from here. An hour and a half. A lot of people with full-time jobs there commute for that long."

"But I never wanted to be one of them. Getting a break in the theater, as in most things in life, is about being there to take advantage of opportunities, like I did with the Treadwell Players. If I hadn't been hanging around as an understudy in January, I wouldn't have gotten the chance to show what I could do with a major role." He put his fork down. "I'll need a place to stay in Washington. It doesn't make sense for me to rent a place in Bayport while I'm in the program. I have accounting clients here, but we mostly communicate electronically."

But he didn't mostly communicate electronically with her. Val's eyes met his across the table. Was this the end of their relationship? No, he'd tell her straight out if it was. "You can come back on weekends or whatever days off you have. I don't think Granddad would mind if you stayed with us." She hoped that was true.

He reached for her hand across the table. "I'd like you to come with me. The place I rent in Washington won't be as large as your grandfather's house, but it'll be big enough for the two of us."

She was too stunned to say anything for a moment. She drank some wine. "I'm more tied down than you.

I can't run the café electronically." Or keep an eye on Granddad from afar.

"Your assistant manager wouldn't mind taking over your café contract. She wanted it to start with." Gunnar studied her face. "I can see you're not enthusiastic about that. The contract ends in the summer, right? You could finish it out and then move."

"The contract goes until September." Val didn't want to barrage him with all her objections to his idea. She ought to at least give it a few days' thought. One objection would suffice for now, the one he'd understand best. "What would I do in Washington?"

"You have a lot of talent, and there are many more jobs there than here." He paused, apparently waiting for her response. When she said nothing, he continued, "And we need to spend more time together to know if we're right for each other."

If neither of them had reached that conclusion yet, would a change of venue make any difference? "This is a little sudden."

"You don't have to decide right away. It's just that if you're going to join me, I'll rent a bigger place, and you could help me pick it out."

In other words, *Take your time, but hurry up about it.* "Give me a few days to get used to the idea. For now, let's talk about something else."

"You mean murder?" His eyes twinkled. "It's your favorite topic."

Sometimes murder was easier to understand than love. "No, food is my favorite topic."

It struck her as she looked at the cold dishes on the table that this meal and the similar one they'd shared last summer were the bookends of Gunnar's stay in

Bayport. He would never move back here, not while he was pursuing acting as his midlife career, not as long as he was successful at it. And she hoped he was, because he'd waited many years to follow his dream.

Her appetite gone, she pleaded fatigue and cut the evening short.

As Val went into the sitting room, Granddad looked at her, pointed the remote at the TV, and muted it. "What's wrong?"

That obvious, huh? She flopped onto the worn tweed sofa. "Gunnar's moving to Washington, D.C., and he wants me to go with him." Granddad listened without interrupting as she gave him the details. "So I have a decision to make."

"One you're not happy about."

Was that a clue to what her decision should be? "Like most people, I resist change." She'd stayed engaged to Tony longer than she should have.

Granddad stroked his chin. "Don't resist change because of me. It's been good having you here, but I'll get along without you." He patted her hand, which rested on the sofa arm. "You know that I wanted your mother to marry someone local."

Val nodded. "Chief Yardley."

"Right, but when she decided on your father, I was happy for her. She chose the life of a Navy wife, moving from one place to another. We missed her a lot, but we were happy to see what a good marriage she had. And she gave me the world's best granddaughter." He squeezed her hand. "You can be anywhere, Val, as long as you're with the right person. Is Gunnar the one you want to spend the rest of your life with?"

A simple yes-or-no question, but Val had a different one-word answer: *maybe.* "I've imagined Gunnar as part of my life here, but I never thought about the two of us being together elsewhere."

"He didn't ask you to marry him. I guess he hasn't made up his mind either."

Val shrugged. "Couples don't jump into marriage as fast as they used to."

"Gunnar jumped into the empty spot after you ended your engagement. Didn't you tell me he was also coming off a broken engagement?" At her nod, Granddad continued, "A few months apart might help both of you decide how you feel. What's the rush?"

She decided against telling him why Gunnar had set a timer on her decision—so he'd know how large an apartment to rent. The aspiring actor couldn't shed his training as an accountant. Her delayed decision meant he'd have to pay higher rent for a larger apartment he wouldn't need unless she joined him. Or else he'd have to forfeit money to break the lease on a small place if she did join him. The economics of romance.

Granddad had given her good advice, by which she meant he'd reinforced her own leanings.

She sat up straighter on the sofa. "Enough of that. Did you find anything interesting in your online research?"

"No connection between Cheyenne and Damian. Nothing at all about Damian's early life. As for the rest of them, they didn't grow up anywhere near each other. I wrote down where they came from and the schools they went to. It's on a sheet of paper next to the computer. I'll show you." He levered himself out of the lounge chair and groaned. "Sitting too long."

They went into the study.

Val glanced at the notes he'd jotted on a scratch pad. One bit of information popped out. Stacy had graduated from Virginia Tech, the school Otto's half sister was attending when she died.

Could Otto's sister and Stacy have been at the same university at the same time?

Chapter 20

Val pointed to the line in Granddad's notes that listed Stacy's degree from Virginia Tech. "Stacy told me Otto's sister was a student at Virginia Tech and died after falling off a balcony railing."

Granddad's eyebrows shot up. "Like the young girl in Otto's mystery. Did Stacy know Andrea?"

"She didn't say so. Let me work out if they *could* have known each other. Andrea was a sophomore, nineteen years old, and Otto about ten years older when she died thirty years ago. The newspaper said he was fifty-nine when he died." Val jotted numbers on a clean sheet in the scratch pad. Based on what Stacy and Trey had told her, she knew how old Otto was when Stacy married him, and how long ago they'd divorced. She worked out Trey's current age and Stacy's age when he was born.

Granddad looked over her shoulders. "Got a bottom line?"

"Uh-huh. Stacy would have been a year or two ahead of Andrea at Tech. It's a huge state university. They overlapped there, but that doesn't mean they knew each other." Something to ask Stacy, along with why she'd snapped a picture of the Browns' wedding portrait.

Val skimmed the other notes Granddad had taken. Otto grew up in Annapolis, served in the Navy after college, and eventually earned a law degree from Tulane University. Cheyenne grew up in West Virginia, but Granddad had no notes about where she'd gone to school. Louisa came from rural Southern Maryland and graduated from the University of Delaware.

Val was intrigued by the absence of information about Damian, in contrast to the details about the others. Based on his mild drawl, he must have come from farther south than the rest of them. Louisa could fill in the missing information about him, but Val wouldn't ask so soon after the shooting. Tomorrow she'd take Louisa a casserole or another dish so she'd have at least one meal for herself and visiting family.

Val might as well cook it right now. After today's shooting and tonight's dinner with Gunnar, she was too troubled to fall asleep. Measuring and mixing ingredients would calm her down. Better than tossing and turning in bed.

She went into the kitchen, checked the refrigerator and pantry, and decided to make a quiche. On second thought, two quiches. One for Louisa, and one for Cheyenne.

At three o'clock on Thursday, Val rang the bell at Cheyenne's house. A gray-haired man in neat, casual clothes opened the door.

A neighbor or relative of the Warbecks? Val smiled. "Hi. Is Cheyenne home?"

The man opened the door wider. "Yes. Please come in. Cheyenne's upstairs, giving my wife a house tour. I got a bum knee, so I didn't want to climb."

Val went into the living room with him. "I brought Cheyenne something for dinner." She set the quiche down on the glass coffee table and sat on the sofa.

"My wife made a chicken pot pie for her. Such a nice tradition, to feed the bereaved." He sat in the side chair across the room. "We were away for a few days and came home to the sad news about Otto. By the way, I'm Jerry Kindell. I used to work with Otto."

The name struck a chord with Val. Jerry Kindell and his wife were the couple Cheyenne said Otto had intended to invite to the *Titanic* dinner. Val introduced herself and said, "I catered the dinner on Otto's yacht Saturday night. You'd have been there too, I guess, if you hadn't been away."

He frowned, puzzled. "We went away Sunday. We would have gone to the dinner if we'd been invited. I really wanted to see Otto's yacht."

It was Val's turn to be puzzled. Cheyenne had told her that Otto had invited Damian and Louisa to the *Titanic* dinner because the Kindells couldn't come.

Jerry stood up as his wife and Cheyenne came downstairs. He turned to Val. "We'll have to be on our way. Good to meet you."

"I enjoyed talking to you," Val said. Very much.

He'd given her an important bit of information, though she wasn't yet sure what to make of it. She knew only that either Cheyenne had lied to her or Otto had lied to Cheyenne about the reason Damian and Louisa had been invited to the dinner. They were the intended guests, not last-minute fill-ins for another couple.

After Cheyenne bid the Kindells goodbye in the hall, she joined Val in the living room. "A reporter called this morning and said Damian Brown was dead. How awful is that? Such a *nice* man."

Val searched Cheyenne's face for a hint that Damian was special to her. No sign of it. "Why did the reporter call you?"

"Because of the coincidence. Damian was on the boat with us when Otto was shot. A few days later, Damian was shot too. Do you know anything about that?"

Val chose her words carefully to comply with what the police had made public. "Damian was shot in his house, apparently by accident."

"You mean he was cleaning a gun and it went off?"

"That happens a lot." True, though misleading in this case. To forestall more questions, Val pointed to the quiche on the coffee table. "I brought you a quick meal you can heat up."

"Aren't you nice? And Bethany too. She brought over a pizza last night for us to share. I'll put the quiche in the fridge. Would you like something to drink?"

"No, thank you."

Cheyenne picked up the dish and took it through the dining room to the kitchen. Val followed her as far as the dining table. Most of the photos that had been strewn on the table two days ago were gone. Now there was only a small stack of them—probably the ones Cheyenne had selected for Otto's memorial service. Val shuffled through the pictures, looking in vain for one of Andrea. She found a photo of Otto as a boy in a baseball uniform, his bat poised for a hit, and a more candid shot of him at the plate when he was older. Viewing the two photos side by side, Val noticed his stance was different. The bat was over the boy's right shoulder, which made sense because Otto wrote right-handed, but over the young man's left shoulder. Maybe someone had scanned an old photo of him and accidentally flipped it, creating a mirror image of the original.

Cheyenne came into the dining room. "I decided to have a get-together on the yacht in honor of Otto. I'd like to do it tomorrow night and invite everyone who was at the *Titanic* dinner."

Yipes. "I thought you never intended to go back on the yacht."

"I don't want to be afraid to go on a boat. Bethany convinced me it was like falling off a horse. You have to get back on it right away, or you may never ride again." Cheyenne went into the living room, sat on the sofa, and motioned for Val to join her. "I'll have a bigger get-together for the people Otto knew in Washington, but all of us who were on the boat Saturday night need to find closure. And I'd like you to cater, and your grandfather and Bethany to help. Just the way you did last time."

No way. "You mean a ten-course meal?"

"Nothing that fancy. Just a light meal. Will you do it?"

Val hesitated. Chief Yardley wouldn't like the plan, probably fearing a murderer might be in their midst, but she could see its value. The get-together might dredge up memories of what had occurred after Otto left the table and make it clear who did and didn't have the opportunity to shoot him. "What kind of food do you have in mind?"

"Nothing you have to fuss with. Cold platters. Cheese is fine, but no garlicky meats."

Cold platters, cold comfort, like Val's dinner with Gunnar last night. "We could do a high tea, with small sandwiches and desserts."

"Perfect."

"Any idea how many guests will be there?"

"I don't know yet, but I'm hoping they'll all come. Otto had gifts for them that he forgot to bring to the dinner. Personalized party favors, I guess. I'll give them out tomorrow night to anyone who comes."

"Do you know what Otto meant for them to have?"

"He didn't tell me. They're sealed in envelopes decorated with images of the *Titanic*. A small envelope for Trey, a larger one for Stacy, and a bulky one for Homer and his wife."

Could those envelopes contain what he'd promised them for attending the *Titanic* dinner? They might accept Cheyenne's invitation if they thought so. "Nothing for Damian and Louisa?"

"Otto put *Titanic* labels on two bottles of wine. He said one of them was for you and your grandfather. The other one must have been for the Browns." Cheyenne chewed on her lower lip. "I feel I should ask Louisa, but I dread talking to her so soon after her husband died."

Val wasn't sure Louisa would accept an invitation from the woman she suspected of having an affair with Damian. But the larger the gathering, the better the chance of getting to the truth about Otto's death. "Louisa may be too upset to come tomorrow night. But if you like, I can talk to her and encourage her to come. We know each other from the athletic club."

"Would you? I'd really appreciate it. The police

released Otto's body. I'd like to spread his ashes on the bay."

"It may not be legal to do that."

"I'll check. If it isn't, we'll throw rose petals over the side. I still need to find someone to pilot the yacht. Do you know anyone who can do that?"

Val did. Someone who should also be there. "Would it be okay if I asked Jerome? He needs closure too." And sitting at the controls might jog his fuzzy memory. "If you have any concerns, I'll try to get you a more experienced pilot to sit next to him."

"No, I'm fine with Jerome."

"I'll call you after I talk to Louisa and let you know if she's coming." Val stood up. "I almost forgot. I brought the invoice for the catering balance. My grandfather said you were waiting for it."

"I'll write you a check now."

Val left with the check, drove to Louisa's house on the other side of Bayport, and rang the bell. A woman in her sixties opened the door. Val introduced herself and said she'd brought Louisa a quiche.

"She's upstairs resting. She didn't get much sleep last night. I'm Linda Zaharee, her aunt. I expect she'll be down before long if you can wait a bit. Come to the kitchen. I just made a fresh pot of coffee."

"Thank you." Val followed her to the kitchen. Like Louisa, her aunt had thick hair, though hers was darker, with a frosting of white. Looking barely more than a dozen years older than her niece, she must have been the much younger sister of Louisa's father or mother.

"I'm glad you brought us this," she said as she put the quiche in the refrigerator. "We can have it tonight. Louisa's not much on cooking, and neither am I."

Val sat at the counter. "Are Louisa's children on their way?"

"Her son is taking a year off from school and hiking in Australia. We haven't reached him yet." Linda poured coffee into two glass mugs with roosters on them. "Her daughter lives in California. She has a big job interview tomorrow. Then she'll take the red-eye and get here Saturday morning. Louisa's parents are also due back from Hawaii then."

"What about Damian's family? Are they local?"

"He comes from southern Virginia, an old mining town. His folks are dead. He never got along with his brother, and they lost touch." Louisa's aunt took a quart of milk from the fridge. "How about some of this for your coffee? We don't have cream."

"Milk is fine." Val splashed some into her coffee. "My condolences. It's a difficult time for all of you."

"The kids will take it hard. My sister and her husband, not so much. They never cared for Damian." She sat next to Val at the counter. "I hate to speak ill of the dead, but . . ."

In Val's experience, that phrase usually preceded trashing the dead.

Linda sipped her coffee. ". . . Louisa's well rid of him. She brought him home with her from college one summer. She refused to go back to school—just wanted to marry him. She finished college eventually, in Delaware. He got one of those online degrees. Her parents paid for everything."

Linda talked nonstop while Val drank coffee. Louisa's parents subsidized the houses she and Damian bought, paid for their grandchildren's education, and tried to find a place for Damian in the family business. He was too lazy to succeed. On his own, he never held

down a job for long. He lost one of them because of
an affair with the boss's wife. Louisa forgave him because she didn't want to admit her parents were right
about him.

Val wondered why Louisa's aunt was confiding these
details to a stranger. Maybe because she would rather
talk about family history than yesterday's shooting.

The floor creaked above them, a sign that Louisa
had woken up.

She came into the kitchen, her eyes bloodshot from
crying or lack of sleep; possibly both.

"Your friend here just brought us a quiche for
dinner," Linda said.

Louisa's eyes glistened with tears. "Thank you, Val.
People have been so kind. The neighbors and two of
the gals from my yoga class brought us food too."

Her aunt poured her a mug of coffee, said goodbye
to Val, and went upstairs.

"Linda's a good egg." High praise, given Louisa's
esteem for poultry. She leaned toward Val and said in
a low voice, "Did you mention the anonymous letter
to her?"

"No."

"Please don't tell anyone about it. The police said
they'd keep it under wraps and notify me before they
made it public so I could break it to the family myself.
I don't want to tell my children if I don't have to."

What was worse than hearing your father was accidentally shot dead by your mother? Finding out that
he too might have shot and killed someone. Sympathy
for Louisa and her children flooded over Val.

She told Louisa about Cheyenne's planned memorial

on the yacht. "She hoped you'd come. She asked me to invite you."

Louisa shook her head. "I can't go."

Val wasn't surprised, but she also wasn't ready to give up. "What the anonymous letter said isn't necessarily true, Louisa."

"The part about the gun was true. Are you saying Damian didn't shoot Otto?"

"Exactly. The letter could have been a sick hoax. Tomorrow on the yacht, I'm sure we'll talk about what happened Saturday night. Now that a few days have passed, people might remember something that would rule out Damian as the shooter."

Louisa's eyes widened. "That would make this whole horrible mess easier on my son and daughter."

With a little more coaxing, Louisa agreed to go.

When Val left Louisa's house, she spotted Stacy half a block away, in front of the house her son was minding. She was leading Gretel on a leash. Too good an opportunity to pass up.

Gretel's tail wagged as Val joined them.

Stacy looked less enthusiastic to see Val, managing only a ghost of a smile. "I just got an unexpected call from Cheyenne. She said you were catering her little memorial to Otto on the yacht tomorrow night. Gathering the suspects together?"

Val leaned down to pet the dog. "Cheyenne views it as a celebration of Otto's life, not an assembly of suspects."

"How do *you* look at it?" Stacy didn't wait for an answer. "I've been doing research today, and not just for my book. This isn't the first time you and your grandfather have dabbled in amateur detection." Her tone was matter-of-fact, giving no hint of her attitude toward amateur sleuthing.

Val smiled. "Then it won't come as a shock that Granddad and I have researched you. Did you know Andrea at Virginia Tech?"

Chapter 21

Stacy took a long moment to answer Val's question about Otto's sister. Nothing unusual about that. Otto's ex-wife never spoke without thinking. "I met Andrea when I was a senior. We knew each other as neighbors rather than friends. She and I lived on the same floor in an off-campus apartment complex."

"Was that where she fell from the balcony?"

"No. That happened at another apartment building during a party Andrea and her friends attended. I dropped in, but didn't stay long. Lots of drinking and some drugs. Not my scene. Before cutting out with my boyfriend, I tried to convince Andrea and her roommates to leave with us. They didn't." Stacy tugged gently on Gretel's leash and led the dog in the opposite direction from Louisa's house. "I found out about Andrea's death the next morning, my graduation day."

That would put a damper on the celebration. "Any witnesses to what happened at the party?"

"No sober ones. Dozens of people saw Andrea on the balcony, but no one had their eyes on her at the

moment she fell. The police wanted to interview a
townie who'd crashed the party, but couldn't locate
him. He'd peddled ecstasy and come on to Andrea. I
saw a sketch of the guy on TV before I left town after
graduation. Handsome dude with a great body. I'd
noticed him, but not talked to him." Stacy stopped
walking as Gretel inspected a tree. "I found out weeks
later through one of Andrea's roommates that she had
alcohol and ecstasy in her system. After circulating the
sketch, the police identified the missing man as a drug
dealer called Demon. They never found out his real
name or where he lived."

Val's heart quickened. *Demon* could be a nickname
for Damian, a handsome dude even in middle age and
the man assigned the role of drug pusher in Otto's mystery game. "Did drugs play a role in Andrea's death?"

"Not in the sense that she died of an overdose or
from tainted drugs. Alcohol and drugs in her system
probably contributed by making her careless. Her
death was ruled an accident."

"Otto must have known you were at that party."

Stacy shook her head. "I didn't meet him until
more than ten years later. When he found out where
I'd gone to college, he asked if I'd ever run into his
sister. Andrea became a bond between us, though I
hadn't known her well." Gretel turned the corner to
search for new smells, and Stacy followed. "The grieving brother blamed the drug dealer and was obsessed
with finding him. Otto had a copy of the police sketch
and showed it to me regularly. He was convinced that
someday one of us would run into the man who caused
Andrea's death."

Val now knew why Otto had invited the couple he'd

just met and the wife who'd divorced him. "Did Otto tell you he'd seen that man at the Protect the Bay Barbecue? That's when he met Damian."

"Otto didn't say that, but the timing fits. We'd had almost no contact for eight years, since our divorce. About two weeks ago, he called me out of the blue and invited me and Trey to dinner on his yacht. He asked me to let him know if one of his guests looked familiar."

Otto, the lawyer, had been careful not to lead the witness. "Did you recognize Damian as Demon?"

"My memory of the drug pusher is hazy, but I'd looked at Otto's sketch enough to say that Damian could have been the man in that sketch. I thought hard about whether to tell Otto even that much, because I wasn't sure what he would do with the information. I even considered saying I recognized no one, but Otto would have known I was lying. He was good at reading people, and I'm not a good liar."

Val remembered Bethany's comment that Stacy had been distracted at the table. Possibly she'd been pondering what to tell Otto. "You must have realized, as Otto's game went on, that he planned to expose Damian at the end."

"So it seemed, but I didn't understand the point of it. After three decades, Damian couldn't be prosecuted for selling drugs, much less held responsible for a girl's accidental death. Thirty years ago he was younger than Trey is now. Young men do stupid things."

Like drugging the pilot of a yacht, as Val suspected Trey had done. "Did you say that to Otto?"

Stacy nodded. "I also told him that even if Damian was Demon, he'd turned his life around and become a family man with a responsible job." Stacy stopped walking as the dog sniffed around a bush. "I find Damian's job as a poultry industry lobbyist repugnant. I thought he should be nailed for condoning cruelty to animals, not for breaking the law years ago."

When could Stacy have given Otto her thoughts about Demon? Before dinner, she could have whispered yes or no about recognizing the drug pusher, but she hadn't been alone with her ex long enough to give him a complicated answer. The first time she could have spoken to him in private was after he left the table and she followed him out of the saloon. She'd lied by saying she hadn't seen him outside.

No point in confronting her about it. Val wanted to stay on good terms with Stacy to find out why she'd snapped a picture of the wedding portrait. "After the shooting at the Brown house yesterday, you were staring at Damian and Louisa's wedding picture. Did that settle the issue of whether Damian was Demon?"

Stacy wrapped the leash around her hand. "I didn't need to stare at the groom in the portrait. One glance at it told me Otto was right about him. I was focused on the bride."

Val took a stab at what had interested her about the bride. "Louisa has changed. Her hair is different now, and her cheeks are fuller, but her eyes are the same, don't you think?" When Stacy nodded, Val sensed more to come. "Why did you snap a picture of the portrait?"

Stacy glanced sideways at Val. "I needed that photo to research Louisa. She was at the party thirty years ago."

Val stopped dead. Granddad had noted that Louisa graduated from the University of Delaware. Maybe she'd visited Virginia Tech or started college there and then transferred. Val caught up with Stacy at the corner. They crossed the street. "Did you know Louisa back then?"

"I'd seen her a couple of times hanging around the building where Andrea and I lived, but I didn't know her name. After I saw the Browns' wedding picture, it occurred to me that one of Andrea's roommates might remember Louisa. I e-mailed the photo of the wedding picture to Jackie, the only roommate I could locate."

"Did she remember Louisa?"

Stacy nodded. "Jackie called me and gave me an earful. In her freshman year, she was assigned a triple dorm room with Louisa and Andie. That was Andrea's nickname in college. Louisa was the odd one out. She started calling herself Louie so she'd have a name that sounded vaguely masculine, like Jackie and Andie. She joined the same clubs as Andrea, bought the same clothes, enrolled in the same classes, and tagged after her everywhere."

Val shuddered. "Creepy."

"Exactly the word Jackie used. Jackie and Andrea moved off campus in their sophomore year and shared an apartment with two other girls. Louisa was disgruntled at not being included and continued to dog Andrea, who called her the *little woman.* Can you guess why?"

"Because she's not very tall?" Nor was Val, and she wouldn't care to be referred to that way.

"Also because her name was Louisa May Purty.

The only Louisa May anyone has ever heard of is the one who wrote *Little Women*." Stacy stopped at a street corner to let a car go by. "Thirty years ago at that party, when I was urging Andrea to leave, Jackie said, *Here comes the little woman again.* Andrea refused to leave because she wouldn't give the *little woman* the satisfaction of ruining her evening." Stacy crossed the street. "Andrea's death hit Jackie hard. She didn't want to go back to Tech for her junior year, but her parents insisted. She was also afraid Louisa would glom on to her next, but Louisa didn't return to Tech."

That fit with what Louisa's aunt had said. "I heard Louisa came home from college one summer with Damian and refused to go back to school. That explains why the police couldn't locate the drug dealer. He'd fled the state and ended up seven hours away." One thing puzzled Val about Stacy's story. "You didn't recognize Louisa as someone from college because she looks so different now. Didn't she recognize you?"

"I doubt it. The only time I got a good look at her was at the party, and she was focused on Andrea. I left right after Louisa arrived."

The similarity between Andrea's fall from the balcony thirty years ago and the situation in Otto's mystery game must have been obvious to Louisa. "Are you going to tell the police about Otto's sister and her connection to Damian and Louisa?"

Stacy smiled. "I assumed you would."

Val now understood why Stacy had shared so much information. She thought the police should know what she'd discovered, but preferred to avoid them because she'd lied to them, claiming she hadn't seen Otto after he left the saloon. Why had she lied? Maybe she assumed that the last person who admitted to talking to Otto would be a suspect. She'd rather the police believe that Otto had killed himself before either she or Trey left the saloon. But the sooner Stacy told the truth, the better for her.

"I'll pass on your information to the police," Val said. "If it's related to their investigation, though, they'll want to talk to you. After Otto disappeared from the yacht, we were all under a lot of stress and not thinking straight. I think the police would understand if you wanted to correct your initial statements. They'll be less forgiving if you don't correct them." Val gave Stacy time to let her words sink in. "Are you going to accept Cheyenne's invitation for tomorrow night?"

"I've already accepted. I want to say farewell to Otto."

"I'll see you then." Val gave Gretel a goodbye pat and returned to her car.

She called Chief Yardley from her car, hoping to drive straight to his office. He was too busy to see her and suggested she stop by at six thirty. That gave Val ninety minutes to make arrangements for tomorrow night's food.

She drove to the club, went into the Cool Down Café, and sat on a stool at the eating bar. Irene Pritchard, her sixtyish assistant manager, was busy behind the counter, assembling the ingredients for tonight's special: creamy chicken and vegetables over egg noodles.

Val eyed the huge quantity Irene was making. "That's a ton of food. You're expecting a busy evening?"

"I sell a lot of take-home meals on Thursdays. Folks get tired of cooking this late in the week. Friday's a lot slower."

"On Friday nights, everybody would rather go to happy hour on Main Street than exercise here and get a take-out dinner." Tomorrow Val could keep Irene busy and give her the chance to earn more than usual on a Friday. "I got a last-minute catering request for tomorrow night, a light meal like high tea for eight to ten people. If you'd be willing to make up some plat-ters, you can set the price and include a twenty percent tip for yourself."

Irene's eyes narrowed. "Are you gonna take a cut?"

"I'll add my fee for serving the meal. The rest is yours, Irene."

"I'm surprised you're getting any catering jobs after somebody died at one of your dinners."

Val bit back a protest that her food wasn't to blame for Otto's death. She'd rather show Irene that her barb hadn't stung. "Actually, I'm getting more catering requests than ever."

"Huh. People sure are strange." Irene cocked her head toward the café entrance. "And here comes one of your friends." Her intonation suggested she consid-ered the friend strange.

Chatty hurried into the café and sat next to Val at the eating bar. "I've got a vacancy in my schedule if you want a massage."

"A massage sounds wonderful, but I don't have a vacancy in my schedule."

Irene left to wait on a man who'd just sat at a bistro table.

"Normally I'd be giving Louisa Brown a massage.

This is her usual time spot. I didn't expect her to show up a day after her husband was shot. You know anything about that?"

"Not much. I can't wait to hear what the police have to say." Val was grateful the chief had suggested she sneak out the back door of the Browns' house. Otherwise, she'd have to answer questions from the media and from Chatty, Bayport's ace gossip. "Speaking of Louisa . . . did you see her on Monday after you gave me a massage?"

"Uh-huh. She has a standing appointment on Monday and Thursday afternoons."

"Did you happen to mention to her that I was going back to the yacht to pick up the scripts for the mystery game?"

Chatty ran her fingers along the edge of the granite counter. "Hmm. I think I did. You didn't say it was a secret."

"True." But if Chatty had kept quiet, Val could rule out Damian and Louisa as people who might have shoved her into the trunk. Changing the subject, Val said, "I've been getting calls about catering *Titanic* dinners, proving that there's no such thing as bad publicity."

"Themed costume parties are all the rage. You can have a niche market, catering disaster-themed dinners."

Val rolled her eyes. "A small niche, probably disappearing once Otto Warbeck's dinner party is no longer in the news."

"But you should capitalize on it and expand your repertoire. You could put on a Last Dinner in Pompeii with the guests in togas, lolling on cushions and eating peeled grapes. Or a Last Dinner before Prohibition, with the women dressed like flappers. Eat, drink, and be merry, for tomorrow we're dry."

Val laughed. "I'd have to put liquor in every dish. Prohibition was certainly a disaster for some people, though not on the scale of Pompeii or the *Titanic*. But thanks for the suggestions." She didn't expect to act on them.

Irene came back from waiting on the man at the bistro table. She grumbled that he'd only ordered a coffee and would probably nurse it for an hour while he read his e-mail.

"That reminds me. I should check my messages." Val took out her phone.

Chatty slid off the stool. "I'm going to spend some time on the stationary bike before my next client comes in. Don't forget we have a tennis team practice on Saturday, Val."

"I'm looking forward to it." If everything went as she hoped tomorrow night, the police would have a murderer in custody by then.

Val glanced at her messages. Bethany had texted, asking if she needed any help with the food for the memorial gathering on the yacht. Val texted back that Irene would prepare the food, though Bethany could make s'mores again.

For the next fifteen minutes, Val and Irene discussed the menu for high tea on the yacht. Irene came up with a list of sandwiches and other finger foods she'd serve. Val suggested tarts for dessert. Irene also wanted to serve scones with clotted cream. Fine with Val. As she was leaving, Irene handed her a bag of four scones, two for her and two for Granddad. He and

Irene had something in common—a gruff exterior that almost, but not quite, hid the soft spot inside.

Val filled a large insulated cup with coffee for Chief Yardley. On her way to the car, she spotted Althea in the club parking lot and asked how Jerome was doing.

"He's remembered bits and pieces about Saturday night," Althea said. "He's still foggy about most of it."

"There may be a way to lift the fog faster." Val told her about Cheyenne's plans for tomorrow evening. "If Jerome is willing to go back on the yacht, sitting in front of the controls might jog his memory."

Althea frowned. "Inviting all those people back on the yacht is playing with fire. One of them might not want Jerome to remember anything. You know what drug they found in his system? Rohypnol. Also known as the date rape drug. It relaxes you and makes you forget everything that happened."

"Shouldn't that convince the police that he didn't drug himself?"

"Not necessarily. It's a party drug. High school and college kids take it to enhance the effects of alcohol. First it makes them high, and then they sleep well."

So Jerome was still on the hook as a pilot who took drugs on the job. Val was convinced Trey had drugged Jerome. The proof of that might be locked away in Jerome's memory. "I understand your concern about Jerome, but I think returning to the yacht will help him figure out who drugged him and why. If I can get Chief Yardley to give him a police bodyguard, will that ease your worries?"

"A little. I'll tell Jerome my concerns, but it's his

decision whether or not to go. I think he'll jump at the chance of a redo."

Val hoped so. Now to talk the chief into allowing that redo. She climbed into her car and drove to the police station.

Chapter 22

When Val went into the chief's office, she handed him the coffee and gave him a bag of scones, minus the two she'd left in the car for Granddad. "Blueberry scones, baked by Irene."

"So it'll be her fault, not yours, if I break a tooth? I've crunched down on some hard scones in my life."

"Eat at your own risk." She grinned as he gave the scone in his hand a doubtful look. "Just kidding. Irene makes good scones."

"You bring sweets when you want to ply me with questions. And today I get decent coffee too. You must have a lot on your mind."

"This time I have some answers, not just questions. I've figured out who shoved me into the trunk. Louisa found out I planned to take the script booklets from the yacht Monday evening. Yesterday when I was with her, she said she was afraid Damian would shoot her, throw her in the trunk, and dump her body where no one would find her. Being thrown in a trunk was on her mind because she knew it happened to me."

The chief raised a skeptical eyebrow. "People killed by the mob end up in trunks too. Are you saying she pushed you into the trunk?"

"No. I glimpsed a dark figure a split second before the trunk lid came down. Someone tall. She's shorter than I am. She told Damian I was picking up the booklets. He's the one who pushed me into the trunk. He wanted what was inside his booklet—Otto's business card with the note about meeting him on deck."

"You don't know that the card fell out of *his* booklet."

Val hoped the police could settle that issue. "Did you check for fingerprints on the card?"

"We found some smudged partial prints, but nothing good enough to be used as evidence in court. It wasn't worth fingerprinting everyone on the yacht for an inconclusive result." The chief sipped his coffee. "We can take another look at the card, now that we have Damian Brown's prints to compare with what's there."

A step in the right direction. "What I learned today convinced me that Otto planned the party and adapted the *Titanic* mystery game with Damian in mind because of something that happened thirty years ago."

Val summarized what Stacy had told her about Andrea, Damian the Demon, and Louisa, Andrea's harasser.

The chief, who'd jotted notes on a pad while she was talking, put his pen down. "The incident thirty years ago might explain why Otto changed the mystery game, but what does it have to do with his death? Do you think Damian or Louisa had any idea that Otto was Andrea's brother?"

Val shook her head. "They wouldn't have gone to the dinner party if they'd known."

"Otto sprang that game on his guests after they were on the yacht. Why would Damian have brought a gun with him? Even if he always carried a gun, he wouldn't have risked a murder rap to cover up a drug sale that no one would ever prosecute."

Val agreed with the chief. "Otto realized that too, so he took justice in his own hands. He set up a meeting with Damian, confronted him about Andrea's death, and pulled a gun. Damian grabbed it and turned it on Otto."

The chief sipped the coffee. "Possible. How do you explain the anonymous letter?"

Val shrugged. "No matter how I put the pieces of this puzzle together, I always have that one piece left over. It doesn't fit anywhere. The only people who could have seen Damian shoot Otto would have gone to the police with the information." She studied the chief's face. Had he made sense of the letter?

He twirled his pen. "Got anything else to report?"

Val told him about Cheyenne's planned gathering for Otto's *Titanic* dinner guests on the yacht.

"Not a good idea." He touched his forehead as if a migraine had attacked him. "One of them might be a murderer."

"But the rest of them aren't and could help figure out who killed Otto. Granddad, Bethany, and I brainstormed about what occurred after Otto left the table, but we were busy with the meal and might have missed something. The others were at the opposite end of the saloon. We couldn't hear what they were saying with the music on. I hope to get the whole group talking about what happened or, better yet, going through the motions." Val could tell the chief hadn't changed his mind. "It's like crowd-sourcing to solve a problem. You can get to the truth faster than if you interviewed them separately."

"We interview suspects alone so they can't influence each other. Crowd-sourcing an investigation isn't standard operating procedure."

Val threw up her hands. "Okay. If you don't want to be there, I'll tell you what happens."

"No, no, no." He slapped his desk. "If it's going on, I want police there."

"Not in uniform, I hope. That will stifle the conversation. Could the officer who pilots the patrol boat sit next to Jerome on the upper deck? Althea told me he's getting back his memory little by little. Being at the helm of the *Abyss* again might help him fill in the gaps."

The chief crossed his arms. "Anything else?"

Just a few questions. "Did Otto's autopsy results come in?"

"The findings aren't complete yet. Specimens from the body still need to be tested. I heard from the medical examiner who performed the autopsy, but until the final report comes in, I'm not making any public statements about it."

But he might answer a specific question in private. Val gave it a stab. "Did the medical examiner mention that Otto had Alzheimer's?"

The chief's eyebrows rose. "Examining the brain after death is the usual way to confirm that diagnosis. The medical examiner looked at the brain. He said nothing about Alzheimer's. Why do you ask?"

"Otto's father had Alzheimer's. Stacy said Otto told

her he'd commit suicide if he ever found out he had the disease."

"That tells me something about Otto's character, but it doesn't explain his death." The chief laced his fingers behind his head, elbows out. "People who deliberately shoot themselves generally do it with their dominant hand. Otto Warbeck wrote right-handed, but his wound was on the left side. That's why I was skeptical of suicide from the start, but I can't rule it out. Your granddaddy called today to tell me what he observed in old photos at the Warbeck house. When Otto played baseball, he was a switch hitter."

A man who batted from either side could shoot himself with either hand. Val gave herself a mental kick for not coming to the same conclusion about Otto's baseball photos as her grandfather had. "Granddad's a better sleuth than I am."

"He's sharp." The chief pushed his notepad to the side. "You don't have to worry about him if you decide to leave Bayport. He gave me a lot of support after my father died. I'll be there to help him if he needs anything. He has a whole community here he can rely on."

So Granddad had confided in the chief about her possible move to D.C. "Did he tell you to say that?"

Chief Yardley shook his head. "I know him well. He'd want you to make the decision that's right for you."

"I will." She'd already done it, but hadn't told anyone. It was time to do that. She stood up. "Thanks, Chief."

"I'll call you tomorrow after I speak to the widow."

Val hoped he wouldn't talk Cheyenne out of the gathering.

She drove from the police station to Gunnar's house, wondering how to explain her decision to him. It didn't matter to Gunnar where he lived, but it mattered very much to her. He could plop down for a few months or years in one location and then move on. He'd done it before and he'd do it again, without looking back. Not the life she wanted. Growing up in a military family, she'd lived in a lot of different places, but the place she called home was where she'd spent her summers, in Bayport with her grandparents. This was where she belonged.

Explaining that to Gunnar was less difficult than she'd anticipated. When they sat down in his living room, he apologized for pressuring her to move. It wasn't fair to ask her to make a commitment when his life was in flux. They agreed they'd had a transitional relationship, rushing into it after broken engagements. A separation would give them both a breather.

She left his house relieved and convinced that he felt the same way.

Back home, she told Granddad what she and Gunnar had decided.

"I'm glad," he said. "You should settle into one of the bigger bedrooms upstairs, instead of staying in the small room you had as a kid."

She could handle a move down the hall.

When Chief Yardley called Val at noon the next day, she expected to hear that he'd talked Cheyenne into abandoning her plan for the gathering on the yacht. Instead, he said he would also be on the *Abyss* that evening. Based on the medical examiner's report and other evidence, he wanted to test a theory about Otto's death. He wouldn't tell Val anything about his theory or the evidence that led to it.

She proposed an experiment to pin down the time of Otto's shooting. She'd need a prop Gunnar could borrow from the local theater group.

"I could use a prop too," the chief said. "I'll contact the theater group. They won't turn down a request from the police. Gunnar can be in charge of props if he's available."

"I have a role for him in my experiment. What about Jerome?"

"He'll be sitting at the helm this evening with a police officer who has a captain's license."

Everything was falling into place for a fitting memorial to Otto. Val hoped it would end in an arrest for his murder.

Val peeled off the last piece of static-cling film covering the saloon's windows on the *Abyss*. With the opaque film gone, she could clearly see the dock on one side of the yacht and the river on the other. With the aft deck visible through the sliding glass door, everything would be out in the open for this gathering, unlike the last one.

Bethany came in from the aft deck, toting two large soft-sided coolers. She wore a black skirt and a white top, suitable for catering a memorial gathering. Her outfit mirrored Val's, though they hadn't coordinated. "Irene had all the food packed and ready to go. Where do you want it?"

"On the counter. I'll arrange the tea sandwiches

and put them in the fridge until we're ready to serve them. You're in luck, Bethany. Everything we're eating tonight is on your diet, all cold food. Or have you already given up that diet?" Usually it didn't take more than a few days for Bethany to abandon a fad diet.

"I've given up eating ice cubes. They make my teeth ache, and they're not very filling. I'm still sticking to cold food for now, but I crave a steaming bowl of soup." She unzipped a cooler. "Where's Cheyenne?"

Val pointed up with her index finger. "On the open deck, where we'll have cocktails. Granddad's up there with her and Gunnar, who'll be serving as bartender." He'd also have an essential role as a stand-in for Damian later in the evening.

Bethany took the sandwiches out of the cooler. "I'm glad your grandfather doesn't have to run around as much as he did on Saturday. It wasn't easy keeping everyone's glass full. Do you need any help here?"

"No, but you could go to the upper deck and prepare the grill and the ingredients for s'mores."

"More s'mores. I'll never eat those again without thinking of this." She made a sweeping gesture around the saloon. "I see Cheyenne peeled the film off the windows."

"I did that. She put off coming aboard as long as she could. I borrowed the key so I could get the food ready."

Before Cheyenne's arrival, the chief had shown Val where to position the props, how to handle one of them, and where to hide them in the engine room.

Bethany picked up the cheese board and crackers. "I'll take these upstairs."

Val arranged the crustless sandwiches on a platter. Irene had cut them into attractive shapes—rounds for cucumber, ovals for egg salad, squares for ham, and triangles for smoked salmon. As she put the sweets on a tiered serving tray, Val glanced occasionally through the sliding glass door at the aft deck where the hostess greeted her guests as they boarded. Cheyenne then sent them to the upper deck.

When Val felt the vibration of the engines, she knew all the guests had arrived and the yacht would soon leave the marina. She set the table in the dining area, put the sandwiches and sweets in the center, and snapped a photo to show Irene how attractive her high tea on the yacht looked. Then she refrigerated the sandwiches and the clotted cream. She'd serve them after everyone was at the table.

Gunnar came into the saloon just in time to help her bring the rest of the cocktail snacks upstairs. He took the platter of crudités with artichoke dip. She followed him out of the saloon and up the stairs, carrying the macadamia nuts and dried fruit. The yacht glided on smooth water.

Cheyenne tapped on her wineglass with a spoon. "Thank you all for joining me this evening. We've come together to celebrate Otto's life and to extend sympathy to Louisa Brown, who also lost her husband suddenly. Once we're out in the bay, we'll have a brief remembrance ceremony. Then we'll have a light meal in the saloon. Tonight, we have some extra people who weren't on the yacht last Saturday. Our bartender, Gunnar."

He waved. "Hi, everyone."

Cheyenne pointed to the bridge, where three men sat with their backs to the open deck. "The pilot from Saturday night, Jerome, is in the middle seat. On his left is Captain Zach, and on his other side is someone you may know." She rapped on the glass door to the bridge.

The man on Jerome's right stood up, turned around, and joined them on the open deck. Chief Yardley had kept out of sight until now. Val studied the faces around her. Louisa looked surprised, Trey nervous, Stacy wary, and Homer puzzled.

"Bayport Police Chief Earl Yardley asked to be here this evening," Cheyenne said. "He'll explain why."

The chief positioned himself so he could see all the guests. "Those of us investigating the death of Otto Warbeck are trying to piece together what happened on this boat six days ago. At the time you might have been too upset to remember details. Tonight, we'll try to stimulate those memories. If you recall anything you didn't mention when I talked to you individually, please speak up." He added, "Or you can tell me in private, if you prefer."

After the chief finished talking, Homer came up to Val. "I have a copy of my script with me." He patted the inside pocket of his jacket. "If you brought copies of the others with you, we could exchange."

"Sorry. I don't have them with me tonight." She decided against telling him the police had taken them. "You said Otto had promised you a *Titanic*-related gift for coming to his dinner party."

"Yes, I'd despaired of it, but Cheyenne said she has what Otto planned to give me."

"And you were supposed to give Otto something in return." Homer looked taken aback, but didn't deny it. Val took a guess at what Otto had demanded. "He wanted to know if any of his guests had ever visited your shop."

Homer ran his finger under his paisley bow tie as if

it had suddenly tightened. "Yes, indeed. He thought one of them might have brought me something to sell. I'm afraid I disappointed him. As I told him, I can describe the decoration on a pillbox I saw a year ago, but I have a bad memory for faces."

Hard to believe he could have totally forgotten the man who'd brought him a possibly stolen vase. He'd dashed Otto's hopes of confirming Trey as the thief. The antique dealer hadn't fingered Trey, either because he couldn't, as he claimed, or because he wouldn't, with his own reputation as an honest businessman at stake.

Homer drifted toward the snack table, where Grand-dad was talking to Stacy.

Val approached Trey and said, "You might want to spend a lot of time on the bridge with Jerome this evening."

Trey's eyebrows lowered. "Why?"

"On Saturday night you left the saloon shortly after Otto. You were gone longer than anyone else. You said you were on the bridge with Jerome, but since he doesn't remember, he can't confirm your alibi for the time when Otto was shot. Seeing you there might help Jerome regain his memory. It's in your best interest if he does." Correction. It was in Trey's best interest, assuming he'd told the truth. But if he'd left the upper deck to shoot Otto, he wouldn't want Jerome's memory to return.

"Okay. I'll sit with Jerome. Maybe if I remind him, he'll—"

"Don't do that. The man sitting next to him at the controls will hear what you're saying. It will sound as if you're trying to plant information."

"You mean I should just sit there and hope Jerome remembers something?"

"You can jog his memory without telling him what to say. Do what you did on Saturday night. Talk about the same navigation instruments. If you took a drink or s'mores with you on Saturday night, do the same this evening. You never know what might bring back memories."

He looked skeptical, but he ambled toward the table where Bethany was assembling s'mores with marshmallows she'd just toasted. Louisa was already enjoying the sweet treats, as she had on Saturday night. Trey filled a plate with them and carried them toward the glass door to the bridge.

Granddad waylaid him. "Don't forget to take a drink with you. I remember you had a root beer Saturday night." He thrust the soft drink into Trey's free hand and opened the door for him.

Val spoke to Granddad in an undertone when he closed the door. "Did you really remember what Trey drank?"

"Not until the chief told me to make sure he had a can of root beer. Jerome was also drinking root beer Saturday night. You know what that means?"

"The drug Jerome took was probably in the root beer." Not in the s'mores. Slipping Rohypnol into a drink was the classic way to drug someone. "Trey must have put the drug in his own root beer and then switched the cans when Jerome wasn't looking."

Val noticed the chief standing alone and joined him. "Did the lab find traces of Rohypnol in the root beer?" At his nod, she continued, "Any fingerprints on that can?"

"Both cans were wiped clean of prints. It would have made more sense to toss the cans overboard."

"Trey wouldn't have done that, not with his passion

for saving the bay from pollution." Val noticed a lack of motion under her feet. She looked out over the water. A few other boats were visible, but they weren't nearby. "The ceremony is about to begin."

Stacy called her son back to the open deck.

Cheyenne spoke for a few minutes about Otto's career as a maritime lawyer and his love of all things related to the *Titanic*. "It's fitting that on the day he died, he was reliving a moment of history that had great meaning for him. I wanted to spread his ashes on the bay, but there are restrictions against that, so I'll toss rose petals."

She took a glass bowl of white rose petals from a built-in cabinet on the deck, threw a handful of petals over the railing, and invited her guests to do the same.

As Val waited her turn, she thought about the planning that had gone into the dinner party last weekend. Otto had interwoven his *Titanic* obsession with his fixation on his sister's death. Val realized now why he'd approached her—not because she was the best caterer around, but because she, along with Granddad, had doggedly pursued the truth about suspicious deaths. Otto wanted them to dig into his sister Andrea's death. To make sure they saw the parallel between her death and Annie's in his mystery scenario, he'd have made it explicit in his solution.

Val didn't need the envelope with the solution to solve Otto's mystery game, but it bothered her that she couldn't find it. As she watched the rose petals she'd thrown in the water drift away, she remembered Otto's challenge to her and Granddad before dinner: *Where would you look for the conclusion to a Titanic mystery?*

It came to her in a flash where he'd hidden that envelope. As the others lingered on the upper deck, she rushed downstairs to the galley. She opened the freezer and found the envelope under the icemaker. Otto's little joke, ice cubes as miniature icebergs. She opened the envelope and read the solution to the game. No surprise. Otto had named Damian as the culprit in the young woman's death. With her brain addled by the drugs he'd given her, she'd climbed on the *Titanic*'s railing and lost her balance. But in Otto's solution, the victim's name wasn't Annie, but Andrea. The name substitution might have ignited some fireworks at the table last Saturday. This evening's re-creation of Saturday's events would definitely make a bang.

Chapter 23

High tea on the *Abyss* would have been somber and silent without Homer, who regaled the table with fascinating, though possibly fictional, tales about *Titanic* artifacts, survivors, and collectors. Val wondered if he was rehearsing for his new business venture of hosting *Titanic* dinners to hawk his antiques.

Chief Yardley was on the phone through much of the dinner. When it was over, he suggested everyone move to the seating area of the saloon.

Instead of trying to squeeze onto the sofa, Val sat on the arm of Granddad's easy chair.

The chief stood at the other end of the room, near the sliding door that led to the aft deck. He addressed the group. "I'd like you to tell me exactly what happened after the host left the table and went out to the deck."

Granddad pointed to the CD player. "Cheyenne cut off the old-time music that had played during dinner. She pressed a button and out came something with no tune and booming beats."

Cheyenne smiled. "My rap workout music."

"Why did you choose that to play?" Chief Yardley said.

Cheyenne didn't miss a beat. "Otto had set up the CDs in the tray on Saturday afternoon. Right before he left the table to go on deck Saturday night, he told me to flip to the next CD and to play it loud like I usually do."

Granddad's furry eyebrows rose in disbelief. He hadn't abandoned his theory that Cheyenne had chosen the music so no one would hear the gunshot when Damian killed Otto.

Chief Yardley's face remained impassive. "I'd like everyone to do exactly what they did that night. Please turn on the music, Mrs. Warbeck."

Cheyenne went over to the player and put on the rap CD.

Stacy shook her head. "It was louder than that."

The chief waited until everyone agreed Cheyenne had matched Saturday night's volume. "What happened next?" He had to raise his voice to be heard over the music.

Trey raised his hand. "I left the saloon, stopped at the bathroom right outside, and then went up to the bridge. I expected Otto to be there, but he wasn't. Jerome looked out of it. I thought I could help him navigate. So I stayed up there."

Val hoped Jerome's memory would come back so he could confirm or deny Trey's statements. If they were together, they'd both have alibis.

The chief told Trey to go up to the bridge and stay there until summoned. He went out the sliding door.

Stacy spoke up. "I left next. Otto had asked me to meet him outside at eight thirty-five." With her lecturer's voice, she could be heard over the music. "When I went out, I glanced up at the pilot deck and glimpsed someone in a tux. I thought at first it was Otto, but it must have been Trey. Otto was waiting for me down the stairs on the swim platform. We spoke briefly and then I returned here."

Chief Yardley jotted in a small notebook. "How long were you out on the deck?"

"Three or four minutes. After I came inside, Damian left."

The chief stopped writing. "I talked to Damian Brown earlier this week. He told me that he went into the head on the deck. Tonight Gunnar is going to stand in for him." When Gunnar went out the glass door, the chief continued, "What happened next?"

Noting that Louisa looked distracted, Val said, "Louisa, I think you went down those stairs." Val pointed at the curved staircase near the dining area.

"Cheyenne said we could use the downstairs bathroom," Louisa said, as if she had to justify her actions.

The chief said, "Would you mind going there now, Mrs. Brown? Stay there about as long as you did on Saturday night."

After Louisa went down, Val stood at the top of the stairs until she heard the bathroom door close. Then she ran down the stairs, opened the door to the engine room, and dashed through it. On her way to the swim platform, she grabbed the two props Gunnar had borrowed. She arranged the life-sized dummy face-down on the deck. Then she aimed the prop gun over the water, as the chief had suggested, and pulled the trigger.

The shot was louder than she'd expected. She dropped the gun on the swim platform near the dummy's left hand and retraced her path through the engine room. As she crossed the hall to the interior staircase, Louisa came out of the head.

She stopped short. "What are you doing here? You weren't down here that night."

"I was looking in the engine room for the envelope with Otto's mystery solution." Technically true, since Val had searched it earlier in the day. "I didn't find it there. Did you hear any unusual noises when you were in the bathroom?"

Louisa looked blank. "No." She started up the stairs to the saloon.

Understandable that she wouldn't have heard the shot inside the guest head, with the engine and the storage rooms between it and the swim platform.

When Val returned to the saloon, rap music still blared from the CD player. No one in the saloon mentioned hearing a gunshot.

Gunnar, Damian's stand-in, burst into the room looking flustered, as Val had coached him to do. Their eyes locked across the saloon. He touched his ear and nodded, the signal that he'd heard the shot while in the head on the aft deck.

Granddad went over to the CD player and lowered the volume. "I'm turning the music down now so we can hear each other. But on Saturday night I turned it down later, after Cheyenne left the room."

Bethany spoke up. "When Damian came in, he said something. I couldn't hear him across the room."

"I heard him," Stacy said. "He got very agitated and shouted, *Where's Louisa?*"

Startled, Val nearly missed the arm of Granddad's chair as she went to sit on it. She could imagine Damian being distressed after shooting Otto, but why would his wife's absence make him so anxious? Was it possible he hadn't shot Otto and had only heard a gunshot? In that case, he might have feared Louisa had been shot. Who could have pulled the trigger? Trey had been the only one who'd gone out on deck earlier and hadn't yet returned.

Cheyenne said, "I heard Damian ask about Louisa too. He definitely looked anxious. He calmed down after I told him Louisa had gone to the guest head on the lower deck. He joked about her hogging the bathroom."

Val glanced at the table, where the scripts had remained during the break in the dinner. When Damian returned from outside, he could have gone back to the table, picked up his booklet, and removed the card on which Otto had written their meeting time. He hadn't done that, suggesting he wasn't concerned that meeting his host would make him a suspect in a shooting.

"Who left the room after Damian came back?" the chief said.

Homer spoke up. "When Louisa came upstairs, I went to the loo on the lower deck. I'd been feeling queasy, but down there the motion wasn't so bad. When I came back here, I felt seasick again. I saw Cheyenne leave by the door to the aft deck. Then I went—"

"One step at a time." The chief turned toward Cheyenne. "Mrs. Warbeck, please show me what you did when you went out on deck." He opened the sliding door for her and went out.

Val hurried to join them. Granddad and Homer followed.

Cheyenne pointed to the head on the deck. "I went in there."

Homer shook his head. "I think not. When you left

the saloon by this door, I was on my way out the door to the side deck. Within seconds, my stomach was roiling even worse. I didn't want to be sick over the railing, so I hurried along the side deck to get to this loo. The door was open and I went in."

Val watched him and the woman he'd contradicted. Which of them was lying? He looked unblinkingly at Cheyenne.

Her eyes darted around. "Yes, of course. I forgot. I went to the master stateroom to use the head."

Val exchanged a look with Granddad. They both knew Cheyenne hadn't returned to the saloon and used the indoor staircase to the stateroom. The only other way was through the engine room from the swim platform, where Otto had planned to meet someone.

The chief said, "Mr. Huxby, please go back to the saloon and make sure no one else comes out here."

"Delighted. I was afraid you'd want me to stay in the loo for the next ten minutes." Homer went into the saloon, closed the sliding door behind him, and stood with his back to it like a guard preventing prisoners from escaping.

"How did you get to the head in the master stateroom, Mrs. Warbeck?" The chief pointed to the staircases leading to the swim platform. "Which stairs did you use to go down to the lower deck? Port or starboard?"

She gaped at him. "Does it matter?"

"In an investigation," he said, "small details often matter. Try to remember what was on your mind Saturday night when you came out here, and go through the motions of what you did."

Cheyenne stood still, her eyes closed. Val peeked over the railing at the swim platform. In the twilight, the mannequin dressed in black looked like a sprawled dead man. The chief had told her how to position the dummy without revealing what he hoped to prove, but obviously Cheyenne was his target.

She took baby steps toward the starboard staircase.

She looked down at the swim platform, yelped, and covered her eyes. "Someone's down there. Who?"

The chief waited a moment before answering. "It's a 3-D version of the chalk outline that marks a body's location. That's where we figure Otto was."

Cheyenne's shoulders sagged. "You're right. I can't keep this up any longer."

Val glanced at the chief. He must have suspected Cheyenne of lying and hoped the dummy would unnerve her into telling the truth faster than an interrogation would. His ploy had worked.

Chapter 24

Cheyenne collapsed onto the deck's built-in bench, her back to the swim platform below. Val sat down beside her.

Granddad lowered himself onto the bench next to Val and gave her an I-told-you-so look. He must have taken Cheyenne's reaction as proof that she was behind Otto's death. Val suspected Otto's wife was about to confess to something, but possibly not murder.

Chief Yardley loomed over Cheyenne. "What did you see when you went down to the swim platform?"

"Otto was lying there dead. He'd told me he was going to commit suicide, but I didn't expect him to do it that night. He had untreatable cancer and decided to die on his own terms."

Val glanced at the chief. He didn't look surprised or skeptical, but he rarely showed much emotion. He would have known about Otto's illness from the medical examiner's report. That must have tipped him off that Cheyenne had abetted Otto's suicide.

Cheyenne wiped away a tear. "I respected Otto's

decision to die as he wanted to, not helpless and in pain. He said that when the time came, he'd make sure his death didn't look like suicide so I could collect on his life insurance, but he'd need my help."

The chief folded his arms. "What kind of help?"

"I was supposed to get rid of any sign that he killed himself. He said he might make the house look like someone had broken in and shot him. Then I'd have to wipe off any fingerprints and dispose of the gun. I begged him to come up with a way that left me out of it. If he drove off a bridge or into a tree, I wouldn't have to break the law."

Didn't she know filing a false insurance claim was breaking the law? Val assumed Otto hadn't mentioned that.

Cheyenne sniffed. "The way I found Otto, it didn't look like an accident. It was either suicide or murder. And if it was murder, I'd be a suspect. People would think that I was lying about him wanting to commit suicide and that I killed him to put him out of his misery. So I decided to turn it into an accident."

"What did you do?" the chief said.

Cheyenne shivered as a cool breeze swirled around them. "I pushed him overboard. Burial at sea. I just hoped he'd stay under. I looked all around for the gun. It wasn't there. The way the boat was rocking, it must have slid off."

Or his murderer threw it into the water. Val stared at the dummy on the swim platform. Why would a murderer throw the gun overboard and leave the body? Though Otto wasn't a large man, maneuvering his body into the water while the boat was rocking would have taken time and strength. It couldn't have been easy, even for a strapping young woman like Cheyenne.

The chief put his hands on his hips like an angry parent. "You could have come clean about his suicide after he was pulled from the water."

Cheyenne looked as if she'd aged ten years in the last five minutes. "Otto took out life insurance less than a year ago. It wouldn't pay out if he committed suicide. He had a lot of debt and warned me I'd have barely enough to live on unless I collected that money."

"Mrs. Warbeck, I'd like you to go to the swim platform and position the dummy so that it resembles how your husband looked when you found him."

After the chief and Cheyenne went down the steps, Granddad whispered, "He's testing her to see if she told the truth."

She motioned for Granddad to move away from the stairs so they couldn't be heard. "You still think she killed Otto?"

"She didn't pull the trigger. We'd have heard the shot, because I turned off the music as soon as she left the saloon. She could have gotten Damian to do it, turned up the music to muffle his shot, and gone out to clean up the traces of murder."

Val shook her head. "If Damian had killed Otto in collusion with her, she'd have stayed inside the saloon so she'd have an alibi."

"*If* she was thinking straight. You believe what she said?"

Val shrugged. "I think she believes it. She expected Otto to kill himself in the near future, but someone may have saved him the trouble."

Cheyenne came up from the swim platform and

pointed to the saloon. "I owe everyone in there the truth. I need a minute to fix my hair and my face." She went into the head next to the sliding door.

The chief poked his phone and put it up to his ear. "Anything new? . . . Okay, you can send him down now."

Seconds later, Trey came bounding down the stairs from the upper deck. "The music reminded Jerome I was there. It was so loud that we could hear it through the floor Saturday night and tonight. He remembered we talked about it."

"What do *you* remember about the root beer?" the chief said. "You've got thirty seconds to tell me."

Trey didn't hesitate. "I wanted to space out at Otto's stupid party, so I put a roofie in my soda before dinner. It did nothing for me. I couldn't understand why until I went to the bridge and saw Jerome nodding off. He had a root beer too and must have drunk mine by mistake."

Val gave Trey credit for a convincing story. It would save Jerome from prosecution.

Cheyenne came out of the head. "Let's get this over with." She went into the saloon.

Bethany made room for her on the sofa. Louisa huddled at the other end of it. Trey stood behind his mother's straight-backed chair.

Gunnar whispered to Val, "Is this the show's final act?"

"Not sure. It's improv from now on." She heard the hum of the engine and felt the yacht moving. They were on their way back to the Bayport marina.

Val sat on the arm of Granddad's chair again.

Cheyenne asked for everyone's attention. "I want to apologize for misleading you and the police about what happened Saturday night. A month ago Otto found out he had an aggressive and incurable cancer.

He told me he would choose when and how he died, but when he took his own life during our dinner party, I was shocked."

Her guests looked shocked now, except for Stacy, who'd known her ex would kill himself under certain circumstances.

Cheyenne continued, "I found Otto dead on the swim platform. He must have thought he'd fall into the bay after shooting himself. He didn't, so I lowered him into the water."

Trey glowered at her. "Why didn't you say that Saturday night? We were all murder suspects."

Cheyenne winced. "I'm sorry. I should have told the truth sooner."

Bethany patted Cheyenne's hand. "But you don't know the whole truth. You can tell us what you did, but not what happened to Otto before you found him. He thought about committing suicide, but did he really go through with it, or did somebody kill him?"

Bravo, Bethany. Val turned toward the chief, who stood near the sliding door to the deck. "Is there any hard evidence that he committed suicide?"

"Some evidence. According to the medical examiner, Otto Warbeck had advanced cancer. His business card with a note on it turned up here on the yacht. He'd scrawled on the back of the card, proposing an eight forty-five meeting. Experts confirmed the note was in his handwriting. He intended to meet someone on the deck. The card had partial fingerprints on it, belonging to him and Damian Brown."

Louisa flicked her wrist. "Otto must have dropped the card and Damian picked it up."

The chief shrugged. "Be that as it may, multiple

witnesses said your husband went on deck at about that time."

Cheyenne nodded. "Just before Otto left the saloon, he told me he wanted to talk to Damian privately and said I should try to keep anyone from leaving the saloon and interrupting them. I had no idea if they ever met, so I didn't say anything about it."

The chief moved away from the sliding door toward the sofa, like an actor going from the wing to center stage. "It's too late to ask the two men if they met or what words they exchanged. But in the week leading up to the *Titanic* dinner, Otto Warbeck took some actions that speak louder than words about his intentions. Five days before the dinner, he bought two identical guns. One of them is probably at the bottom of the bay, minus the bullet that killed him." The chief shifted position to stand in front of Louisa. "You found the other gun under the passenger seat of your husband's car. Two days before the *Titanic* dinner, Mr. Warbeck sat in that seat, when your husband gave him a ride to the golf course."

Though the chief was only giving facts, their significance was obvious to Val. Otto planned to kill himself and frame Damian for murdering him.

Louisa broke the stunned silence, her eyes flashing with anger. "Otto planted that gun. It's his fault Damian is dead."

"He didn't pull the trigger, Mrs. Brown." The chief let that sink in for a moment and then continued, "But he did something else that led indirectly to your husband's death. You may not know this, but many color laser printers leave codes, nearly invisible except under special light. The codes indicate the printer's serial number and a time stamp showing when a page was printed. Otto Warbeck had that type of printer. On the morning of the *Titanic* dinner, he printed the anonymous letter you received."

Louisa blinked, looking dazed. "Otto wrote that letter before the dinner? It said Damian shot him." Her eyes widened. "Otto killed himself and tried to make it look as if my husband did it. That's evil!"

"Why would he do such a thing?" Bethany sounded outraged.

Stacy looked up at the chief, who nodded to her.

She talked about Otto's sister's death, his obsession with finding the man he blamed for it, and the sketch he had of Demon the drug dealer. "A couple of weeks ago, Otto met Damian for the first time and recognized him as Demon."

"No way." Louisa's high-pitched voice reached new heights. "He didn't know how Damian looked when he was young."

"That's why Otto asked me to confirm his suspicion." Stacy's low, calm tone contrasted with Louisa's. "Thirty years ago I saw Demon. Two days ago I saw the same man in your wedding picture. I was at the party the night Otto's sister went off the balcony. And so were you . . . *Louie*."

Louisa gasped. "Andie fell. Damian didn't push her."

Gunnar leaned down and whispered to Val, "The lady doth protest too much, methinks."

Stacy's eyes narrowed as she stared at Louisa. "It never crossed my mind that anyone pushed her . . . until now." She looked around the room. "For those of you who don't know, Otto's sister's nickname in college was Andie, short for Andrea. Louisa called herself Louie in those days."

"Louie," Homer muttered.

Bethany turned to Louisa at the other end of the sofa. "When we were playing the mystery game, you called the girl who fell from the *Titanic* Andie, but her name was Annie. Otto corrected you."

That slip of the tongue had tipped Otto off that Louisa had known his sister. Based on Val's brief acquaintance with him, she knew he'd have reacted to this information, but how?

Louisa crossed her arms. "I don't remember that. You must have misheard."

Trey stepped toward the chief. "I remember it . . . and something else that happened at the table. I was sitting next to Louisa, and I saw Otto slip something to her. It looked like a business card. That was just before he announced we were taking a break."

Louisa sat perfectly still, her lips trembling. Several seconds passed. Then she said, "Yes, that's right. I'd asked what kind of work he did, and the business card was his answer."

Val might have believed that explanation if Louisa hadn't taken so long to come up with it. Could Otto have scrawled a note to her on the back of a business card, as he had to her husband?

Homer cleared his throat loudly. "I found something Saturday night that might be of importance, though I didn't realize it at the time. When I went to the loo downstairs after Louisa came up, I spotted a bit of paper on the floor. It was Otto's business card with a message on the back. It said *Louie, 8:40 on deck re Andie.*"

Val felt a tingle like a mild electric shock. Otto's note to Damian had specified only a meeting time, but his note to Louisa also made clear what they would discuss. If she'd known about the route through the engine room, she could have taken it to meet Otto on deck, five minutes before his planned meeting with her husband.

Louisa stared at Homer, wide-eyed. "I had no idea Otto wrote on the back of the card. I glanced at the front of it. I would have slipped it into my purse, but that was across the room. I tucked the card under my belt. It must have fallen out when I went downstairs."

Val pictured the wide satin belt on Louisa's dress. In the absence of pockets, which the dress lacked, the belt made a good hiding place for something as small as a business card. But why not leave the card on the table? Val could think of only one reason—because Louisa didn't want anyone to see the note Otto had scrawled on it. She didn't want to explain who Louie and Andie were.

The chief turned from Louisa to Homer. "Do you still have the card, Mr. Huxby?"

"I put it in a pocket in my tuxedo. I imagine it's still there."

"Don't touch it. I'll send someone to pick it up."

Louisa chewed her nails.

Val felt the vibration from the motor lessening. The yacht must be leaving the bay for the river. They'd dock at the Bayport marina before long, but would the truth about Otto's death have come out by then?

"We'll soon be on land, so I'll wrap this up quickly." the chief said. "The autopsy report on Mr. Warbeck has information about his wound. The bullet's angle of entry suggested someone shooting upward into Mr. Warbeck's head. He wasn't a tall man. Of the people who left this room after he went out, only one was shorter than him."

Val and everyone else looked at Louisa. Would she crack?

Louisa shrank from their intense gaze. "You don't understand. Otto forced me to shoot him!"

Chapter 25

Cheyenne broke the stunned silence that followed Louisa's disclosure. "What do you mean Otto forced you? How?"

"I wanted to meet him on deck at eight forty, like he said in the note. After a couple of people went out, Cheyenne blocked the door to the aft deck and said to use the bathroom on the lower deck. I knew I could get outside from there by going through the engine room."

Cheyenne nodded. "When I gave her and Damian the yacht tour before dinner, I pointed out the engine room door and said it led to the swim platform. I never dreamed anyone would go that way."

"I was just doing what Otto asked," Louisa whimpered.

"What happened next, Mrs. Brown?" the chief said.

"I thought Otto would be on the deck outside this room, but he surprised me on the swim platform. He backed me against the low railing." The words tumbled out of Louisa's mouth. "He told me that he was Andie's brother and that Damian caused her death. I swore Damian was nowhere near her when she fell. Otto accused me of lying, pulled out a gun, and threatened to kill Damian and me. I had one way to save myself, he said. He stuck the gun in my hand, guided it to his head, and told me to pull the trigger."

Louisa shuddered. "No sane person would do that. I thought it was part of his mystery game and the gun wasn't loaded, but I was scared. The boat was rocking, and my hand was slipping on the railing. I had to do something." Louisa squeezed her eyes shut as if to erase her memories. "I pulled the trigger, and he fell."

An hour ago Val wouldn't have believed the story. But after hearing about Otto's illness and his attempt to frame Damian, she could imagine Otto coercing Louisa into shooting him.

The chief's face revealed nothing about what he was thinking. "What did you do after you shot him, Mrs. Brown?"

"Threw the gun in the water and ran back through the engine room to the guest bathroom. I was a nervous wreck. I stayed in the bathroom until I stopped shaking." She hugged herself as if the memory of it gave her chills.

"Did your husband know you'd shot Otto?" the chief said.

"He didn't see me do it, and I didn't tell him. He said he'd heard what sounded like a shot while he was in the john, but since no one else mentioned it, he just let it go." Louisa lowered her head, cradled it in her hands, and sobbed.

As the chief made a quick phone call, Val gave Louisa a glass of water. She'd have offered something stronger, but she thought Louisa would need a clear head for the next few hours.

Two Bayport police officers met the yacht when it docked and whisked her away while the others remained on the boat.

The chief cautioned the group in the saloon against talking to the media, in the interests of justice and out of consideration for Louisa's family.

Cheyenne looked profoundly unhappy. Her celebration of Otto's life had exposed his dark side. She pulled herself together enough to remember the gifts he'd left behind for his guests—actually, bribes to induce them into coming to his dinner. She gave Trey a business envelope, Homer a thick manila envelope, and Stacy a thinner one.

Homer tore into his envelope and announced that it contained the entire set of scripts from Otto's mystery game. Not the *Titanic* collectible Otto had hinted he'd give him, but Homer looked pleased anyway. Trey took a check from his envelope, stared at it wide-eyed, and put it in his shirt pocket. Val guessed it was Otto's donation to the Protect the Bay Fund. Stacy looked inside her envelope and smiled, her eyes tearing. Apparently, Otto had made good on his promise to return her great-grandmother's letter.

What a strange man. He'd manipulated people and destroyed lives with his last acts on earth, but Otto's word had been his bond.

Cheyenne handed Val a check. "This isn't just for catering. You did what I asked. You helped prove that Otto didn't commit suicide. That's worth a lot to me."

Val was stunned by the amount. Once she gave Irene the money for preparing the food, there would be enough left to cover the termite repairs at Grand-dad's house. Would Cheyenne ever collect on Otto's life insurance policy? Technically, he hadn't committed suicide, but the insurance company's lawyers could argue that forcing someone to kill him was the equivalent of suicide.

As Val cleaned up after the meal with Granddad and Bethany, the chief beckoned her to the aft deck.

She joined him at the railing. "It was a brilliant idea to put a dummy on the swim platform. You must have expected a strong reaction from Cheyenne."

"I hoped for one. Otto's illness, his gun purchase, and the anonymous letter he printed all pointed to suicide with an intent to frame Damian. His wife was the obvious person to remove any evidence of suicide." He leaned against the railing. "Louisa's role wasn't as obvious. Did you figure out she shot Otto before she told us that?"

"Not until tonight. When I fired the prop gun on the swim platform, ran back inside, and saw her coming out of the guest head, I realized she'd had the time and the opportunity to kill Otto, but only if she knew about the path through the engine room." She caught the chief's eye. "The report about the angle of the shot must have tipped you off about Louisa. Did you just get that news by phone tonight?"

"I had the report earlier, but it wasn't conclusive. A taller shooter could have knelt or held the gun low. Or Otto could have shot himself at that angle." The chief looked up at the stars for a moment. "Louisa confessed before I got around to saying that."

"She was on the verge of confessing because of what came out earlier. Everyone contributed details they hadn't previously realized were important." Val ticked off the examples on her fingers. "Stacy mentioned the girls' nicknames. That jogged Bethany's memory about Louisa's tongue slip about Andie. Then Homer realized the significance of the card he'd found with the names Andie and Louie on it, and Trey remembered the note Otto passed to Louisa."

The chief smiled. "Okay, you've made your point about crowd-sourcing. But I'm not adopting it as an investigation method, though it worked tonight."

"Do you think the state's attorney will prosecute Louisa for killing Otto?"

"Tough case to win. She convinced everyone in the saloon that she was coerced. Her defense attorney will put Otto on trial and make her look good next to him." The chief's voice rumbled with anger. "She was on the scene of *three* suspicious deaths. She shot two men. Still, she may walk around free."

Val felt a chill at the thought of Louisa at large. "It was odd how Louisa declared Damian didn't push Otto's sister off the balcony, when no one suggested he did. Maybe pushing Otto's sister was on Louisa's mind because *she* did it."

"Possible. I got a call tonight from the investigator on that case. He said some students on the balcony heard Otto's sister yell, *Get away, Louie.* Then they heard a scream, and she was on the ground. The police couldn't find a man named Louie or Louis who'd been at that party. They assumed that was Demon's real name."

Val snapped her fingers. "Otto must have recognized the name Louie. After Louisa said Andie's name by mistake, he realized Louie could have been her nickname. He then tweaked his suicide plan."

The chief leaned on the railing, looking out at the river. "People intent on suicide often can't pull the trigger. Otto might have had that problem if he'd stuck with his original plan, killing himself while Damian was out of the saloon. He couldn't have forced Damian to shoot him, but it was easy to overpower a little woman."

Val paced the deck, thinking about Damian's death. "Louisa might have lied when she said her husband didn't know she'd shot Otto. If Damian knew, he had a hold over her, and she had a reason to kill him besides her jealousy of Cheyenne. Is there any proof they struggled over that gun?"

"We can poke holes in her story, but the evidence against it isn't overwhelming. She'd claim she was distraught when she first gave her statement and now she's so traumatized she can't remember the details. A jury would feel sorry for her unless we can prove premeditation."

Val flashed back to the scene in the kitchen after Damian was shot. Nearly hysterical, Louisa had explained what had happened and produced the anonymous letter. Then she left the kitchen to meet the ambulance. On her way to the front door, she stopped in the powder room and ditched her apron. An apron with big patch pockets.

Val stopped pacing. "Is it possible for a gun to pick up fibers from material, say if I carry it in my pocket?" When he nodded, she continued, "Louisa was wearing a cobbler apron when she shot Damian. It was four in the afternoon. There was no sign of cooking she'd done or intended to do. Why the apron? Maybe she'd found the gun in Damian's car earlier that day or even the day before. She lured him into the garage, pulled the gun from her pocket, and shot him."

"Why wouldn't she just put the gun in her pants pocket?"

"Because women's pants usually don't have pockets." Val thought about the pants she owned. "That gun would be a tight fit in the back pocket of my jeans. You'd see the outline of it, and I couldn't pull it out fast. An apron pocket doesn't have those problems."

"Fibers from it on the gun *would* suggest premeditation. Let's hope she didn't burn that apron."

The chief called Monday evening to tell Val that her hunch had been correct. The fiber evidence from the gun was enough to charge Louisa with her husband's murder.

Val put down the hall phone, relieved that a killer wouldn't go free, but sorry for the families touched by Otto's and Damian's deaths. Before she could return to the sitting room to tell Granddad the news, the doorbell rang.

Bethany stood on the porch. "I've just had dinner with Cheyenne at the Bugeye Tavern. She got a surprise package that might interest you."

"Come in."

They went into the sitting room. Bethany greeted Granddad and plopped down on the sofa near his lounge chair. "Cheyenne found a box on her doorstep today. It contained three *Titanic*-era souvenirs, stolen from Otto eight years ago."

Val curled up on the other end of the sofa. "Someone's conscience woke up." Trey must have felt guilt pangs after receiving Otto's donation.

She told Bethany and Granddad the news about Louisa's apron.

"The apron's not the only sign that she planned to kill Damian," Granddad said. "She came over here on Tuesday afternoon pretending she was worried that her husband was a murder suspect. Her real reason for coming was to plant the seed that he'd shot Otto. Then the police wouldn't suspect her of shooting Otto and would accept her yarn about fighting Damian for the gun."

Bethany squirmed on the old sofa, possibly feeling a spring poking through the cushion. "Louisa was a victim too . . . of Otto. He planted the gun and sent the anonymous letter to ruin Damian's life, but it destroyed hers too."

Granddad folded his arms. "You can't excuse Louisa. Otto forced her to shoot him, but killing her husband was her own idea."

Val couldn't argue with that. "No way Otto could have guessed that Louisa would react to the letter by shooting Damian, though I don't think Otto would have been unhappy about it."

"I can't figure out Louisa," Bethany said. "She seemed to love her husband, so why did she want him dead?"

"Jealousy." Granddad took off his bifocals. "I saw her spying on Damian when he paid Cheyenne a long visit on Tuesday afternoon. Louisa thought her husband was having an affair and would throw her over for a younger woman."

"She was wrong about that, Mr. Myer. Cheyenne said Damian came on to her that day. She told him she wasn't interested, and he dropped it. They drank tea in the kitchen and chatted."

The kitchen: the one room Granddad couldn't peek into when he'd spied on Cheyenne and Damian.

He waved away Bethany's defense of Cheyenne. "Doesn't matter what they did, but what Louisa believed."

Bethany frowned. "Why didn't she tell the truth right away about what happened with Otto on the swim platform?"

"No one would have believed it," Val said. "Her story was plausible only after we found out that Otto intended to commit suicide and make it look like murder."

Bethany grimaced. "Otto and his *Titanic* dinner have left a bad taste in my mouth."

Granddad leaned back in his chair. "To get rid of it, eat something that tastes good. Not ice cubes."

"That diet is history. I didn't lose weight on it." She turned to Val. "Speaking of history, you should expand your catering menu to include themed historical dinners, like the *Titanic* one. Dinner with Queen Victoria, for example. The hosts and guests could cosplay as their favorite Victorians."

"Cosplay?" Granddad frowned in puzzlement. "What does that mean?"

"Dressing like a character from a story. It's very trendy. At a Victorian table, you might see Count Dracula, Sherlock Holmes, Alice in Wonderland, and Miss Havisham in her tattered wedding dress."

Granddad stroked his chin. "I don't know about cosplay, but the themed dinner party has legs. Dinner on the Orient Express. Dinner at Washington's Mount Vernon. Not many caterers offer that. What do you think, Val?"

Better than the disaster dinners Chatty had suggested. Val would enjoy researching the meals served in various historical eras. "If you take the *Codger's Cookbook* off my plate, Granddad, I'll add themed dinners to my catering menu."

To her surprise, he agreed.

"Let's put the cookbook on the back burner," he said. "Now's the time to ride the wave of publicity from the *Titanic* dinner and take your business in a new direction. And I'll help."

Val suspected he'd help by cosplaying the chef.

FIRST-CLASS DINING SALOON MENU
R.M.S. *Titanic*, April 14, 1912

Hors d'Oeuvres Variés
Oysters
Consommé Olga   Cream of Barley

Salmon, Mousseline Sauce, Cucumber

Filet Mignons Lili
Sauté of Chicken Lyonnaise
Vegetable Marrow Farci

Lamb, Mint Sauce
Roast Duckling, Apple Sauce
Sirloin of Beef, Château Potatoes
Green Peas   Creamed Carrots
Boiled Rice
Parmentier & Boiled New Potatoes

Punch Romaine

Roast Squab & Cress

Cold Asparagus Vinaigrette

Pâté de Foie Gras
Celery

Waldorf Pudding
Peaches in Chartreuse Jelly
Chocolate & Vanilla Éclairs
French Ice Cream

VAL'S *TITANIC* DINNER MENU
on the *Abyss*

Hors d'Oeuvres

Consommé

Salmon, Mousseline Sauce, Cucumbers

Stuffed Zucchini

Roast Beef, Château Potatoes
Green Peas, Creamed Carrots

Sorbet

Cold Asparagus Vinaigrette

Mushroom Pâté
Celery

Waldorf Pudding

Cheese and Fruit

Note: Val served sorbet as a palate cleanser in place
of the similar Punch Romaine, which is a half-
frozen mix of fruit juice and wine, eaten with
a spoon.

THE
CODGER COOK'S
RECIPES

CHICKEN LYONNAISE

The menu in the Titanic's *first-class dining room was inspired by French cuisine. While no recipe for the Sauté of Chicken Lyonnaise served on the* Titanic's *last night has survived, this is a simple, quick, delicious version with few ingredients. The vinegar and onion sauce in this recipe is popular in Lyons, the gastronomical capital of France, renowned for its poultry.*

- 3 tablespoons olive oil (or 2 tablespoons oil and 1 tablespoon butter)
- 1½ pounds chicken tenders
- 3 large shallots, chopped small, or a medium onion, finely diced
- ½ cup red wine vinegar
- ½ cup crème fraîche or heavy cream
- salt and freshly ground pepper to taste (optional)

Lightly salt and pepper the chicken pieces if desired.

Heat the oil (or oil and butter) at medium high in a skillet large enough to hold the chicken in a single layer. If the chicken won't fit in a single layer, use two pans, with the fat divided between them, or cook the chicken in two batches in the same pan.

Sauté the chicken pieces for 3–4 minutes until brown. Turn the pieces over using tongs and sauté them on the other side for 3–4 minutes, until the internal temperature is 165 degrees Fahrenheit. Remove the chicken to a serving dish and loosely cover it with aluminum foil.

Add the shallots or onions to the pan and sauté them until lightly browned. Stir the vinegar into the skillet little by little and boil the liquid down until it's no longer watery.

Stir in the crème fraîche or cream. Cook until the mixture is blended and has turned light brown, about 5 minutes.

Return the chicken to the pan and heat the pieces in the sauce, rotating them to make sure all sides are in the sauce.

Serves 4.

CHÂTEAU POTATOES

The name of this dish comes from its popularity among the French nobility. In the Titanic *kitchen, a crescent-bladed paring knife called a turning knife would have been used to cut the potatoes into fancy eight-sided shapes. I'm guessing they taste about the same as potatoes with four sides.*

Preheat the oven to 375 degrees.

   6 medium to large potatoes
   3 tablespoons melted butter
   2 tablespoons olive oil
   ½ cup flour
   ½ teaspoon salt
   parsley sprigs (optional)

Peel the potatoes and cut each of them into eight pieces. All the pieces should be about the same size. Spread them out to dry.

Pour a mixture of melted butter and olive oil into a glass baking pan (13 x 9 x 2 inches).

Mix the flour and salt together and sift over the cut potatoes until they are lightly coated. Turn the potatoes over and sift flour on the other side. Repeat until the potatoes are coated lightly on all sides.

Put them in the pan, flat side down, in a single layer with some space between the potatoes.

Roast the potatoes for half an hour and turn them to brown on the other side. Total time in the oven: 60 minutes. The potatoes should be soft and browned.

Note: The smaller the size of the potato pieces, the shorter the roasting time.

Serve them in the baking pan prettied up with parsley sprigs.

Serves 6.

ROASTED ASPARAGUS VINAIGRETTE

The asparagus vinaigrette on the Titanic *probably would have been boiled, cooled, and served cold. The roasted asparagus in this recipe can be served warm, cold, or at room temperature.*

Preheat the oven to 400 degrees.

1 pound fresh asparagus with tough ends
    snapped off
3 tablespoons olive oil (two for roasting and
    one for the vinaigrette)
½ teaspoon Dijon mustard

1 tablespoon lemon juice or champagne
   vinegar
kosher salt and freshly ground pepper

Toss the asparagus in a large bowl or pan with 2 table-spoons of olive oil. Sprinkle with three pinches of the salt and a few grinds of pepper.

Spread the stalks in a single layer on an aluminum-covered baking sheet. Roast until tender, approximately 10 minutes for ½-inch diameter stalks, and less time for thinner stalks.

Make the vinaigrette by whisking the mustard with the lemon juice or vinegar. Slowly add the remaining olive oil while whisking. Season with salt and pepper to taste.

Toss the asparagus with the vinaigrette and serve warm or cold.

Serves 4.

CLASSIC S'MORES

8 sheets graham crackers, broken into
   16 squares
2 milk or dark chocolate candy bars (3–4 ounces
   total), broken into rectangles that fit the
   crackers
8 standard size marshmallows

Preheat a grill to low-medium heat, or use a grill or charcoal fire that is cooling down.

Put a cracker on foil and top it with chocolate. Put it at the edge of the grill until the chocolate softens, usually less than a minute. Remove it from the grill.

Put a marshmallow on a stick or long skewer. Hold it over the heat, close enough to toast but not burn the marshmallow. Rotate it until the marshmallow turns golden brown, about 1–2 minutes.

Put the marshmallow on your chocolate-topped cracker and use another graham cracker to squash it and hold it down while you remove the skewer. You should now have a sandwich with melted chocolate and gooey marshmallow filling.

Yield: 8 s'mores of 2¼ inches

S'MORES TARTLETS

These treats bake in a mini muffin pan, no campfire or grill needed. They're more buttery than the classic s'mores, and less messy. You're likely to have crumbs instead of gooey marshmallows on your fingers and clothes.

Preheat the oven to 350 degrees.

> 1 cup plus 2 tablespoons graham cracker crumbs
>
> 3 tablespoons sugar
>
> 6 tablespoons melted butter
>
> 2 milk or dark chocolate candy bars (approximately 1.45 ounces each), divided into rectangles
>
> 12 standard size marshmallows, each cut in half to make two circular pieces

Combine the crumbs and sugar in a medium bowl. Stir in the melted butter and mix until blended.

Lightly grease 24 cups (1¾–inch diameter) in a mini muffin pan.

Divide the crumbs among the cups. Press the crumbs down and around the sides with a tart tamper, a spoon, or your fingers.

Bake 4–5 minutes.

Remove the pan from the oven. Put one chocolate rectangle in each cup and a marshmallow, cut side down, on top of it. Return the pan to the oven for 3 minutes or until the marshmallows are softened. To brown the marshmallows, put the pan under the broiler for a minute.

Cool the pan on a rack for 15 minutes. Carefully lift each tartlet from its cup. Serve warm immediately or serve at room temperature after the tartlets have cooled down.

Yield: 24 tartlets

SAVORY CHEESE S'MORES

20 whole wheat or rice crackers
¼ cup sun-dried tomato pesto, homemade or
    store-bought
1 package Brie bites in sealed cups, 5 per
    package; or 10 Brie wedges cut from a wheel
    to the size of the crackers

For each s'more, spread a cracker with a teaspoon of pesto.

Spear a Brie bite or wedge on a long stick or skewer. Hold the cheese over an open fire or hot grill. Cook for about 2 minutes, turning the skewer to heat the cheese evenly.

Slide the Brie bite off the skewer with a fork and slice through the middle of it to make two rounds.

Place each round on a cracker with pesto. Top with a second cracker to make a sandwich.

Eat while warm.

Yield: 10 pieces

Connect with

Visit us online at
KensingtonBooks.com
to read more from your favorite authors, see books
by series, view reading group guides, and more.

for sneak peeks, chances to win books and prize packs,
and to share your thoughts with other readers.

**facebook.com/kensingtonpublishing
twitter.com/kensingtonbooks**

Tell us what you think!

To share your thoughts, submit a review,
or sign up for our eNewsletters, please visit:
KensingtonBooks.com/TellUs.